Searching for Gildeen

28 medical stories inspired from 40 years
of emergency medicine

Philip L. Levin, MD

Published by
Doctor's Dreams Publishing
P O Box 4808
Biloxi, MS 39531, USA

Prepared in the United States of America

Acknowledgements:

Cover photo by Isabelle Parker, taken at the Museum of
Contemporary Art in Houston

Special thanks to Lisa Pinkowski for proofreading and editing
suggestions

The quote from and the existence of "American Short Stories" are
fictional

Table of Contents

Story	
Introduction	
The Stomach Ache	Appendicitis
Quinn	Meningitis
Take Your Medicine	Schizophrenia
In the Waiting Room	Drugs & Death
Asclepius	Faith healing
Fielder's Choice	Prostate Cancer
The Rash	Child Abuse
Brave Heart	Lymphoma
By the Numbers	Death in the E.R.
Rebecca	Melanoma
The Sacrifice	Obstetrics
Chamber of Salvation	Gun Shot Wound
Overdose	Suicidal ideation
You're Going to Die	Aneurysm
The Corpse Who Wasn't Dead	Forensics
Crying Baby	Car accident
The Old Biloxian	Stroke
New Year's Eve Celebration	Leg fracture
Heart Broken	Heart attack
Searching for Gildeen	PTSD
The Sore Toe	Endocarditis
The Drug Raid	Institutional Safety
Mississippi Farmer	Organic Brain Syndrome
Christmas Eve in the E.R.	Renal Failure
Old Dog	Esophageal foreign body
Roger's Back Pain	Aneurysm
The Headache	Brain Tumor
Ready or Not	Burns

Introduction

In the emergency room, that ever-open sanctuary of desperate need, people bring their battered bodies, their suffering souls, and their flagging spirits. For nearly forty years I've plied my trade as an E.R. doctor, from small-town, five-bed understaffed outdated converted wards to fifty-bed, modern mechanized mayhems. I've seen the comedy and the pathos, saved lives and held the hand of someone taking a last breath.

Each story in this collection draws from these dramas; each is based on a different disease or aspect of medicine. Told from the perspective of those involved (the physician or the patients or the family), the characters find their lives disrupted by their sudden ill health, the dangers of death always a thread in the fabric of their lives. Following each story I've added a short discussion of the disease represented in the story and a discussion of the framework around which the story evolved.

I've always been a writer, from grade school, when I wrote a syndicated comic story I shared with my friends, to producing a college newsletter and later paying my way through medical school with travel and professional articles. I started writing medical stories as a medical student, the first of these related here as "Mississippi Farmer." Though most of these stories are based on real events I've experienced, some of them are a bit bizarre, such as the sci-fi "Asclepius."

These stories have all been fictionalized, and events have been altered. Yet in all of them the story tells of what happened, or could have happened, and brings to life the world of the emergency room.

The Stomach Ache

Mariam looked around the deserted ward, making her way to the one cubicle with closed curtains. It'd been several months since she'd had occasion to visit her husband here at his workplace in the pre-surgical suite, and now, instead of standing as physician he was lying as patient. Pulling back the curtain, she studied him as he reposed on the chrome-railed stretcher, his face drawn in pain. A blonde nurse on the far side of the bed was wrapping a brightly-colored tourniquet around his upper arm.

Under the fluorescent lights, Roger's face appeared pale and gaunt. The array of medical equipment and beeping monitors gave the room an otherworldly look, a stark contrast to the luxurious office furniture and subtle paintings in which Mariam usually dwelled. She stepped up and planted a kiss on his cheek.

"How are you feeling, dear?"

Roger gave her a wan smile. "Not so good, stomach's killing me." He looked her over. "You sure look sharp; sorry I had to pull you away from the benefit."

"Thanks." She twirled slowly, showing off her evening wear. "I was having fun. Not to worry, though. There'll be another event somewhere else next weekend." She rested her hand on his shoulder as she watched the nurse prepare to stick a needle in his arm.

Miriam asked, "How does it feel to be on the receiving end of the pokes?"

Roger turned to observe the nurse. "Gwen wouldn't hurt me, now would you, Gwen?"

The nurse looked up, first at Roger and then at Mariam. Mariam was startled by the woman's cold eyes. "You're his wife?" the nurse asked.

"Yes. Thank you for taking care of Dr. Prince." She offered a friendly smile, which went unreturned as the nurse turned back to her work. Mariam admired the smoothness with which Gwen guided the needle into Roger's arm, a flush of red blood flowing back. From this line, she filled a series of tubes, each with a teaspoon's worth of body serum. Her actions were smooth, experienced. Mariam studied the young woman's face, its cheekbones high and minimal make-up. She had a natural beauty, though worry lines had left their memories across her forehead.

"You've worked here long, Gwen?"

Gwen glanced at her before returning her concentration to the IV she was preparing. Snagging a bulky plastic bottle onto a shining ceiling hook, she uncoiled its tubing and attached it snugly to the needle in Roger's arm. Not a drop of blood went awry. She stepped back, crossing her arms across her chest. "Ten years. I know Roger better than do you." The woman had a gruffness to her vowels. Miriam placed the accent as Eastern European.

Roger chuckled weakly. "Gwen means that when two people work together every day they get that impression. No one can replace a spouse's intimate knowledge."

Gwen allowed a bare nod. "Of course that's what I meant."

Roger grunted, and Miriam noticed his knuckles white on the rails. "Have you had anything for pain?" she asked.

He shook his head, and Mariam turned to Gwen. "Dr. Prince is hurting. Could you please give him something?"

"I'll check Dr. Keyes' orders." The nurse came around the stretcher, stopping to study Mariam, looking her up and down slowly, as if she were a specimen in a museum. "Dr. Prince talks much about you. It is true you are the richest woman in the city?"

Mariam felt her face flush. "Well, one of them I suppose."

Gwen smiled enigmatically and slipped out of the cubicle, pulling the curtain closed behind her. Still staring in that direction, Mariam commented, "Not very friendly, is she?"

"Ah, don't pay any attention to her," Roger said. "Gwen's got personal problems. Debt up to her armpits. Probably angry she has to stay late."

Mariam reached over and smoothed her husband's hair, rewarded with his contented sigh. His mouth pulled to one side in that impish grin Mariam loved so much. Despite being a respectable anesthesiologist, sometimes he seemed nothing more than a little boy. "So what's up, honey? Stomach ache you said?"

"Dan Keyes says appendicitis," Roger reported. "You just missed him. He rushed in between cases, felt my belly, and plans to take me to the O.R. at midnight. What time is it now?"

Mariam checked her watch. "Ten. When did you get sick?"

"Started this afternoon. At first I thought it was lunch – I brought in that left-over   casserole you made and thought it tasted funny. Maybe I shouldn't have left it out on the counter all morning. Anyway, shortly after eating I began feeling nauseous, vomited a few times. And now … under the knife I go."

She lowered herself into the worn-through fabric chair sitting by the stretcher. Taking a tissue from her purse she wiped off a light film of sweat from his brow. He smiled at her, closed his eyes, and settled back into his pillow. She loved his handsome face, from the crinkling of his eyes that had first attracted her, to the strong Harrison Ford chin. By the time she'd met Roger, six years ago, she'd given up on getting married. And then he came into her life. Like a prince in a fairy tale, he swept away nearly fifty years of loneliness. It'd only taken two dates, and she'd thrown all caution to the wind. Though nearly ten years her junior, with his sweet nature, appreciation of her lifestyle, and gentile manners, he was her Prince in more ways than just name.

A green flush washed through his cheeks, and he sat up, grabbed a blue bag, and vomited a few tablespoons of bile to the half cup already inside. Mariam grimaced and looked towards the curtain again. "What's taking that nurse so long?"

She rose and stepped around the stretcher, peeking out through a gap in the curtains. About a dozen yards away Gwen stood at the nursing station, locked in animated conversation with a dark-skinned woman sporting a fancy hairdo. Their faces were close, their voices hushed, and their looks furtive. The dark woman wrote furiously on a pad in front of her.

Mariam stepped out into the hallway and called, "Hey! Are you bringing Dr. Prince's pain medicine?" They startled apart, shoving the pad away. Mariam watched Gwen walk over to a machine and poke at the keypad. After it beeped, she pulled open its plastic door and extracted two bottles. The other woman started to say something, but Gwen shook her head and indicated toward Mariam with her eyes. Gwen fiddled with some materials at the work station, before heading back to the cubicle carrying a trio of syringes.

Mariam regained her post at Roger's right as Gwen, on his left, injected the medicine from one of the three syringes into his IV. Dropping the empty tube into a storage case behind her, she turned back to look down on Roger, her expression strangely haughty. "He sleep now."

Mariam watched, and, as promised, his expression softened, leaving behind a dreamy smile. His breathing slowed, and he seemed to be resting comfortably. She looked up at Gwen. "Thank you."

Gwen snorted, a single unpleasant syllable of derision. "No need to be grateful. I have my own agenda."

Mariam's attention shifted with the sound of the cubicle's curtain being thrown back. The other woman entered, her large hoop earrings dancing on either side of her brightly rouged cheeks. She held up a clipboard holding a stack of papers.

"You be Mister's wife, no?" she asked.

Mariam nodded, trying to analyze the woman's accent. She decided it might be Caribbean. "I'm Mrs. Prince, yes."

Mariam held out her hand as the woman approached, but instead of shaking it, the woman put the chart into it. "My name Raweena. Lady must sign these." There were a dozen forms, insurance information, hospital smoking policies, and such. Mariam scanned each one before signing, page after page. The last one was titled "Permission for Surgery," a long one with lots of fine print. Under "Risk of complications" a scrawled line read, "Bleeding, Allergic Reactions, and Death." Mariam looked up in alarm.

She saw Raweena staring down at Roger, a hateful expression distorting her face. Mariam reached up and touched Raweena's arm, and the clerk startled, quickly blanked her expression.

"Raweena, what's wrong?"

"Nothing, Lady." She took the chart and started to back away, but Mariam held her wrist.

"There's something more. Something personal. Please tell me."

Raweena looked at the ground a moment. When she turned her gaze back to Mariam, her lips were curled in anger. "You rich Lady, no can understand. Mister look at me, see only black skin. To Mister, we be insects, bugs you step on. Mean nothing."

Mariam recoiled at the viciousness in her voice. "What are you talking about? Roger's not prejudiced, certainly no racial bigot."

Raweena removed Mariam's hand and stepped back. "You have children, Lady?" she asked.

Mariam shook her head.

"I had three. Now one be gone."

Mariam watched Raweena squeeze her eyes tight, a hint of wetness forming on their edges, and the clerk raised her sleeve to wipe them.

"My son, B'sheetah, he would be four-year-old next month." She stopped, her eyes staring above Mariam's head. Mariam stood and stepped towards Raweena, but the clerk waved her off.

Softly, Mariam implored, "Tell me what happened, Raweena. Please."

The clerk took several slow breaths. When she spoke, her voice sounded distant, as if relating a ghost story. "Was two year ago, deep of winter. B'sheetah, he have ear infection. Many ear infection. Always sick; fever, crying. Doctor say get surgery. I bring him here."

She paused, and Mariam glanced at Gwen. The nurse stood quietly, her lips taut.

Raweena continued. "He go surgery. They say 'one hour.' One hour pass. Two. I wait here, this very room. Four hour. Finally your Mister come, take me small room. Tell me much hoo-hoo. B'sheetah have 'accident' he say. 'Accident?' No!"

She glared at Mariam. "Dead and buried now. B'sheetah's soul back with ancestors'." Raweena shook her fist at Roger. "You never pay for murder." She spat on the floor next to his stretcher and ground it with her shoe. "Murder," she murmured.

Mariam shuddered. Roger rarely talked about his work, and had never mentioned this case to her. "I'm certain this must have devastated Dr. Prince. I'm so sorry, Raweena."

"Sorry? Lady no understand sorrow. How you know, you with fancy jewels and satin dress? What you know of Raweena's life? Lady ever hide under bed, gunshots outside window? Lady ever sell herself so can feed children? Lady ever have Mister come home drunk and beat you for fun?"

Raweena glared at her. "Lady not sorry, but soon will be. Lady see Gwen and I talk? She no want tell you, but I say we must. Lady must know, or justice not done."

Gwen sighed. "Are you certain, Raweena? I still think we should just keep our mouths shut."

Raweena turned on her, her face twisted in anger. "No! Lady must know!" Raweena faced Mariam and sneered. "We plan revenge many, many months. Tonight, we kill Mister."

Mariam grabbed at her neck. She whispered, "What?"

"You think your husband has appendicitis, don't you?" Gwen asked with a smirk.

Mariam looked from one to the other but didn't answer.

Raweena put her head back and laughed, her harsh utterances bouncing off the walls. She stopped abruptly and turned her wide eyes at Mariam. "It not appendicitis. We poison Mister, and now he die!"

Mariam jumped up. "You … you're both crazy. I'm going to get some help." She started to run out, but Gwen called out.

"Hear us out. If you leave, he'll die."

Mariam turned, standing with her back to the curtain, eyeing them warily. "Go on then."

"Why don't you come sit down?" Gwen said, indicated the chair. Mariam shook her head and Gwen shrugged. "You've been married five years, Mrs. Prince?"

Mariam nodded. "About that."

"Did Roger ever tell you about his past sex life?"

Mariam felt resentment at her familiarity. "You should call him Dr. Prince. Of course we talked. He said he'd had a few girlfriends. Nothing serious. What are you getting at?"

Gwen laughed bitterly. "'Nothing serious,' he said? Well, Mrs. Prince. I was one of those 'nothing serious' women. Roger used me, told me he loved me, talked about marrying me. And then he met you, and *jetzt,* I am nothing to him. A used toy to be thrown away. Oh, and throw me away he did. Not answering my calls. Not giving me time of day. 'Get over it,' he said. Can you imagine, Mrs. Prince? 'Get over it,' as if a broken heart is like a stubbed toe."

She glared at Roger, her nostrils flared, her breath heavy. "So I pretend I was over it. But I planned. And I recruited a friend." Here she indicated Raweena whose face still held an angry glare.

"What are you trying to say?" Mariam whispered.

"We put arsenic in his lunch. You see, Mrs. Prince, acute arsenic poisoning mimics appendicitis. It causes vomiting and makes the belly very tender, just the same. When the surgeon cuts open your husband's belly, he's going to be surprised to find the appendix completely normal. Of course, then it will be too late. Roger will die on the table. Everyone will think it was just an accident, just one of those rare complications of surgery one can't predict. Like with Raweena's child. Clever isn't it? We'll get away with murder!"

Raweena spoke up, "Just like he murder my little B'sheetah."

Mariam felt her legs giving out and hurried over to collapse in the chair. She took a few deep breaths. Reaching over she stroked her husband's face. It had a gray pallor. "I don't believe you. This is utter nonsense. It has to be." She stood again. "Of course it is. You're just trying to scare me with this cock-and-bull story. Dr. Keyes is an experienced surgeon. He wouldn't be fooled. Besides, there must be lab tests."

Gwen shook her head. "The surgeon decided without tests. You saw me draw blood when you first came in. Lab tests don't prove appendicitis. But ... since you're still suspicious ...." She turned to Raweena. "Go see if the test results are back." Raweena nodded and walked out of the cubicle.

Mariam bent over her husband, gently pressing on his stomach. He moaned, but continued to sleep under the heavy sedation. She looked up when Raweena returned. The clerk shuffled through the paperwork and handed Gwen one of the sheets. The nurse laughed and held up the report.

"You want proof?" she asked. "Here!" She passed the page to Mariam.

Mariam read, its edges crumpling in her grip. "Arsenic level? You ran an arsenic level? Why would you do that? It will just incriminate you."

Gwen snorted. "Raweena will delete it from the system. We wanted to be sure the level was high enough to kill him. We just guess the dosage."

Mariam looked at the page again and the stated toxic dose. She calculated that his level was twenty times beyond the deadly limit. She jumped when Raweena jerked the page from her hands, leaving little slivers in each of her fists.

"So, you see, Mrs. Prince," Gwen continued. "We're perfectly serious. We both hate your husband, plot his death, and now we did it."

Mariam shook Roger's shoulder, but he didn't stir. She felt her heart pounding. Wetting her lips, she managed to ask, "What … why … why are you even telling me this?"

Raweena kept staring at her, but Gwen shuffled her feet before looking up again. "We weren't going to tell you. Probably shouldn't have. But I felt sorry for Raweena. She really does have a hard life. We decided that we'd give you a chance to buy your husband's life."

Mariam's eyes grew wide. "What are you talking about now?" She stood up again. "This is crazy. I'm going to go get some help. Now that I know what's wrong I'm sure a physician can cure him."

Gwen, standing behind the stretcher with Roger's IV tubing in one hand, held up two syringes in the other. "I recommend against leaving. In the smaller syringe, I have the antidote. In the other, enough medicine to kill him. You go along with us and Roger lives to get his normal appendix taken out. You cause trouble, he dies right here."

Mariam eyes widened. "How can you possibly think you'll get away with this? You think I won't report this whole thing to the police? This is absolutely absurd!"

"Oh, I no think Lady call police," Raweena said. "Lady no want to go to jail."

"Me?"

Raweena held up the lab report. "Arsenic. Police will say Lady poison Mister. It be in food he bring from home. That how we give poison. And we save meal. We give to police, they arrest Lady."

Mariam's mouth went dry, her head spinning. It seemed that these women had created the perfect trap. "How … how do I know your antidote will even work?" she whispered.

Gwen took the smaller syringe and injected some of its content into Roger's IV. "This should be enough for a few seconds," she said.

Roger moaned, his eyes flickering open. "Ow. My stomach!" He looked at Mariam. "Honey? What's going on?"

Mariam jumped up and leaned over him, kissing him repeated. She pulled back just a few inches, staring into his eyes as they closed again. "Roger! Roger! Can you hear me?" In a moment he was snoring again. Mariam put her head on the bed and sobbed.

Gwen cleared her throat. "Raweena and I want one million dollars apiece. She has an account in a Dominican bank where she's been sending money to her family. Hand her the information, Raweena." The clerk took a card out of her pocket and passed it to Mariam.

She stared at the card. "Two million dollars? Do you really think someone can come up with two million dollars in the middle of the night?"

"Roger loved to talk about the millions of dollars you move around the world. He said you could come up with as much money as you want any time, day or night." She held up the larger syringe and waved it back and forth. "Let's hope he was right."

Feeling dazed, Mariam took out her cell phone and popped it open. She looked from Raweena's cold stare to Gwen's smug grin. "How do I know you'll keep your end of the bargain?"

"I would rather have the money," Gwen said. "Revenge is sweet, but money better."

"And you?" Mariam asked, turning to Raweena.

Raweena tilted her head. "I have two other children, Lady. You pay Mister's ransom, I be satisfied."

Mariam pushed one of her phone's speed dial buttons. She listened to it ring. Once. Twice.

"Put it on speaker phone," Gwen ordered. Mariam complied. "Hello?"

Mariam held the phone in front of her. "Hello? Carl?"

"Mariam? Glad you called. Shame you had to leave the party so early. How's Roger?"

She glanced at the two women, both watching her closely. "Turns out to be his appendix. He'll be going under the knife soon."

"Appendicitis? Well, what do ya' know? You holding up okay?"

"That's a definite no." Mariam forced her hands to shop shaking. "Listen, Carl. Are you home yet?"

"Yeah. Left just after you. Got an early meeting tomorrow. I'm checking the Asian markets on my desktop before turning in. Sounds like you're on speaker phone. You alone?"

"No. Listen, Carl, I need you to play along with me a little, okay?" she pleaded. "Would it be possible to transfer two million dollars to a Dominican bank account tonight? Like right away?"

She waited, as his silence proved his hesitation. "Two million dollars? That's a lot of money. What's this about, Mariam?"

She squeezed the phone tightly as she forced out a semi-cheerful laugh. "Oh, it's the wildest thing. Roger made some sort of crazy commitment, and I've got to take care of it tonight. You know how he can be."

She listened to the extended silence from the other end. "It's due by midnight, Carl. You think you could possibly? You know I wouldn't ask if it weren't an emergency."

His answer came out in hesitated steps. "I don't think it can be done, Mariam. How about you come into the office tomorrow, and we'll talk about it."

Gwen cleared her throat and held up the larger syringe. "Make him do it," she said with a snarl.

Mariam took a deep breath. "Listen closely Carl. I need your help with this right now. Let's use the same money we were spending at the benefit tonight."

"That money?" The sounds of him taking several deep breaths came through the speaker phone. "You sure you want to use that money?"

"YES!" She shouted. "Now you're getting the idea. And, while you're at it, let's get the same people involved too. You know, the people who were benefiting."

"The same people, huh? And you're at the hospital with Roger now? I think I can handle it."

"Good." Mariam read the bank information to him from the card. "You got it, Carl?"

"Sure, I understand perfectly," he replied. "I'll make sure it gets done immediately."

"Oh, and send us a fax when the money is transferred, okay?" She looked at Gwen who told her the fax number, which she relayed over the phone.

"Right. And Mariam ... be careful." He clicked off.

Gwen laughed and even Raweena smiled. "You did good, Lady."

"So now what?" Mariam asked.

"You give us your phone and we wait."

Mariam handed it over and sat down again, stroking Roger's hand. She checked her watch, reading eleven-thirty. She'd only been here an hour and a half, yet it seemed like a lifetime. She closed her eyes, fighting exhaustion. "What next?" she asked.

"We get the confirmation," Gwen said, "and I give Roger the antidote. He goes to surgery, he wakes up, everything is just as it was."

Mariam's eyes snapped open and she sat up. "You think it will be over? You think you can keep on working here, that life will go on as before, except you'll each be a million dollars richer?"

The two other women shared a glance. "I guess we hadn't really thought about it," Gwen said. "The original plan ... well. I don't know. But, with a million dollars, what difference will it make if we have to leave? We can settle elsewhere. I might even go back to Slovakia."

"And how do you plan on collecting your million?" Mariam asked.

Gwen glanced at Raweena who seemed to be studying her nails.

"It's all going to be in Raweena's hands, isn't it?" Mariam observed. "Her account in the Dominican bank. I don't see you ever getting your hands on any of that money, Gwen. Isn't that right, Raweena?"

Gwen's eyes narrowed. "You wouldn't hold out on me now, would you girl?"

Raweena looked at her and smiled. "We be buddies, Gwen."

"You better not." Gwen started chewing on her lip, fiddling uncomfortably with the syringes in her hands. "You just better not. I would give you regrets."

They sat in silence, Mariam slumped in the chair, Raweena leaning against the wall by the curtain, and Gwen holding the syringes and the IV. Eventually the sound of the fax machine penetrated the curtain. "I go," Raweena said, and slipped out. She returned in a moment, her smile stretching cheek to cheek. "Look!

We got money!" She handed the paper to Gwen whose stern face also broke into a grin. Just for a moment.

"So now you'll give Roger the antidote?" Mariam asked.

Gwen laughed. "Antidote? You are a little fool. This isn't an antidote to arsenic poisoning." She held up the two syringes. "The smaller one is called Narcan. When I gave a little to Roger it reverses his sedation, though it wears off quickly. No effect otherwise. This other syringe just holds saline."

"But …" Marian pointed. "The arsenic?"

Raweena laughed, her deep tones echoing off the cubicle's walls. "Arsenic? Where we get arsenic? Lady be silly."

Mariam gripped the rails in front of her. "I bet you never even lost a child."

Raweena's eyes lit up. "Clever story, no?"

"And I never slept with Dr. Prince," Gwen said. "Raweena and I improvised. I thought up the plan when you show up in all that jewelry. Your husband has appendicitis, nothing more. But now Raweena and I are millionaires, and you can't prove a thing, other than that you felt generous and gave us a big tip for taking such good care of him! Isn't that a great joke?"

Raweena held up the paper with the crumpled edges. "And arsenic test? I fake it."

The two women turned at the sound of the curtain being pulled back. Three police officers stood there, each with a hand on his holstered gun. "You all right, Mrs. Prince?" one of them asked.

She stood up and walked rapidly over to them. "Thank God, yes."

Gwen stared at her. "What? How did you arrange this?"

It was Mariam's turn to laugh. "The function I came from tonight was the Policeman's Ball. When I told Carl I wanted their help, I'm sure he called them immediately. By the way, we were using fake money at a mock gambling function there, so I'm afraid your two million dollars doesn't exist."

Gwen held up the fax. "But …"

Mariam smiled. "Clearly Raweena isn't the only one who can fake paperwork. I'll take my phone back now, please."

One of the policemen took out his handcuffs and Raweena stepped away. "I do nothing!"

"I think the judge may disagree with you," Miriam said. "Extortion is illegal in this country."

A couple of young men in red scrubs walked into the room. "We're here to take Dr. Prince to the O.R. if that's okay?" one asked.

"Yes, of course," Mariam answered. "Let's get that appendix out!"

Appendicitis

Typically, appendicitis develops quickly, within twelve hours from onset of a vague bellyache until severe pain, and, if ignored, may go on to rupture. There are great variations in the disease process, both in presentation and in speed of deterioration. In my early years as an E.R. doctor, before CAT scan proof of disease became the standard of care, surgeons made their decision whether to operate based on clinical presentation. About one fourth of the time, the appendix was normal, the pain being from some other source.

I had appendicitis at age 55. On a week's sojourn in NYC, one with a fancy dinner and a Broadway Show scheduled for each night, I began feeling ill at 9 p.m., and by 7 a.m. my companion helped me into a taxi, asking the driver to take us to the nearest hospital. The diagnosis was made without any fancy tests, and by noon I was on the operating table. The procedure went so smoothly that at 7 a.m. the next morning I walked out of the hospital.

Poisoning with arsenic is always a favorite murder mystery technique. It's actually very easy to diagnose at autopsy, so if you're planning on using it, I recommend you be sure you can blame someone else, like in this story. As an E.R. doctor, I know of dozens of ways to kill people, as you'll see in this collection. So, a word of advice. Better say only good things about my book because, who knows, you might end up on my stretcher someday.

Quinn

With one hand on the cubicle's sliding door, Joyce paused to calm her pounding heart. So angry! How could he sleep with Rita? Apparently he couldn't resist her big tits. *Goddamn him.*

She took a deep breath. Checking her watch, she saw it was just shy of midnight. *How am I ever going to deal with seven more hours of this shift?*

Slipping into the room, she forced herself to smile at the young woman dressed in jeans and a button-down shirt. She wore little make-up, just some lipstick and blush. Joyce placed her in her mid-twenties, maybe five years younger than herself. The mother cooed softly to the Sesame Street wrapped bundle in her arms.

"Good evening, I'm Joyce. I'll be your nurse today." She touched the mother's shoulder and peeked into her baby's face. He slept, masked with the peaceful expression of the innocent.

Mom looked up at Joyce and smiled. "Hi, I'm Patty, and this is Randy. He'll be two-months-old next Saturday." She turned back to the baby, love in her voice. "Say 'Hello' to Miss Joyce, Randy."

Joyce pulled out her pen, ready to make notes on Randy's chart. "You're his mother then? What's going on with Randy?"

Patty glanced at Joyce before gazing again into the baby's face. The child slept on. "He had a cold last week, though he seemed to be getting better until this afternoon. When I picked him up from my mom's house after work, she told me he wasn't eating. He took less than half an ounce at six, refusing even sugar water at nine." Her brow wrinkled in puzzlement. "I hate to be a nervous first-time mom, but something just doesn't seem right."

Joyce made notes. "Stays with your mother, huh?"

Patty sighed. "Randy's father is out of the picture – the bastard."

Joyce put down the chart and placed her hand on Patty's shoulder. "Oh, I'm sorry. You want to tell me what happened?"

"It's an old story. He said he loved me, but once I got pregnant, he realized maybe I wasn't the right one after all. One day I found out he had screwed my best friend and I told him to get lost."

Joyce snorted. "Men! The fellow I've been with the last few months just did the same thing to me! Of course, I wasn't pregnant like you. Still, I know how that hurts."

"No! Well, Miss Joyce, sounds like we're going to be friends."

They laughed and Joyce picked up the chart again.

Joyce looked at the child's vital signs. Fever of one hundred and two was common this time of year; lots of kids with colds and flu. "When was the last time you gave Randy medicine for his fever?"

"He took a little ibuprofen at six, but wouldn't take anything when I tried at nine."

"Let's get Randy out of that blanket, okay?" Joyce suggested.

When laid onto the stretcher, Randy let out a weak cry. Joyce noticed a bluish tinge to his tiny hands and feet. Taping the monitor lead to his toe, she recorded his slightly low oxygen reading onto the chart. She hooked up a nail-sized tubing to the oxygen jet on the wall and gently fitted its plastic prongs into his nose.

Patty held the baby's arm as Joyce started an IV and filled some small tubes with his blood. As they worked together they talked, Patty telling of her work as a legal secretary, Joyce of how she'd been a nurse for seven years, but only in the E.R. for two.

"You like your work?" the mother asked.

Joyce forced a smile. "I usually do. Sort of having a hard time concentrating tonight. See, I just found out about him and Rita an hour ago." She felt herself welling up and turned away. Patty placed her hand on Joyce's shoulder.

"This too will pass."

"Thanks. I know it will. Just, I thought we had something going these last five months. We were talking long term plans, you know, maybe eventual marriage. But if you can't trust someone, what's the point?"

Patty nodded. "Can I hold him?" she asked, pointing to her baby.

"Yes, of course." Joyce helped bundle him up and Patty cuddled him lovingly.

"What do you think's wrong with my baby?"

Joyce gave her a reassuring smile. "Lots of babies run fever; could be anything. Doctor Quinn will be here in a few minutes."

"What's the doctor like?" Patty asked. "What? You just got the strangest expression."

Joyce cleared her features. "Sorry, still upset about my personal life."

"Hey, we're friends now, Miss Joyce. Is there something you're not telling me?"

Joyce forced herself to smile. "No, really. Quinn's a fine doctor."

"Is this Quinn the guy who cheated on you?"

Misery draining the light from her eyes, Joyce nodded.

Patty stomped her foot. "I don't want that S.O.B. taking care of my baby!"

Joyce forced a smile. "He's a good doctor. Really. This is just a personal thing between him and me."

"Would you let him take care of YOUR baby?"

A dreamy look settled into Joyce's eyes. "Just last week, after, you know, while cuddling, we talked about having some babies. He's so kind to the kids here. Sometimes he even acts like one."

"Sounds like you really love him."

Joyce shook her head. "Loved. Past tense."

Patty extended her arm and drew Joyce into a three-way hug.

"Maybe you should go home?" Patty asked.

Joyce shook her head. "Only two nurses tonight, just me and Becky. I'll be all right in a moment." She hurried out of the room and down the hall. Locking herself in the restroom, she startled at the face staring back from the mirror; red eyes, wrinkled brow, and pinched lips. *No wonder he's grown tired of me.*

When she returned to the central area, she found Quinn leaning against the counter, talking with the new ward clerk. Joyce studied him, his athletic build, thick curly black hair, and piercing eyes. So handsome. So skilled. So self-absorbed. The young clerk clearly was enthralled.

Joyce came up behind him and spoke near his ear. "New patient in Pedi-5."

He glanced at her. "Moment." He turned back to the clerk. "You understand what I'm ordering now? C.T. with and without contrast, abdomen and pelvis, on Miss Trevino in Med-12. Got that?"

Joyce watched him lower his hand to rest on her shoulder. The girl noticed too, touching it there lightly as she looked up at him and smiled. "Oh yes, Doctor Quinn. I'll be happy to do it for you."

He stepped away and took the chart out of Joyce's hands. "What's up with the baby?" With his free hand he reached to touch her arm, but she stepped back.

"Eight-week-old with fever of 102. I started an IV and drew blood." She showed him the tubes.

"Okay, let's go."

He carried the chart as he led her down the hall. She came up close behind him and whispered in his ear, "'Oh yes, Doctor Quinn, I'll be happy to DO IT for you.' Now what do you suppose she was thinking about?"

Quinn stopped abruptly and turned to her, his face grim. "She's only a teenager. Come on, Joyce. I messed up. I admit it. I said I was sorry. Give me a break."

She glared at him. "You messed up? Is that what you want to call screwing around? You tell me you're at a medical meeting when really you're out boinking Rita."

"It was a medical meeting. Afterwards we went out for drinks and got carried away. I told you I was sorry. You know Rita doesn't mean anything to me."

Joyce kept her face stony. Through clenched teeth she said, "Just go see this baby."

Joyce slid the door shut behind them, following Quinn with his grand presence. He flashed that huge smile, the one that brought out his dimples and crinkled his nose. *He thinks he's so cute.*

"I'm Doctor Quinn. You must be Randy's mother?"

"Patricia Tucker." She nodded a stiff greeting, cuddling her infant in both arms.

"Joyce tells me he's got a bit of a fever. Let's see what we can find."

Joyce closed her eyes, savoring the rich sounds of his confident voice. She had fallen in love with its deep timbre the first time she heard it. She shuddered, thinking of him using it with Rita.

Quinn paused to splash his hands at the sink, asking Patty to lay the baby on the examining table. He applied his stethoscope to the child's front and back, looked in his ears, and prodded the boy all over. While he worked he talked with the mother. Joyce watched his face; his compelling half smile never wavered. The way he moved his hand or tossed his head flashed images in her brain: Quinn standing naked in her bedroom or in a robe on her balcony, a drink in hand, looking at the stars. She felt her heart lurch.

When he'd finished examining the child, he returned to the sink and scrubbed his hands again. He turned to Joyce, making sure she was ready, and rattled off a string of orders. She wrote them on the chart as he dictated. When he finished, she passed it over to him to review. Quinn studied what was there, scribbled some notes, signed it, and handed the chart back to Joyce.

Turning to Patty he said, "One of the usual tests on babies this young is a spinal tap. Basically it's similar to a blood test, but instead of putting a needle in a vein, I'll place one into Randy's spinal canal. I'll only take a few drops of spinal fluid."

The mother tented her brows and turned to Joyce. "What does that mean?"

Joyce stepped forward and took her hand. "Doctor Quinn will put a tiny needle in Randy's lower back. It'll be okay, Patty; I've seen him do it before. I'll bring a permission slip for you to sign which includes a diagram of what he's doing and why."

Patty let loose of Joyce's hands and picked up Randy, cuddling him lovingly. "Is that test absolutely necessary?"

Quinn studied her, his lips pursed. "I think it is."

Joyce laid her hand gently on Patty's arm. "Doctor Quinn wouldn't do anything to hurt your baby."

She frowned at Joyce. "No? He hurt you didn't he?"

Joyce lowered her gaze to her feet and took a breath. "That was personal." She looked up, her eyebrows knitted. "Doctor Quinn is an excellent doctor. If he says this needs to be done, then you have to trust him."

Patty searched Joyce's face, and the nurse smiled gently. The mother nodded and turned to Quinn. "I want to be here."

Quinn glanced at Joyce before answering. "Usually I don't have mothers in the room for this procedure. Are you sure you want to watch me put a needle in your son?"

Patty cocked her head. "Why not? I held him while Miss Joyce did it."

Quinn grimaced. "Okay, you can watch if you'd like. I'll be back once Joyce gets everything set up." He left the room. After reassuring Patty once more, Joyce followed.

He was waiting for Joyce just down the hall. "What the hell did you tell that mother?"

Joyce's face flushed, and she stared at the floor. "I'm sorry, Quinn."

He put his hand under her chin, lifting her face until their eyes met. "You can't be talking me down to the patients. Let's keep our personal life out of this."

She smiled weakly. "I said I was sorry. It won't happen again."

Quinn looked deep into her eyes until Joyce had to close her own. "Familiar words," he murmured. "Didn't I just say them to you?"

She stepped back, anger flushing her cheeks. "Don't even go there."

Quinn's hands curled into fists, slowly relaxing again. "Okay. Let's just get through this. Let me know when you've got everything ready."

She followed him into the nursing station where he turned to the other nurse. "Becky, is that pelvic ready yet?"

"Just about. Give me a few minutes and I'll have her in the stirrups."

"Okay, I'll be there in five." He pulled another chart out of the rack and rifled through the lab reports on it. Becky went to set up her patient, and Joyce gathered the paperwork and equipment she needed for the spinal tap.

She explained the procedure to Patty, showing her the diagrams, and having her sign the form.

"I'm not really that worried about the procedure," Patty said. "I just have bad feelings about this guy 'cause of the way he treated you."

Joyce shook her head. "Actually he's very nice. It's just that…" Joyce closed her eyes, bowing her head over the sink. A single tear rolled off her nose and down the drain. "I feel so … betrayed."

"Men! When they cheat, you gotta get rid of them."

"I wish I could, but I have to work with him. Now, tomorrow, next week, next month, next year. I've got to see him smile at other women, and watch them fawn all over him, and wonder why the hell I ever fell in love with him in the first place."

"And are you still in love with him?"

Joyce looked out towards the hallway, to somewhere out there where every day Quinn brought comfort to a sufferer, hope to the ill, and sometimes even saved a life. It wasn't just his being a doctor that made her head swoon, or his amazing charm and good looks. It was the way he had always treated her, valued her, made her feel as if she was the most important person in the world to him. She'd given her heart to this man, believed in him as her shining knight, her perfect match.

She turned her focus back to Patty. "Yes, I still love him. Yet, right now, I hate him, too. Oh my God, it hurts."

She wiped her eyes with a paper towel and took a deep breath, forcing herself to smile. "But none of that matters right now. What's important is that we think about Randy, and get him better. I'll tell Doctor Quinn that we're ready."

When Joyce left the room, she found Quinn, Becky, and Charlotte, the aide, in Med-10 taking care of an elderly man in heart failure. She slipped into the room, helped start an IV, and mentioned to Quinn that the spinal tap tray was ready. He grunted his acknowledgement as he concentrated on the current crisis. Joyce went back to the nursing station and took the opportunity to catch up on some paperwork left over from an earlier patient.

About an hour later, after dealing with a couple of other patients, Quinn told Joyce he was ready. They entered Pedi-5 and Quinn donned the sterile gloves Joyce had set out on top of the tray.

"You sure you want to stay for this?" he asked Patty.

She nodded and backed into a corner, out of the way, but still able to watch the action. Joyce sat the baby up, holding him curled forward so his back arched towards Quinn. He painted the child's lower spine area with orange Betadine, applied sterile drapes, and picked up the long spinal needle.

He glanced at Patty who nodded. After injecting a wheal of numbing medicine, Quinn guided the metal tube into the space between the backbones. In a few seconds he was rewarded with the return of a lightly milky fluid.

He glanced up at Joyce, whose eyes grew large. Quinn let two drops fall into each of four small test tubes. He sealed them and withdrew the needle, cleaning the wound and applying a Band-Aid. He handed Joyce the tubes and snapped off his gloves.

"That wasn't so bad," Patty said.

"Miss Tucker," he said slowly, "Randy's spinal fluid should have been crystal clear. Instead it looks a little cloudy."

"And what does that mean?"

Quinn's face tightened in concern. "We'll have to wait for the laboratory to look at it under the microscope, but it might mean there's infection in the spinal fluid."

She titled her head. "What are you saying?"

"Infection in the spinal fluid is very serious. Fortunately, I've already had Joyce give Randy antibiotics, so that will help." He glanced over at Joyce who had turned pale.

Quinn's frown stiffened. "We'll be back in a bit, Miss Tucker. I'll need to call the neonatologist – that's the specialist for infants. Joyce, please talk to me when you're done here."

He grabbed the four tubes with the child's spinal fluid and exited the room, leaving Joyce to clean up the tray. She cautiously sifted through the instruments, picking up the needles and placing them in the thick-walled red disposer.

"Hey, Miss Joyce, what's going on?" the baby's mother asked.

Joyce folded up the rest of the tray as she explained. "Doctor Quinn is concerned that your baby might have a very serious infection called meningitis. I need to run out and get some antibiotics for him. I'll be right back."

She slipped out of the room and hurried to the chart rack, finding that the slot for the Tucker chart empty. Turning around she saw Quinn studying it. He glanced up at her, his expression grim.

"Could we talk in private a moment, please?" he asked.

She nodded, and followed him into an empty exam room where he shut the door. He shook the chart at her.

"Did you forget to document when you gave the antibiotics?" he asked, his eyes drilling into her.

Joyce cringed. "I wrote down every order you gave me. You never said a word about antibiotics."

He pointed to where he'd written an order for Rocephin, a strong antibiotic. "Didn't you see this?"

She stared, feeling her face flush in horror. "When did you write that? Just now?"

"WHAT? Are you accusing me of falsifying records? I wrote this in the room when I first saw the child."

Joyce felt her heart pound. She remembered him scribbling on the chart, but thought they'd only been notes. Had she missed a critical order?

"I … I don't remember seeing this."

"Hell. It's been over an hour. Timely antibiotics are critical for an infant with meningitis. You know that. What the hell is wrong with you?"

"You Son of a Bitch! What do you THINK is wrong with me? We had five months of happiness, long enough to let down my barriers and trust you. Then you go off and fuck Rita. You're a filthy BASTARD!" She used her sleeve to wipe at the tears streaming down her cheeks.

Quinn stepped back, holding up his hands. "Joyce! Stop it. I messed up. We all make mistakes. We can talk about that after work. But, Good God, this is a baby with meningitis! Go get that Rocephin and …"

The ward clerk's voice on the overhead intercom interrupted. "Doctor Quinn, you're needed in Pedi-5 stat."

The two rushed out the door and down the hall into the baby's room. Randy was seizing, Becky and Charlotte holding him against the stretcher. The baby's little arms and legs shook in rhythmic fashion, his eyes jerked up into his skull. His skin turned blue as his diaphragm spasmed preventing it from bringing in oxygen.

"Give him a half milligram of Versed, stat," shouted Quinn. "Bring the Broselow Tape and the pedi crash cart. Now!" He turned to Patty. "Maybe you better wait outside."

"No, I don't think so," she said, jutting her chin defiantly.

Joyce stepped up and took her hand, turning to face Quinn. "She stays."

Quinn grunted and turned to the cart the aide had just rolled in. He snapped off the plastic locks and grabbed the tiniest intubation equipment. The laryngoscope blade was as small as a wood screw, the tube like a coffee stirrer. Becky returned with the Versed, injecting it in the IV. The seizures stopped. A respiratory therapist arrived and began preparing his equipment.

Quinn looked over to Joyce, still standing against the wall holding Patty's hand. "Why don't you make yourself useful and go get those antibiotics?" he snapped. "And have the ward clerk call the neonatologist stat."

Joyce couldn't release her stare into Patty's eyes. The mother dropped Joyce's hand and gave her a push. "Go."

Joyce rushed out of the room and into the nursing station, jabbing at the buttons on the medication machine with trembling hands. She kept messing up the codes, managing to get the drawer open on the fourth attempt.

She grabbed the bottle, but it slipped out of her hand, crashing against the wall. Praying it hadn't broken, she rushed over and scooped it up, examining it carefully for cracks. Finding none she resumed breathing.

Joyce pulled down the small saline bag she needed. Forcing her hand to be steady, she measured the exact dose into a syringe and transferred the medication into the bag, giving the fluid a yellow hue.

Looking around the station Joyce noted that everyone but the ward clerk was in with Quinn. Dressed in a magenta jumpsuit, the teenager sat with the phone in one ear while keeping one eye on the monitors. Joyce called out, and the girl glanced at her, mumbled into the phone, and hung it up.

"You need something, Joyce?"

"Doctor Quinn wants the neonatologist stat," she called. "Intercom into Pedi-5 when he answers, please."

She rushed back into the room to find the respiratory therapist pumping oxygen into the mask he held against the baby's face. Joyce looked up to the monitor, noting that the baby's heart rate raced at hummingbird's cadence.

Quinn hunched near the boy, watching the oxygen readings creep upward. 85%. 90%. 92%.

"Good enough," Quinn said. The therapist took the mask away and Quinn bent over the boy's mouth, searching the back of that tiny cave for the eighth of an inch opening to Randy's windpipe.

"This was easier on the kittens," Quinn muttered.

Joyce had only seen an infant's intubation once before, eight years ago when she was a student. That time had been by an anesthesiologist who specialized in newborns. She watched Quinn struggle.

"Don't worry," Joyce said to Patty as they grabbed each other's hands. "Quinn's the best."

Patty pulled her into a tight hug and whispered in her ear. "It's his third try."

Joyce gasped involuntarily and turned to watch Quinn. Sweat beaded across his forehead. He dropped back, indicating for the technician to resume the bagging.

"Damn it! Where's the cavalry?" He turned to Joyce. "You did remember to call the neonatologist and the anesthesiologist didn't you?"

Joyce shook her head. "I told the clerk to call the neonatologist, but you didn't say anesthesiologist. You want me to do that now?"

His shoulders drooped. "I didn't ask for the anesthesiologist? Oh God. Okay, I'll give it one last shot then we'll page her stat."

He pointed to Joyce's hand. "Could you please start those antibiotics?"

She looked down, startled to realize she still held the bag. Jumping across the room, she slipped the needle of her medication into the baby's IV. "Antibiotics running," she called. Becky, standing in the corner with the chart, repeated the words as she noted the time on the medical record.

Quinn nodded to the respiratory therapist who backed away, giving the physician his space. Joyce held her breath, counting the seconds to herself.

One. Two. Three. She glanced at the monitor, watching the oxygen level fall.

Six, seven, eight. How long dare he go without pumping oxygen into the baby?

Eleven, twel' ...

"I'm in," Quinn announced.

The therapist confirmed the placement, and took control of the baby's respiratory needs. The clerk's voice came on the intercom, announcing that the neonatologist was on the phone.

Quinn's face lifted. "Cavalry on the way!" He nodded to the nurses, "Hold the ship steady, mates. I'm going to take this one in my cubby." He grabbed the chart and strode out of the room.

Becky looked at Joyce who shifted her eyes to the door. She took the hint. "Call if you need me." Having attached the ventilator, the technician followed her out, leaving just the two women with the baby.

Patty pulled Joyce into a tight hug. She whispered, "Is my baby going to die?"

Joyce held close, struggling to keep her sobs in check. Quinn's infidelity seemed meaningless in the face of Randy's problems, of Patty's heartaches. She whispered back, "I don't know, Patty. I trust Quinn."

Patty leaned away to look into her eyes. "You really trust this man?"

Joyce's stomach squeezed. "As a doctor? Absolutely. He's the best." She broke from Patty and went over to Randy, placing her stethoscope on his heart and lungs, checking his reflexes. He seemed to be sleeping comfortably.

Quinn came back in the room, his eyes shining. "Neonatologist happens to be in the house – says he'll be right down. Becky's bringing in the loading dose of Phenobarbital he ordered."

He checked out the baby again, and turned to Patty. "Miss Tucker, I know how worried you must be about Randy. I promise you we have done everything we can, and we'll continue to do so. In just a few minutes the specialist will be here. If you have any questions at any time, both Joyce and I will be here until seven in the morning. Do you have anything you want to ask right now?"

Patty looked at him, her eyes narrowed. "You swear you've done everything you could?"

Joyce held her breath as she watched Quinn. His expression never changed. "Yes, Miss Tucker. Everything."

"Yet, a few minutes after you stuck a needle in my baby's back he had a seizure. I can't help but think there's a connection."

Quinn shook his head. "I can see why you might think that, but I assure you, the seizure was due to the infection, not to the spinal tap." He stepped forward, offering his hands to her.

She stared at them, and then looked up into his eyes. He smiled, comfortingly, hopefully. She took his hands and held them. "Pray for my son, Doctor Quinn."

He nodded and gave her hands a gentle squeeze.

Becky came in with the dose of medicine. "Doctor Quinn," she called. "The patient in Med-10 has a pressure of seventy. Can you get over there?"

He nodded and slipped out of the room. After attaching the little container of medicine, Becky followed him.

Moments later, the neonatologist entered. Tall and lanky, he wore a tie decorated with Disney characters, Mickey and Donald cavorting on a field of pansies. He introduced himself to Patty and examined Randy as he listened to Joyce give a brief rundown on what had been done so far. An NICU nurse dressed in bright pink scrubs wheeled in an isolation unit.

Patty asked, "Is my baby going to be okay?"

The neonatologist raised his bushy eyebrows in uncertainty. "Babies are pretty resilient. The next twenty-four hours will be crucial, but we may not know if there's any long-term complications for a couple of months."

"Months?" Patty's eyes squeezed shut. "You mean he's going to have to be in the hospital for months?"

The physician scratched his ear. "We'll see. Too soon to really predict."

Patty picked up Randy, hugging him tightly. "What's the worst scenario?"

The doctor hesitated and reached to touch Patty lightly on the shoulder. "Children with meningitis sometimes have serious complications, ranging from simple deafness to severe mental retardation. As I said, time will tell." He held out his arms and Patty reluctantly handed Randy to the physician who placed him in the isolation carriage.

Patty turned to Joyce, and pulled her into a hug. Joyce rubbed her back as the mother sobbed quietly.

The NICU nurse and the doctor wheeled Randy out the door, with Joyce and Patty right behind. Just outside the door, Joyce spotted Becky charting at the station.

"Can you spare me for a few more minutes?" she asked Becky. "I'd like to go with them upstairs."

Becky looked at the tracking board. "Suppose. We've only got three patients, but don't be gone too long."

At the door of the NICU, the neonatologist paused a moment for Patty to kiss Randy. She laid him back in the transporter and watched the NICU doors close behind him. Joyce led her into the nearby waiting room, where a few other parents were watching FOX news, reading a rumpled magazine, or stretched out on blankets on the floor. The two women sat next to each other and held hands.

"I'll need to get back to the E.R. in just a moment," Joyce said. "Is there anything you need before I go?"

Patty leaned across the chair arms and hugged her. "Thank you for being here, Miss Joyce. It's as if God delivered you to help me through this crisis. If it weren't for you, I'd be a screaming nut right now."

Joyce returned the squeeze. "God works in mysterious ways, you know. This crisis has given me a different perspective on my own problems; that's for sure."

The television's drone and a sleeper's snore provided a dull background to the darkened room. Crumpled fast food bags and a half-made jigsaw puzzle occupied a table in the corner. The smell of cleaning products competed with that from body odors permeating the room. There was a feel of bored terror here, the dull fright of prolonged unknown outcomes. The parents waited, camped out, hoping that their babies would get better, would somehow overcome the odds and heal enough to graduate home. Or perhaps die. Either way would be better than sitting in purgatory.

Joyce started to get up and Patty grabbed her hands. "Please. You have to tell me one more thing before you leave. Was Quinn telling the truth? Did he really do everything he could?"

Joyce collapsed slowly back into her seat. She found her tongue wouldn't work. Finally she croaked out, "Yes."

Patty stared into her face. "You promise?"

Joyce closed her eyes and took a deep breath. She opened them slowly and forced herself to return the mother's gaze. "Yes, Quinn did everything right." She dropped her eyes to her hands clenched tightly in her lap.

Patty laid her hand on Joyce's. "What aren't you telling me?"

Joyce thought back to those moments when Quinn had scribbled on the baby's chart. She looked into Patty's eyes, not wanting to tell, but knowing if she didn't she'd never be able to live with herself.

"Remember when Doctor Quinn first saw the baby? He gave me some orders which I wrote down. Well, later he wrote an order for antibiotics, and I didn't see it. So an hour passed when Randy could have been getting the needed medicine. It's my fault – all mine, not Quinn's."

Patty stood, turned away, and walked to the door. Joyce watched her stare down the hallway to the NICU entrance. Joyce came up behind her and placed her hand on Patty's shoulder.

Patty continued to look down the hallway. "An hour without antibiotics, and then my baby had a seizure." She turned to look at Joyce. Her expression seemed blank, as if in shock. "Would that hour have made a difference?"

Joyce bit her lip. "I ... I really don't know." She felt her heart pounding, tears blurring her vision.

Patty took her in both arms and hugged her tightly. "My baby. My sweet baby. Pray for my child, Miss Joyce." They held that hug for a baby's eternity.

Joyce murmured, "I wish I could stay, but they need me downstairs."

"Yes, of course."

Joyce stepped back and looked into Patty's tear-filled eyes. "I can't ask you to forgive me. All I can do is say I'm sorry."

Patty tilted her head and let a feeble smile come to her sad face. "Thank you for telling me, Miss Joyce. Knowing the truth is the first step towards forgiveness."

Joyce closed her eyes, images of her months with Quinn flashing through her memory. Kind and brilliant at work, around her apartment he was gracious and funny. And in bed, ah, in bed, so gentle and loving. He had cheated on her, but ... he had promised to never do it again.

Joyce took Patty's hands for one last moment, one last smile. Turning, she hurried down the hallway.

Meningitis

Prior to the introduction of the H. flu vaccine in December 1987, bacterial meningitis struck infants frequently, their immune systems too immature to fight off the infection. Perhaps weekly I performed a spinal tap on an infant with fever, often admitting these little tykes to the NICU for a twenty-four-hour observation, even when their taps came back clear. For those children who we did discharge, it became routine to administer a dose of Rocephin to any child under six months with fever, just as a precaution.

The H. flu vaccine changed all that. While other causes of meningitis still strike, such as meningococcal and certain viruses, in the past twenty years I've needed to tap fewer than five infants. Prophylactic Rocephin shots have also gone by the wayside. Still, meningitis does exist and, as in this case, can often follow a routine infection from which the child seemed to be recovering. When Meningococcal meningitis strikes, nowadays more often in adults, all the medical personnel exposed to the patient will take prophylactic antibiotics, typically just one pill.

Even though soap operas portray the hospital setting as a hothouse of passion, relationships between doctors and nurses are as typical as relationships between any other co-workers. Sometimes people who work together fall in love. Sometimes lovers make mistakes. In the emergency room, nurses and doctors mustn't let their personal issues distract them, though, of course, we'll all only human. I remember one time when one E.R. doctor's husband was having an affair with a nurse. That E.R. doctor found she couldn't work, missed some shifts, and eventually was fired. Ten years later the husband (an Internist) was still on duty and still propositioning nurses.

Take Your Medicine

Cynthia felt her heart lurch when she read the name on the next chart: Tom Reynolds. She realized she hadn't seen her ex-husband since she'd him committed to the state hospital six years before. She'd remarried, this time to a stable man – dull perhaps, but stable.

She peeked around the cubicle's curtain to study Tom. Her ex-, who once had been so handsome with his crew-cut and bare chin, now showed the ravages of his disease. His scraggly facial hair and tangled locks tumbled to his shoulders in a dangerous, dirty look. Scratches marred his face and arms, deep self-inflicted wounds that oozed around the scabs.

He looked up at her and smiled, showing teeth yellowed and rotten. Yet despite all this, despite the hair and the scars and the wounded smile, she still felt her heart race at seeing him again, at remembering how he used to look, at how much she had loved him. At nineteen he had shown none of these problems. They'd attended school together, he for his degree in computer graphics, and she for hers in nursing. Now she had her nurse practitioner degree while he was down and out.

She pulled the curtain closed behind her and leaned against the wall. "Hello Tom."

"Hey there, beautiful. You're a doc now, huh?"

She shook her head. "Still just a nurse." She glanced at the IV running vitamin-enriched fluids into his emaciated body. Now thin and tortured, she remembered when those arms had been muscular, holding her tenderly.

He laughed. "I figure you'll be running the show soon enough."

She checked the level of the IV bag, half infused already. "What are you doing these days?"

"Live high on the government, that's my fortune. Got my own place, just off the wharf, don't you know; complete with lumpy mattress, broken toilet, and all the roaches and rats you can catch. You should visit some time."

Cynthia closed her eyes, trying to block out the images. When he'd first developed the schizophrenia, she freaked out, frightened by his screaming at the hallucinations, the weird pacing and gesticulations. Despite how much it hurt her to do so, she had turned him out, "for the safety of their child."

"I'm sorry, Tom. Truly sorry."

He grimaced and looked away. "I suppose I was hard to live with." When he looked back at her she recognized the familiar twinkle in his eyes. "Tell me about Brent."

She took out her cell phone and pulled up a photo. "Look. He's into baseball now; plays in the church league." She watched him studying the picture, the broken-tooth smile coming easily to his lips. Though most people said Brent looked just like his mother, that was because they'd never seen his real father. Tom handed the phone back to her.

"How are you doing, Tom?" she asked.

He shook his head. "Not so good. The voices are pretty strong these days. Aliens, don't you know. They're eating me." He held out his arms, pointing to all the scratches. "See?"

She ran her finger gently along the scabs and fresh cuts. "Tom, you're doing this to yourself. It's called formication, the feeling of bugs crawling under the skin."

He laughed. "Sounds like fornication. Remember those days? You were one sexy bitch, by golly."

Cynthia felt her cheeks flush. "Stop that, Tom. I'm a married woman."

Tom held up his hands. "Sorry. Sometimes the voices make me say stupid things."

Lifting up his shirt, she found marks all over his back, too. "How are you scratching way up here?"

"It's the aliens I tell ya. They got pointy whiskers and long hairy tails. You think you can get me into the psych hospital? Sure could use a real bed and some fresh meals. And away from the aliens. They live on human flesh, don't you know. At night, passed out on my slab, I wake up as dessert. It's scary as shit."

Cynthia considered if she could get him admitted. On a Saturday afternoon it would be practically impossible, except for a true emergency. Besides the alien delusion and self-mutilation, Tom appeared to be functioning adequately. Giving him these vitamins and fluids would have to hold him through the weekend. Even if she ordered tests, it'd be unlikely anything abnormal would show up.

Too bad there wasn't a lab test that could show how bad the schizophrenia was.

Or how much a broken heart hurt.

"Tom, I'm not going to be able to get you a psych bed right now. They're all full. You know, if you'd just take your medicine, you'd do a lot better. Why don't you take the pills the doctors prescribe?" She held up the bag of bottles he'd brought in. "These are still nearly full from when you got them two months ago."

"The voices tell me not to take them. They're poison, don't you know."

She sighed. She knew that paranoia was typical of schizophrenics, so they skipped taking their medications, and then became even more paranoid in a vicious descending spiral. "I'd like to help you, Tom, but I can't admit you to the hospital today. Maybe I can get you a bed at a halfway house, like the Wilson Ranch? They usually have an opening."

Tom shook his head violently. "No! They steal things and treat you like shit. I'd rather go back to my refuge under the wharf. You're sure you can't admit me?"

Cynthia shook her head. "I'm sorry, Tom." She brought out her wallet. "But if you need some money? I think I have forty dollars."

He yanked the needle out of his arm. "Forty bucks? Jesus Christ. If you can't even help the father of your child, what the hell good are you?"

She reached out, but he shook her off.

"Forget it," he insisted. "I'm out of here."

She stepped back and watched him trudge to the curtain, blood oozing from the torn IV site. He stopped and turned to her, despair riding on his drooping mustache. "Can you at least tell me how to stop those aliens from eating me alive?"

"By taking your medicine."

His deep brown eyes beseeched her, haunting shadows of distant memories. "You promise?"

She handed him the bag with his pills. "Yes. I promise."

He took it, dropping his gaze to the floor.

Cynthia forced her voice to sound encouraging. "I'll make an appointment for you with your counselor for Wednesday morning." She watched him throw back the curtain and walk out of the room. At the end of the corridor, he slumped against the door. A tear showed on his cheek. "Can I ask you something?"

"What?"

"If Brent develops schizophrenia, will you stop loving him, too?"

* * *

Late Tuesday afternoon Cynthia was sitting at her desk dictating some charts when a police officer came into her office. She remembered having seen him before, but didn't recall his name.

"Dr. Allen?" he asked.

"It's Mrs. What can I do for you?"

He held out his hand. "I'm Sergeant Galbraith. You know a Tom Reynolds?"

A heaviness descended on her shoulders. "Yes, of course. He's my ex-husband. Since you're here, I presume he's in trouble again."

"No ma'am. He's dead."

"Dead? What happened?"

The officer grimaced. "Overdose. Had a whole bunch of empty pill bottles around. Nasty."

"Oh my God." Cynthia struggled to breathe. Swallowing hard, she asked, "Will you need me to identify his body?"

Sergeant Galbraith shook his head. "No, I don't think you'll want to. He was living in a sewer. The rats ate his face off."

Schizophrenia

Mental illnesses can be classified into three types: neuroses, psychoses, and personality disorders. Neuroses affect most everyone to some degree, the mildest ones shrugged off as superstitions or idiosyncrasies. The most common neurosis is acrophobia (fear of heights), followed by arachnophobia (fear of spiders). Most neuroses develop in childhood, though any type of major life event can create a neurosis, such as post-traumatic stress disorder. Neuroses can be treated with anti-anxiety pills, such as Ativan, though these won't cure the problem. Cures require counseling to get to the root of the problem, or special techniques, such as bio-feedback.

Psychoses affect the mind in more permanent fashion, schizophrenia (now called schizo-affective disorder) being the classic example. Here the brain itself functions inappropriately, and counseling will have no effect. Schizophrenics typically have auditory and visual hallucinations. Because of the weird input, where the patients are unsure what is real, they tend to develop a "flat affect," a blank expression despite major stress. Schizophrenics generally are not dangerous, though they can be quite scary. Often they feel that either God or the Devil is talking to them, and, if untreated, might wander the streets shouting at their demons. Other psychoses include bipolar disease (manic/depression) and certain severe depressions. Major tranquilizers, such as Thorazine or Haldol, will muffle the disease, though most patients have frequent exacerbations.

I remember a patient early in my career, brought in by her family, who seemed totally normal on my interview. Then the son suggested I ask her about her relationship with the Queen of England. "Yes," my patient told me, "the Queen and I talk every day." This is an example of delusion, which is important to distinguish from delirium. Delirium is a temporary hallucination, often drug induced (like with Spice) or from withdrawal from alcohol (the D.T.s), though other conditions (such as fever or a Lupus exacerbation) can also cause delirium. Frequently people have paranoid delusions, thinking that the CIA is spying on them, or, to the contrary, that they work for the CIA. In contrast to delirium, *delusions can be defined as firm, fixed, false beliefs and may respond quite quickly to medications.*

Every baby is born with a unique personality, and these evolve as we age and are influenced by our environments. Personality disorders, the third type of psychiatric illness, is the hardest psychiatric illness to treat, not curable with counseling and rarely responsive to medication. Examples of personality disorders are obsessive-compulsive disorder, attention deficit disorder, and narcissism. A common misconception of schizophrenia equates it with multiple personality disorder, but there's actually no relationship between these illnesses.

Depression, the most common psychiatric diagnosis, can fall into any of these categories, often caused by temporary stresses, such as illness or divorce, or be a result of one of the more major categories, such as bipolar illness. Medications can help certain depressions, although withdrawal symptoms when the medications are stopped can be severe.

In the Waiting Room

I slipped through the sliding glass doors into the waiting room. With my first breath, I recognized the traditional hospital smell of rubbing alcohol and cleaning solution. Better than the odors of vomit and decay, I supposed.

The aquamarine-walled waiting room held a couple dozen comfortable-looking chairs, mostly empty. One older fellow sat alone, staring past me at the glass doors leading towards the emergency room. Settling into the seat just behind him, I studied the back of his head, noticing tense muscles stretching between his trim gray hair line and the clean collar of his shirt.

"Someone you know sick?" I asked.

The man turned to me, taking a moment to focus. "They got my wife back there in one of those rooms. I sure wish I knew what was going on – it's been nearly an hour."

"I'm in a similar boat," I replied. "The ambulance brought in my son and they won't let me back to see him or tell me anything about his condition."

The man reached out his hand. "Looks like we're friends in need, fellow. Name's Ted Beasley."

I took the man's firm handshake and gave him the onceover. Bushy gray eyebrows gave him an owlish look.

"Rick Lewis. Friends indeed. What happened to your wife?"

Ted's expressive eyebrows sagged. "Hasn't been doing well for the last few months. I've been telling her to call the doctor, but she wouldn't, afraid he'd send her to the E.R. Cleo often said, 'E.R.s are for the dying.'"

"So what happened?"

Ted turned back to stare in the direction of the trauma rooms. "I found her collapsed in the garden."

I let the silence soften. "Why won't they let you back with her?"

"They told me someone would be with me shortly." Ted dropped his head into his hands. "It can't be good."

"Maybe no news is good news," I suggested, patting him on the shoulder.

After another long stare at the glass doors, Ted turned back towards me. "Maybe. Maybe so." He tented his forehead creases. "So what's up with your son? An accident?"

I gave my bottom lip a chew before answering. "I'm afraid he might be on drugs."

Ted nodded in understanding. "A teenager?"

"Fifteen."

"I feel for you, Rick. One of my sons got into drugs for a while. He's clean now, though. What's your boy's name?"

"Andy." I remembered how I'd found him in his room, screaming with hallucinations. The EMS fellow said something about spice. "I'm so mad at him. He knows better than to do that kind of thing. I haven't decided what kind of punishment to mete out, but it's going to be a doozy!"

I saw the hesitation in his lips before Ted asked, "Do you really think that's going to help?"

"Shouldn't it? How did you get your son off drugs?"

Taking yet another glance towards the emergency room door, Ted stood and walked around the aisle to sit in a chair facing mine. "I didn't used to spend much time with Tim. I was climbing the corporate ladder, staying late at the office, bringing home work on the weekends. Then one day I met one of his teachers at a play's intermission. Pure coincidence … or maybe it was fated. She asked what had been going on with Tim, why were his grades plummeting, why was he missing so many classes? Can you believe it? I had no idea."

He reached up and rubbed his pate through his sparse hair. A satisfied smile graced his face. "Yep. I decided that very night his life was more important than my career. I told my boss I was cutting down to part-time, only working weekdays when my son was at school. From then on, I left the office each day in time to pick him up when his school day ended. We spent every evening together, every weekend going places, camping, hunting, hiking. In two months he was a changed man. Heck, I was too.

"And Cleo," he pointed in the general direction, "Cleo and I never missed the lost income. Once Tim got off to college I retired completely. I'd learned how to be a best friend to my son, and was able to turn that into the best marriage a man could ever have."

He sat down again and his eyes lost their focus. "I was eighteen and she'd just turned seventeen when we married. I remember our wedding day like it was yesterday, held at the Beauvoir. We had a canopy of two-hundred-year-old oaks drifting their leaves into the columned chapel."

As he talked, I watched layers of stress drift away from his face. His voice trailed off and a joyful smile of wonderment settled on his lips.

"Good-bye," he whispered.

I took hold of Ted's offered hands as a strange flush passed across his face.

"Cleo's passed," he whispered. "She kissed me good-bye."

We sat in companionable silence for about five minutes until a security fellow came through the doors and beckoned for Ted. He dropped my hands, took a step away, stopped, and turned back. "Love your son," he said. "He's the most precious thing you have."

I watched the sliding glass doors close behind him and the guard.

It was another hour before that same guard came for me. I followed him into a curtained-off stretcher where I found Andy sitting up. His face rested down on his outstretched palms.

"Andy?"

He looked up, darkened sockets holding reddened eyes. "Sorry Dad. Damn. So sorry."

I sat down on the visitor's chair. "What happened?"

His reluctant words dribbled out between extended pauses. "It was a new kid, invited a couple of us home after school. Didn't know his parents weren't home. Someone passed a joint and I thought it wouldn't hurt to take a few puffs. Guess the stuff was messed with. Looked pretty bad, huh?"

"Yes, you did." I watched him drape that sad face back into its palm cradle. He'd grown so much in the past couple of years. From a little boy he'd sprouted into a long-limbed scarecrow, and now muscle was beginning to fluff out those limbs. How long had it been since I'd just sat and looked at him? Months? Years?

"You know that concert you were wanting to go to this weekend?" I asked.

He didn't look up, only murmured. "Suppose that's cancelled."

"Yes indeed." I gave the moment a pause. "Instead you and I are going camping."

Andy sat up, his eyes widening. "Really? You ... don't you have a meeting or something?"

I shook my head. "Consider it cancelled, too. As soon as they release you, we're going to Walmart and stock up on all new gear, a new tent, new bags, fishing poles, everything we need, and heading out early Saturday morning for a weekend at Buccaneer State Park."

"Hot shit! That'll be grand!" He gave me a thumbs up.

I stood and stepped to the stretcher, reaching out my arms. He grabbed me and brought me into a tight hug. In a moment I heard a sob. I'm not sure who it came from, but I think maybe both of us.

Drug Abuse and Death at Bedside

Drug abuse often begins with peer pressure, teenagers experimenting with forbidden fruit. Although the theory of "gateway drugs" has been well debunked, nevertheless, the thrill a teenager finds from perception-altering experiences sometimes entices them to try other items, from alcohol to heroin. While marijuana is relatively benign, and even valuable for certain medicinal purposes, it's incumbent on the physician and our society to promote awareness and education of both the risks and benefits of medicinal substances, those provided by prescription, over-the-counter, and on the unregulated markets. Particularly worrisome are the addictive stimulants, sedatives, and opiates. Parental involvement can have a huge influence on behavioral change.

"In the Waiting Room" tells of a pet peeve of mine, excluding family from the bedsides of their ill loved ones. While it's certainly convenient for the nurses to not have to deal with family members in a small room already crowded with medical personnel helping the patient change into a gown, hook up IVs and monitors, obtain EKGs, draw blood, and obtain background information, the exclusion of the family creates anxiety for both patient and family, and also prevents obtaining important historical information.

In the direst of situations, with the patient on death's door and the medical personnel performing extreme methods, such as intubation, CPR, and major tube insertions, studies have shown that families allowed to witness these events report more satisfaction that the medical crew really did all they could to try to save their loved one's life, as compared to those excluded from the experience, who sometimes fear that the doctor just let their loved one die. I personally have found that if the family stands witness to our efforts, they'll often speak up and ask us to stop much sooner than we otherwise would, usually for the best.

Asclepius

Five candles dance around me, casting shadows on the room's mystical items. For the second time my chants call Asclepius to the physical plane. He materializes, appearing as a huge eye glowing a rainbow of colors. His hum vibrates through the room.

"I again answer your summons, Doctor. Has the power of healing been all you expected?"

"I healed many today," I reply.

The smoke drifts gently, creating wavering curtains in the eye's glow.

"And yet you are not content."

"People mob me in stores and on the streets. They scream, begging me to touch them, cure their illnesses, save their stricken lives. I am fearful."

The magical eye bathes me in aqua light. Calm flows into my tingling hands.

"Do not be frightened. No harm will come to you."

I touch my throat and my forehead, curing the hesitation. "I fear not for myself, Asclepius. Rather, I fear for the imbalance of the world. Afflictions are banished by my touch. Cancerous tumors disappear. The blind see."

I stare into the eye, drawing the fortitude to admit defeat.

"I cannot continue, Asclepius. Every undeserved miracle I bring eats a hole in the fabric of the world."

"You wish for me to take the gift away? You wish to go back to the ways of treating with pills and needles?"

I glance around the chamber. The years I spent devoted to the dark arts brought adornments to every cranny. Mountains of books tumble in the corners. Magical icons hang on walls or gather dust on ancient teak shelves.

"Asclepius, can you help me in another way? Could you provide me with the ability to diagnose, to be able to determine what's wrong with my patients? If I have this knowledge, I can guide them to the best available treatments."

"Yes, I can change your powers. But once I provide this request, we will be done. I will never again return to your summons."

I take a deep breath, steeling myself for the change. "I humbly implore you to grant my request."

The eye's glow penetrates my brain, creating a euphoric shudder sprinting through my spine. As I lose consciousness I hear it say, "Your wish is granted, Doctor. Sleep."

***

When I awake, I feel refreshed. I head to the bathroom where I'm stunned by my mirror image. My eyes glow like smoldering coals. I see plaques and scars and depression and infections and arthritis. I realize that, for the rest of my life, this is how I will see everyone, penetrating their body to their illnesses.

For a moment I feel joy, interrupted by terror. I identify a tumor in my lungs—the untreatable kind—and I know I am going to die.

Faith Healing

Do you believe in Magic? Most people do. From benign remedies of chicken soup for colds, to cupping for evil spirits, to leeching out the bad blood, folk remedies run the course from benign to harmful. It's not just the uneducated or superstitious, even well-informed professionals fall victim to beliefs not supported by science.

Through the centuries, physicians have followed theories that did more harm than good. President Garfield's physicians killed him by digging for a bullet in the wrong place, creating an abscess that resulted in death while the bullet itself was not causing any harm. Even modern medicine is not immune from magical thinking. During my medical school years, the professors taught us to give lidocaine to every heart attack patient to prevent irregular heartbeats., Only later did we discover that lidocaine increased mortality by suppressing heart function. Until very recently physicians believed giving estrogens to post-menopausal women reduced heart attacks, a theory now disproved by appropriate studies.

Who wouldn't want magical powers of healing? This isn't to say that "laying on of the hands" isn't helpful. Statistics show that patients who believe they'll improve enjoy a higher cure rate, including those with confidence in their doctor. On the other hand, as related in this story, disease and death play an important role in the cycle of life. The young replace the old, until they, too, age into death.

I'm proud to be a healer, satisfied with modern medicine's ability to diagnose and treat most illnesses. Physicians don't need to cure everything. We must try our best to discover those problems that we can help, bring hope to those in doubt, and comfort those who suffer.

Fielder's Choice

Jim watched his smoke drift into a gray mushroom above his head. He handed the cigarette to Molly, lying next to him, who took a deep drag and released her smoke to mingle with his. Jim perched up on one elbow and studied her.

"Your body is absolutely magnificent. You know that?"

Molly reached for the sheets and pulled them up to her neck. "Ralph always made fun of my small breasts."

They looked at each other, contented smiles tugging at their cheeks.

"He was an idiot," Jim said, surprised when she turned away. "What did I say?"

With her head half buried in the pillow she murmured, "Nothing."

He pulled the sheet back down and stroked her side. "Molly? What?"

She flipped towards him, mascara streaks running down her cheeks. "I'm sorry, Jim. He really was an idiot. But I loved him. I thought we'd be together forever. When he left, I thought I'd never be with a man again. I feel … sort of like I'm betraying something."

Jim kissed her lightly on the lips. "Don't feel sad. We said we'd try it just this once. Didn't you enjoy it?"

She turned onto her back, staring at the ceiling. "Yes. Very much. Thank you for being so gentle." She pulled the sheet back up to her neck again.

They smoked in silence, while Jim's mind played back the lovemaking. It had been so lovely, except when …. He pushed himself up against the headboard, looking down on her. "Molly?"

"Hmm?"

"Molly, did I satisfy you?"

She breathed quietly until Jim wasn't sure if she was going to answer. Eventually she responded with a deep contented sigh. "Jim, you satisfied me greatly! Why would you ask such a thing?"

Jim shrugged. "It's been six years since I had a lover. And, well, you know. I'm just not able to do what I used to."

Molly reached up and stroked his cheek. "What makes a good lover is not duration, but sharing. You're wonderful."

Jim took her hands and stared into her eyes. He tried to read her expression, to see if her answers were just appeasement. "You're sure?"

"Baby."

He felt a warmth rush through him, a happiness that he hadn't felt in a dozen or more years. Scooting back down, he placed both hands on her head, cupping her ears, and pulling her forward so their lips met. He enjoyed the sweet softness of her kiss.

When she withdrew he placed his hand on her wrist, eager to hold her close. "Molly, we've dated six months, and now making love. How about we think of taking the next step?"

He saw her quizzical look.

"I'm talking marriage. I love you. I want you to marry me."

Her expression froze, and she turned her head away where the bedside clock fell into her vision. She raised her hand to her mouth.

"Oh, look at the time. I've got to get going."

Jim tightened his hold on her wrist, holding her back as she tried to pull out of bed. "Molly!"

She shook off his grip and slipped out of bed, quickly pulling on her panties. Without turning to face him she said, "You know I don't like leaving Kenny at my mom's this late." She slipped her dress on over her head.

He swung his legs out of bed, stood, and reached around to hug her. "Sweetheart, don't run off. Talk to me."

She turned to face him, pushing back away and leaning against the wall behind her. "You're the sweetest man I've ever met, Jim. I'm slowly opening doors to you I thought I'd closed forever. I'm not saying we'll never get married, but I have to be sure everything's right this time. After all, I have an eleven-year-old counting on me. What would he say if I came home one day and announced I was getting married? That would be so unfair to him."

"It doesn't have to happen that way." He stood and reached out to her. "Why not give him a chance to meet me?"

She shook her head. "Kenny is very vulnerable right now. His father used to say mean things to him, yell at him for doing badly at school. I don't think it would be fair to introduce you to him until we're sure this relationship is going to work out."

Jim felt a coldness grip his heart. "Work out? Molly. Are you thinking we're not going to work out?"

"I'm just scared, Jim." She wrung her hands. "I want it to work between us, but … what if it doesn't?"

He sat back on the bed, shaking his head. "You've talked about Kenny since the first day we met, and I'm been asking to meet him. Don't you think it's about time?"

Jim watched Molly's knuckles whiten as she squeezed her hands together. "I don't know."

"Molly. Give us a chance. We can start out with something simple. Does Kenny like bowling? How about we all go out bowling next Saturday?"

Jim watched her standing against the wall, her gaze on her feet. He went to her, raised her face, and kissed her gently. "Molly, I love you. Let me share this part of your life too."

A tentative smile danced across her face. "I suppose bowling would be okay."

Jim leaned in and she reached up, pulling his face to hers. Their kiss lingered, and he could feel himself start to respond. She must have felt it too, because she pushed away and pointed.

"See? I told you not to worry so much about your performance. He'll be fine. Anyway, like I said, it's your gentle touch I love, not how long you last." She strode across the room, turning at the bedroom door to blow him a kiss before stepping out.

He listened to her footsteps disappear down the hallway, followed by the closing of his apartment door. Lighting another cigarette, he lay back in the bed, thinking of how much he loved her. He pulled the sheets up, smelling her aromas. She'd been so responsive to his touch, to his kisses, and his orgasm had been heart pounding.

He touched himself, and it felt good, but soon the softness returned, and he wondered what would happen next time. He remembered that his friend, Bob, had talked about seeing a doctor for something like this. Maybe he'd give him a call in the morning and see if he wanted to get together and talk.

* * *

O'Reilly's had televisions on every wall and around the bar, with sports of various genres playing on each one. Jim and Bob settled in front of the main attraction, the Braves game on the big screen. The waitress brought them their wings and beers, and they settled back, cheering and gabbing.

"I bet it's been a year since I spent a Sunday evening at a sports bar," Bob said. "Whatcha been up to? Hardly ever see you at work anymore."

"Same old, same old. So how's it working out over at management?" Jim asked. "When you first got the promotion you used to drop by every few days to check in. How come you don't anymore?"

Bob shrugged. "They're piling on the work. I'll make a point of stoppin' by." He took a swig of his beer and pointed at the screen. "Watch this. Aaron's gonna throw him the knuckler and Chipper'll smack it over the fence."

They watched the pitch, the swing, and the miss.

"Damn. Strike out. End of the inning."

"It's only the fourth," Jim observed. He grabbed another wing and chomped it thoughtfully. "Say Bob, remember last year when we were all talking about how we were getting older? Didn't you say something about having tried Viagra?"

Bob grinned at him. "That new girlfriend of yours working your pecker to death?"

Jim felt a blush burn his cheeks. "Molly's seven years younger than me. She's not complaining, but I'd sure like to have something just in case."

"Yeah, I know that feeling. Course, an old married man like me doesn't have to perform as much."

"So, did the Viagra work for you?"

"Like a charm," Bob said. "You gotta have a prescription. Here, I'll write the name of my doctor on this napkin. Goldberg. He's an expert on peckers."

Jim examined the name before stuffing the napkin into his wallet. "What's he like? I don't get along with doctors real well. Haven't seen one in years."

"You'll like this guy. Used to play pro ball."

"Really? Okay, thanks. I'll give him a call tomorrow and see if he can fit me in on Tuesday."

Bob pointed up at the television. "Next inning's started."

* * *

Jim studied the dozen framed certificates hanging on the examining room's wall, calculating Doctor Goldberg at two years younger than himself. Besides the certificates, the decorations included anatomical charts, male genitalia mostly. It was sort of embarrassing. *What would make a guy choose to specialize in peckers? Hope he's not queer.*

He walked over and looked out the fourth-floor window. Across the street an ambulance rolled up to the E.R. entrance, red lights roiling in silence. A chubby fellow in a blue uniform climbed out of the driver's seat, walked around to the back, and popped the rear doors. With the help of his buddy they pulled out a stretcher carrying an emaciated man, IV fluids running into his arm. The trio disappeared into the E.R. doors.

"Boy, that guy ain't got much longer," Jim muttered to his reflection.

He turned at the sound of the examining room door opening. Tall and muscular, Dr. Goldberg gave Jim a glistening smile and a firm handshake. Jim looked him over, impressed with the doctor's vitality.

"Welcome, Mr. Norwood. A pleasure to meet you."

Jim returned the amenities. "Got a view of the hospital, huh?" he said, indicating the window.

"Yes indeed. I'm over there at least twice a day, making rounds or consults. Do a bit of surgery a couple of days a week, too."

Jim sat down on one of the two solid wooden chairs, the only furniture besides the examining table and a cabinet. "Thanks for squeezing me in on such short notice. I'm not interested in surgery today, thanks anyway."

Dr. Goldberg laughed. "Good philosophy! I see you like the Braves."

Jim touched the cap with its fancy "A" embossment. "Yeah. My friend Bob told me you used to play pro-ball."

The doctor pulled a framed photograph off a shelf and handed it over. It showed him in Yankees pinstripe, just completing a swing, with a full stadium crowd blurred in the background. Written in pen along the bottom corner were the words "First home run," and a date.

Jim stared at it a long time. "How come you gave it up?"

"It was fun, but I wanted a more reliable profession." He retrieved the photo and returned it to its shelf. "I presume you didn't come to see me about my baseball career?"

Jim felt the blush return to his cheeks. "Well, see, I got myself a new girlfriend. And, well, during our lovemaking session a couple of nights ago, my peter sort of petered out."

"So you were able to get an erection, but it didn't last?"

"Yeah," Jim said with a nod. "I mean, she was satisfied and all that. But I want something just in case it happens again. Bob said you gave him Viagra and it helped him."

"From what you've told me, it does seem Viagra, or one of the other similar erectile dysfunction medicines, would be worth a try. Let me get a history and physical on you first, just to be sure there're no contraindication to the prescription."

Doctor Goldberg indicated for Jim to get up on the stretcher. Picking up a chart, the doctor scribbled notes as Jim answered his questions. "No prior illnesses or hospitalizations? No daily medications? You smoke or drink?"

"I'm not a big drinker, mostly just beer. Not a heavy smoker either. A pack will last me three or four days."

"They're not good for you, you know," the doctor said. "You should give 'em up."

After washing his hands, Dr. Goldberg poked and prodded across Jim's body, looking into Jim's eyes and listened to his heart and lungs.

"You ever use Viagra?" Jim asked.

"Oh, occasionally. It certainly has worked for me." The doctor stepped back and asked Jim to stand. "Now turn around and pull down your pants."

Jim squeezed his legs together. "Can't we skip this part, Doc?"

Dr. Goldberg shook his head. "It'll only take a moment."

Jim sighed, and turned, bending over the table. "So, you're … uh, married?" he asked, through gritted teeth.

"Yes, twenty wonderful years." The doctor finished the exam and Jim jerked up his pants, settling back onto the wooden chair. "Everything A-OK?"

Dr. Goldberg's face had lost its smile. "I'm a little concerned about your prostate."

Jim's mouth went dry. "What are you talking about?"

Dr. Goldberg pulled the other chair up next to Jim, and sat. "Mr. Norwood, your prostrate has a nodule. I think I'd better do a biopsy."

"A biopsy?" Jim drew back. "That sounds like surgery. You trying to be funny here?"

The doctor shook his head. "I never joke about illness. He clasped his hands in his lap. "A nodule on the prostate needs to be investigated. In order to tell what it is, I'm going to have to take you to my small operating room here. It'll only take about five minutes for me to get the biopsy and I promise you won't feel a thing. Afterwards, I'm going to send you across the street for a CAT scan."

Jim stared at him in confusion. "Are you absolutely certain all this is necessary? I just came in for some pills, for God's sake."

Dr. Goldberg leaned forward and placed his hand on Jim's shoulder. "Absolutely. We'll do all this now, and I'll see you at nine a.m. tomorrow to discuss the results."

Jim nodded, because he was too overwhelmed to say anything else. Over the next two hours he felt like a puppet, being ordered this way and that, first the biopsy, and then the CAT scan. At one point someone drew some blood.

By the time he got home dusk had arrived. He climbed up to his apartment and locked the door behind him. Before opening a can of soup for dinner Jim called into work, telling them he'd need another sick day tomorrow.

As he ate he wondered whether he needed to worry. Breaking from his usual resolve not to drink during the week, he picked a six-pack from the refrigerator, and sat in front of the TV, not caring what channel was on. He woke at two AM with the TV still blaring, turned it off, and dragged himself off to bed.

* * *

The next morning he sat impatiently in Dr. Goldberg's office. "Tell me the good news, Doc," Jim said, trying to force cheeriness into his faltering voice.

Dr. Goldberg's smile was nowhere to be seen. "Jim, there's no simple way to say this. You have cancer."

"Cancer?" Jim closed his eyes. He'd known a few people with cancer, and it had always been bad news. He felt the room closing in around him.

Through a haze he heard Dr. Goldberg's voice. "Jim? Jim? Are you okay?"

Clawing back to consciousness, Jim tried to make his voice sound normal. "I'll make it. What now, Doc?"

"You'll have to have surgery, Mr. Norwood. What we call a radical prostatectomy."

"Surgery, huh?" Jim let out a deep breath. "Well, I suppose that's not that awful. You just cut out the cancer and I'm done? I can get on with my life?"

Dr. Goldberg's smile started its return. "That's a good attitude. It may not be quite that simple, but, yes, basically that's the plan. For the next month you'll take a medication called Lupron to shrink your prostate. After that I'll do the radical prostatectomy. Here, have a look."

Jim leaned over the desk to watch as Dr. Goldberg used anatomical drawings to explain the planned procedure. He explained various risk factors, including the possibilities that the cancer may have already metastasized and that, even with the surgery, it might grow back.

"Let's see," Dr. Goldberg said, pulling a calendar from a desk drawer. "How does May eighteen sound? That's a Tuesday."

Jim leaned back in his chair, crossing his arms across his chest. "Let's skip the drugs and just do the surgery, Doc. I don't do well worrying about things."

Dr. Goldberg shook his head. "No, you'll need the month. Besides the benefits of the Lupron, you'll want some time to prepare for your recuperation. Figure out who's going to take care of you; let your work know about your needs. You'll be unable to work for about two months."

Jim felt a desperate need for a cigarette. "Two months? Oh come on, Doc. I'm pretty tough. Why would I have to miss all that work?"

"Well, for example, for the first month you'll have to wear a catheter."

"A catheter? You mean I'm gonna go around with one of those plastic tubes out my dick for a month? You've gotta be joking."

Jim watched the worry lines deepen around the doctor's eyes. "No. The biopsy showed you have a highly malignant cancer.

Without the surgery, your life expectancy would be less than three years."

"Death?" Jim fell back in his chair, grabbing his chest. He tried to take some deep breaths but couldn't get his diaphragm to cooperate. Dr. Goldberg brought him a cup of water, and Jim choked some of it down.

Jim finally squeaked out, "Damn. Well, I guess peeing out a tube for a month is going to have to be got through." He took out his cigarette pack, but put it back when Dr. Goldberg shook his head.

"Well hell, Doc. There's not anything else I need to know, is there?"

The doctor clasped his hands on the table, staring at them almost a minute before looking up into Jim's face. "There are two main complications from removal of the prostate, the first is incontinence. In laymen terms, a leaky bladder."

Jim felt his mouth drop. "Like in wearing Depends? You mean I'm gonna be wearing diapers like some old fart in the nursing home? This isn't funny, Doc. Next thing I know, you're gonna tell me I won't be able to get it up afterwards."

Dr. Goldberg pursed his lips before speaking. "Jim, I'm sorry. You mentioned a new girlfriend so I can imagine how this must be really hard on you."

"Shit!" Jim said, standing up. "You telling me I'm going to end up limp?"

Dr. Goldberg opened his hands. "Even in the best of hands there's some risk. My personal results have been much better, but studies have found some resultant impotence as often as fifty per cent of the time."

Jim felt his throat tighten. Unable to catch his breath he struggled to the door. "I've got to get out of here," he croaked.

"Wait a minute," Dr. Goldberg called to Jim's retreating back.

Jim sprinted down the stairs and out onto the street, running wildly until exhausted. He walked, block after block, until he came to a small park where he collapsed onto a black iron bench. The panic disrupting his thoughts slowly cleared, leaving an empty sensation.

Jim watched the park life. Pigeons pecked near his feet. Mothers pushed carriages or strolled with toddlers in hand. The singing of birds and the startling yellow of spring daffodils felt incongruous with his black thoughts.

Cancer or impotence? What fiendish practical joke was God playing upon him? What kind of life without sex? What would Molly say? She was young and sexually needy. Despite what she said, she'd never accept him as not truly a man.

Jim sat for hours, rousing when the evening chill brought a shiver across his shoulders. He caught the northbound bus, standing and holding a rail in the almost empty chamber. In a seat halfway down the aisle a young couple giggled and kissed. Jim turned to the window and watched a tear trickle down his cheek. He left the bus one stop before his apartment, entering a liquor store and picking up five bottles of vodka.

"Must be a hell of a party you're planning," the clerk said.

Jim looked him over: gray grimy hair, red nose, and saggy cheeks of too much alcohol for too many years.

"You got a girlfriend?" Jim asked.

"Sure do." The clerk flashed a crooked grin.

Jim studied the fellow again: fat belly, bad teeth, and ruddy complexion; surely no Don Juan, this guy.

"What do you think she'd say if you suddenly became sick?"

The fellow looked at him through narrowed lids. "Is this some sort of threat, Buddy?"

"No, nothing like that." Jim waved his hands. "I just got some bad news and I'm trying to figure out what to say to my girl."

The clerk pulled his mouth to one side while he thought. "Well, is she gonna find out anyway?"

Jim nodded.

"What difference does it make, then? Hell, just tell her. Better she find out from you than somebody else."

* * *

That night, and for the next day, and night again, Jim stayed in his apartment, sitting in the dark, drinking vodka, and staring at the walls. When the phone rang he ignored it.

On Friday morning a pounding at the door soaked into his consciousness. He tried ignoring this too, staring at the door as if he didn't understand why it was offending him with all that noise.

"Jimmy? Are you in there? It's Bob."

Jim tried to speak, a hoarse whisper escaping from cracked lips.

"Bob?"

He pushed himself out of the recliner, stumbled, regained his footing, and staggered to the door.

Squinting through the peephole he identified his friend. Managing a nearly normal voice he called through the door, "Hey, Bob."

"You okay there, fellow? You've missed four days of work and wouldn't answer the phone."

Jim slumped against the door rubbing his head. He kept trying to develop some spit to moisten his dry mouth, but none would come.

"Jimmy? You there?"

Jim popped the door lock and stepped back. Bob pushed open the door, took one look and a smell, and shook his head.

"Goddamn, Jimmy Boy. You look awful. Been on a binge, huh?"

Jim followed Bob's stare to the coffee table where three empty vodka bottles lay on their sides. He couldn't remember drinking them, or even whether he had sampled from one this morning. He collapsed onto the couch in front of them.

"Guess so, Bob. I'm having a hell of a time."

Bob leaned against the armchair across from the couch. "You wanna talk about it?"

"It's bad news, Bob. Doc says I got prostate cancer. He says I gotta have surgery."

Bob clucked his tongue. "Tough break, Jimmy, but not worth falling apart over. You never have surgery before?"

"I had my tonsils out as a kid. Wait a minute and I'll tell you more." Jim excused himself and went to the bathroom. He washed his face and brushed his teeth and hair before returning.

He found Bob straightening up the place. "So tell me what sent you over the edge, Jimmy."

Jim settled onto the couch and dropped his face into his hands. "Give me a minute."

He heard Bob knocking around the kitchen and soon smelled the sweet aroma of coffee. Rising to the allure, Jim joined him and took a swig of the offered steaming mug. The caffeine surge cleared his brain cobwebs. "Thanks Bob."

Bob topped off both mugs. "So what's the story?"

Jim placed his cup on the counter and stared at it. "Goldberg says the surgery could leave me impotent and incontinent. You know what those words mean?"

Bob whistled. "Yeah. Think you should get a second opinion?"

A spark of hope flared in Jim, but quickly faded. "That'd be a strike out for sure, Bob. This guy's got certificates out the wazoo."

"So whatcha gonna do, Jimmy? Try to race the cancer to your death with vodka?"

Jim shook his head. "No. But I can't face this surgery. Me and Molly are hitting it off so well. I know she's gonna drop me when she finds out my pecker's gonna be useless. Shit. Any woman would. Well, maybe not a loyal wife like your Debbie. But Molly … she's still got a lot of hang-ups from her divorce."

Bob took Jim's empty and washed out both mugs. "Why not give the girl a chance?" he asked. "Maybe she'll surprise you."

Jim stared into Bob's eyes, seeing only honest hope. Jim dropped his gaze to his feet. "Yeah, maybe. We got a date tomorrow night. Guess I'll find out."

* * *

Jim looked up from the scorecard to give the boy a reassuring smile. "Let's see, you scored a 135 on that game, huh Kenny? That's really good."

"Yeah, thanks for showing me that curve, Mr. Norwood."

Jim watched as the eleven-year-old took a gulp from his drink. Nearly as tall as his mother already, he had the clumsy grace of adolescence. When he placed his drink back on the table, he nearly spilled it.

"It takes practice," Jim said. "Not many people could pick it up as quickly as you did. Only took you three games. I'm very impressed. Keep practicing and you'll hit that soft spot every time."

The two sipped cokes and ate nachos as they waited for Molly's return from the restroom.

"You like my mom?" Kenny asked.

Jim leaned back in his chair, nodding slowly. "I like her very much, Kenny. How do you feel about that?"

Kenny shrugged. "I guess it's okay. She says she likes you, too. You think you might get married?"

Jim felt his hands shaking. He took out a cigarette and knocked it on the table.

"You can't smoke here," Kenny said.

Jim nodded. "No, not down here in the lanes I guess. Anyway, my doctor told me I need to quit."

Jim put his cigarette away, listening to the rolling thunder of the balls and the slamming of the pins.

"Well?" Kenny asked. "You going to marry my Mom?"

Jim shrugged. "I don't know, Kenny. I think she doesn't want to marry me."

"Yeah, she's pretty mad about my Dad."

Jim took another nacho. He chewed it slowly, enjoying the sticky sweet flavoring before swallowing and washing it down with some cola. "And there are other issues."

Kenny looked down at his lap. "Who wants to be burdened with a kid, huh?"

Jim reached over, laying his hand on Kenny's arm. "No, no, Kenny. You're a great kid. I'd be glad to have you in my life. I guess all of us see the world from our own perspective. If things don't work out with your mom, it won't be because of you."

Kenny looked up, his eyes pleading. "Yeah? So how come my Dad left?"

"You mustn't blame yourself that things didn't work out between your parents, Kenny. When parents get divorced it's because of the parents' issues, never their children's fault."

The boy reached over and dropped a jalapeno slice in the middle of a cheese laden nacho. Cheese dribbled down his shirt as he brought it up to his mouth. "Even if I'm not all to blame, I can't help thinking that I'm in the way sometimes. My mom says I'm not, but my teachers don't have much patience with me. I've got dyslexia. You know what that is?"

"Sure." He paused to survey the lanes, all the different people, a mix of ages, hairstyles, races, clothing – everyone living their own lives, yet brought together in this cosmos of a gentle sport. "Life is never perfect, Kenny. Sometimes it pitches us a knuckleball and we strike out. Other times, though, we can connect and really send that old ball flying. All we can do is wait at the plate and try to connect with whatever pitch we get."

Kenny scraped the last of the cheese out of the paper container with a broken chip. "So, you're saying I gotta stop thinking dyslexia is my fault."

Jim nodded. "We all have problems, Kenny."

"You got problems too?"

Jim stared at his soda. "Yeah, Kenny. Me too." He looked up quickly. "But that doesn't mean I'd run out on you. No siree. If Molly and I do end up getting closer, I'll stick with you both like a pitcher keeping that runner on base."

Kenny laughed. "You sure do like baseball, don't you?"

Jim grinned and nodded. "Yep. I like taking kids with me to baseball games, too."

Molly returned, her lipstick and blush freshened. "You boys getting along?" she asked.

"Sure, just fine," Jim said.

"Mr. Norwood says you're not ready to marry, huh Mom?"

Molly glared at Jim who smiled sheepishly and shrugged. She looked away, down the bowling alley. Jim tapped his fingers under the tabletop as he watched her.

Turning to Kenny, she said, "Baby, you're the most important person in my life. I need to be sure that any decision I make will be good for both of us."

"I like him."

She looked at Jim and smiled. "I like him too." She looked into her purse and fumbled for a tissue. Turning away she dabbed at her eyes. "It's time to go," she said. "Mr. Norwood will drop us home and then I'll drive you over to Grandma's for a few hours. You have those movies we rented don't you?"

"You've only asked me four times." He turned to Jim and held out his hand. "Thank you very much for the pizza and the bowling, Mr. Norwood."

Jim took the hand and gave it a warm squeeze. "It was a pleasure to meet you Kenny. I'll look forward to seeing you again."

* * *

He sat on the edge of the bed as Molly kneeled behind him, massaging his shoulders. "Jim, what's wrong? You've seemed so distracted all evening. You hardly spoke to me during the bowling tonight. Are you angry about something?"

He shook his head. "No, I'm not angry. I'm worried."

"Something about work? Something about me?"

"Yes to both. I missed work the last four days this week."

"Oh! I didn't know you were sick. You seem okay now."

He moaned with the pleasure of her touch. "Um, that feels good. Yeah, I'm better now."

Molly stopped massaging, resting her hands on his shoulders. "So what's going on?"

He turned on the bed to face her. He loved looking at her body, so trim and alluring. Her baseball breasts, her sweaty skin, and her curly bush were incredibly sexy.

"Molly, you said one of your biggest concerns was how Kenny would react. We got along great tonight. I told him I'd take him to a baseball game sometime."

She backed up until she was resting against the head of the bed and pulled the sheets up over her breasts. "You had no right to promise him that. He's had enough disappointments in his life."

"I don't intend to disappoint him. I'm hoping this relationship is going somewhere."

Molly picked up the pack of cigarettes from the bedside table, shook one out, and lit it. She inhaled long and deep, holding it captive before letting loose, slowly, in a dual stream of curling ringlets, creating a fog that obscured her face. She offered the stick to Jim who shook his head. She took another puff and ground it out in the ashtray next to the bed.

"I like you very much," she said. "I enjoy spending time with you."

"So you like me, huh? That's it? Is that all we have going? A friendship with some sex thrown in?"

Molly bit her lip. "Jim, I'm sorry if that's not enough. That's all I want right now. You're long over your divorce, but mine is still too fresh."

"Two years is a pretty long time."

Molly shook her head. "Not long enough."

Jim pulled himself up on the bed, kneeling next to her. "Molly … I'm sick."

She cocked her head. "Yes?"

"I'm very sick."

"It doesn't show," she said. "It isn't something contagious is it?"

Jim shook his head vigorously. "No, no. Nothing like that." He got up and began pacing.

He sat back down across from her and reached out for her hands. She tentatively put one out for him. "I went to the doctor on Tuesday," he said. "I was thinking I might get a prescription for Viagra."

Molly laughed. "Is that what this is about? You're concerned about having trouble in bed? You really had me going."

Jim bit his lip. "No, Molly. It's more serious." He held her hand tightly capturing her eyes with his own. "Molly, the doctor says I've got cancer."

He saw her face blanch. For a long time she merely stared.

"Molly?"

Her pent up breath blew out softly across the rippling sheets. "What kind of cancer?"

"Prostate."

"How awful." She took out another cigarette, and fiddled with it. "I don't know anything about these things. What did the doctor say? Can they cure it?" Her words tumbled out. "Are you going to die? Have to take lots of drugs and go bald?"

Jim shook his head. "He says I have to take pills for a month and then surgery." He saw a smile return to her face.

"And that's going to cure it? Doesn't sound that bad."

"Well, I didn't actually talk to him about all the details." He bit his lip, trying to make the next words sound casual. "There may be complications from the surgery."

Molly closed her eyes and hung her head. "Complications? My life is already too complicated. I don't know if I want to hear about this."

"You don't want to hear about what might happen to me ... to us?"

He saw her eyes flash. "Us? What do you mean us?"

"Don't you think that anything that happens to me will affect us?"

She climbed from the bed and pulled on her panties. "Us? There's not just you and me in 'us' anymore. Now there's Kenny, too." She grabbed her dress and dropped it over her head before continuing. "I don't know if you knew about this cancer before we made love last weekend, but you must have known before trying to make friends with my son today."

Jim stood holding out his hands. "I just found out. There wasn't any time to change the plans."

"There was plenty of time to change plans. And there still is." She turned her back to him and strode to the bedroom door.

Jim reached out his hand. "Molly, don't walk out. Please."

She stopped at the door, one hand on the knob. Her head bent.

"Molly. I love you. Can't you see that?"

He watched her standing there, her chest barely moving with her breath, a statue of desire. He spoke again, a whisper in the quiet room. "Don't you love me too?"

She spun to face him, anger flashing across her features.

"Damn it, I DO love you. That's why I'm so hurt. I've tried not to love you, to keep my feelings isolated, boxed away. I kept telling myself that I was just going to get hurt. But I allowed myself to ignore those warnings. Last week when we made love, I felt my heart melt. I imagined I had finally found the man of my dreams."

She shook her head, opening her purse and searching through. Jim picked up a tissue box from the bedside table and brought it over to her. She grabbed the top one and rubbed her eyes.

He leaned forward to hug her but she pushed him away.

"Molly. Baby. You just told me you loved me. Didn't you hear yourself? You said you loved me, and I love you. Isn't that enough to make it all worthwhile?"

She shook her head. "I don't know, Jimmy. Maybe. I have to think about what all this means to Kenny, too. I know you're hurting, and I don't mean to add to that. But right now I'm hurting too, and I need to deal with my pain before I can do you any good. Can you understand that?"

"But ... you do love me?"

Molly tilted her head and smiled. "Yeah, I guess I do."

She leaned forward for a gentle kiss, but stepped back when Jim reached for more.

"Molly, I need you."

He saw fright form in her eyes. "Don't need me, Jim. You can't count on me right now. Please. Just give me some time to think."

She returned to the door and stepped halfway through.

"Molly. I need to see you again. I can't let it end like this."

She paused but didn't turn to him.

"I'll call you tomorrow?" he asked.

The silence stretched, Jim barely daring to breathe. Her answer came softly, sadly. "No, not tomorrow. Give me a couple of days to think this out."

The door clicked closed.

* * *

Jim called in sick again on Monday. When he showed up at Dr. Goldberg's office the doctor interrupted seeing another patient to join Jim in the doctor's office.

"I tried to call you, Mr. Norwood."

Jim shrugged. "I needed some time. That was quite a shock you hit me with last week."

Dr. Goldberg nodded. "Yes, I'm sure it was." He picked up a manila folder that had Jim's name on it. "Let's see. We were talking about putting you on Lupron for a month and scheduling surgery for mid-May. Are you ready now?"

Jim shook his head. "This is messing up my relationship big time. What did you say was the chance of impotence again?"

Dr. Goldberg grasped his hands together, donning a sad frown. Jim got an image of the doctor as a funeral director, offering sympathy to the bereaved. He realized that wasn't far off the mark.

"Unfortunately, the chances are pretty high of at least some impotence. If that does occur, medicine has developed many treatments. Sometimes people respond to medications, like the Viagra you wanted. Some men choose to have implants or pumps inserted."

Jim got up and went to the window, looking down at the busy traffic below. "This is really tough on me, Doc. I just don't know if I can face not getting an erection the rest of my life. Isn't there some alternative? Drugs? Radiation? Anything? Maybe I should get a second opinion."

"You're welcome to do that, Jim. I can refer you to some reputable colleagues. But, realistically, I'm certain other urologists will recommend the same treatment plan. You've got an aggressive tumor. Without surgery you're sure to die within a short time. There's really no alternative."

Jim looked at the floor, shuffling his feet. "How can I be sure that living without sex would be worth it, Doc?"

Dr. Goldberg squeezed his chin as he thought. "I've got an idea."

He lifted up the phone and placed a call. Jim stood quietly, watching the traffic come and go from the hospital across the street while Dr. Goldberg talked in subdued tones, making arrangements. The doctor joined him at the window and pointed to a red brick building two blocks down from the hospital.

"You see that building with the green sign out front? That's the hospice, a place for patients with terminal illnesses. I've arranged for the nurse in charge, a Mrs. Williams, to give you a tour. Here, take this prescription for Lupron with you in case you decide to give it a try. Give me a call in a few days and let me know what you're thinking."

Jim decided to leave his car in the parking garage and walk the two blocks. Mrs. Williams, a trim woman in her forties, met him at the door. Leading him into her small office, she poured them both some coffee.

"A hospice unit is like a medical ward in some ways," she explained. "A patient is only admitted here after all medical hope for cure or recovery is gone. Our patients are all dying, some from cancer, some from other diseases like multiple sclerosis or Lou Gehrig's disease. We only provide what we call palliative care; that is, comfort and pain relief."

Jim sipped his coffee and looked around the office, cheerfully decorated with bright pictures and flowers. "I suppose Dr. Goldberg wants me to see what to expect if I don't have surgery for my cancer."

Mrs. Williams nodded. "Yes, that's what he told me. You're welcome to talk with anybody here."

She introduced Jim to staff, patients, and family members. The patients' ages varied greatly, with as many young adults as middle-aged and elderly. Jim spent over an hour sitting quietly with one fellow dying from metastatic prostate cancer. Even the smallest of movements made the fellow cry out in pain.

"Prostate cancer sets up in every bone in the body," Mrs. Williams explained. "It makes each motion agony, even breathing."

At four o'clock Jim left the unit and walked over to the pharmacy. He filled the prescription and took the first pill.

* * *

"Hello?"

"Hey, Molly, it's Jimmy."

Jim rummaged through his refrigerator as he held the phone against his ear. He hadn't been shopping in over a week, making the choices slim. Closing the refrigerator, he pulled a can of sardines and some crackers from a cabinet.

"So I'm back at work. How are things going with you?"

"Okay, I guess. Have you been back to the doctor?"

Jim popped the top of the sardines and pulled a packet of Ritz crackers from their box. He grabbed a fork and poured some water into a cup, gathering everything at the table to eat as he talked.

"Yeah. All I've gotta do is take pills for a month and have a little surgery. Course, he said it'd take me a month or two to recover. But he seemed pretty confident I'd be cured." Jim wondered how much of this he believed. He'd been trying hard to convince himself that all would be well.

"Did he say he was going to remove your prostate?"

"Yeah. He showed me pictures of how it was done. How about we get together Saturday afternoon? We can take in a movie, Kenny included of course." Jim pulled some sardine onto a cracker and munched while he waited for Molly to answer. The pause became prolonged.

"Molly, you there?"

"Yes. I'm here."

"So ... what?"

"I need more time to sort things out. I did a little reading about surgery for prostate cancer."

Jim paused in his chewing, putting the half eaten cracker back on his plate. He wiped the thick oil off his hands and lips. "Yeah? Go on."

"It's not simple surgery. Most people take months to recover and some have a lot of permanent problems. And sometimes the cancer comes back anyway. Did your doctor tell you all this?"

Jim gritted his teeth. "Yeah. What's your point, Molly?"

"That is my point. I feel like you haven't been honest with me. You took Kenny out after you already knew about the cancer without talking to me first. And now you're trying to make little of a very serious illness. Ralph was just like that, never giving me the full picture."

"Molly. Don't."

"I'm sorry Jim. I really am. But I can't invest time into a dishonest relationship. Maybe it's better if we don't see each other anymore."

He dropped the phone on the table, stood up and stared at it. He walked across the kitchen and pounded on the wall before returning to pick up the phone. As he lifted it he heard Molly talking.

"Hello? Jimmy? Are you there?"

"No." He said. "I'm not here. And I won't be here for you again. I'm going to get through this, Molly. I need people who are going to be a hundred per cent behind me. Good-bye."

He hung up the phone, sat in the chair, and stared at the wall. He looked over at the remaining vodka bottles sitting on the kitchen counter and shook his head.

"I'm going to get through this," he said out loud.

He picked up the phone and called Bob.

"Hey fellow," Bob said. "I heard you got back to work. How you doing?"

"Just fine, just fine. I started my pills and gonna have surgery next month."

"Yeah? You feeling okay, then? Really?"

Jim picked up the sardine again and savored the thick pungent flavor. He pushed away the water and went to the 'fridge for a beer.

"Yeppers, Bob, my man. Life is good. It's going to be a rough road, Doc says, but I expect a clear playing field at the end."

"That's great, Jimmy. You want to meet at O'Reilly's Sunday night, again? We had a blast last time."

Jim piled the sardines onto another cracker. He took a large bite, the juices dribbling down his chin.

"Sounds great, Bob. The game's not over until the fat lady sings, and I plan to be here for the whole nine innings."

Prostate Cancer

Prostate surgery is the third most common cancer in men, behind lung and colon. The incidence increases in age, so that by age eighty, 80% of men will have it. However, most of the time it's slow growing. There's a saying in medicine, "Most men will die with prostate cancer, but not because of it." Radiation implants may adequately treat many of the cancers.

However, as portrayed in this story, sometimes it strikes younger men, and when it does, it is often a very aggressive type. It commonly metastasizes to bones, causing severe pain and fractures. The treatment outlined here was typical in the 1990s, though in the 2010s special robot surgery, called Da Vinci, dramatically changed the techniques, reducing the morbidity and recovery time.

I wrote this story based on a friend of mine, a fifty-year-old physician who had just married a beautiful young wife a few months before he received the cancer diagnosis. They had planned on having a child, and my friend had counted on working another dozen years to build up a nice nest egg. He went through the procedures as described, out of work nearly three months, and ended up both incontinent and impotent. He had to retire from the E.R. and worked part time doing workmen's comp physicals.

As Jim would say, "Sometimes life will throw you a curveball." It's important to take a moment, perhaps every day, and recognize one's blessings.

The Rash

Only the four-year-old's face and scrawny arms showed outside the oversized hospital gown. She clutched her dad tightly, her eyes wide with fright. Dad hugged back, his hair as blond and his blue eyes as huge. He was a big man, with that ground-in look of a laborer. A navy tattoo danced on his muscular arm.

"I'm Doctor Cooper," I said.

The man reached out with one arm, the other holding tightly onto his charge. "Jimmy Gordon, sir."

Glancing at the chart, I said, "You told the nurse that Amelia has a rash on her privates?"

Dad's words came out slowly, stumbling. "It's not ... I mean, it is. But it's somethin' ... worse."

"When did you notice it?" I asked.

"We're divorced, Sally and me. I get Amelia two weekends a month. Picked her up tonight. Soon as I seen it ... I knew it ain't right."

I put the chart down and donned latex gloves. "Okay. Let me have a look."

Dad turned Amelia on his lap so that she sat with her back against his chest and raised the gown. There, on what should have been pale pink smooth labia, glared a dozen angry red ulcers.

Dad had been watching my face. "It's bad, ain't it?"

I tried to quiet my aching heart. "Are there any men in your ex-wife's house?"

I watched his eyes narrow. "Has he done somethin' to my little girl? I'll kill him! I'll beat the shit out of that bastard!"

"This doesn't look good, Mr. Gordon."

"Doc, you gotta level with me. What do ya think?"

I hesitated, but couldn't avoid the truth. "I'm afraid this looks like a case of Herpes."

He turned his daughter and hugged her tightly to his bosom. Gentle sobs leaked out of the bundle. I stepped forward, placing my hand on his shoulder. He didn't look up to ask, "What next?"

I stepped out of the room to gather a nurse and the equipment. I also took the opportunity to have the clerk call for protective services. The nurse helped dad hold Amelia as I obtained the culture. The cotton swab applied gently across the tender lesion made her cry out in pain.

Henson, the social worker on call that Friday night, seemed tired. I explained the situation, about how the father had limited visiting rights, and the possible perpetrator in the mother's home.

"You sure about this, Doc? I just had a case where someone thought Herpes, and it turned out to be just a diaper rash."

For a moment I hesitated, then cursed myself for doing so. "Yes, I'm certain. I've been an E.R. Doc long enough to know what I'm looking at. I presume you'll be calling in the police?"

"A little early for that." Henson sighed. "How do you know it's not the father who's the abuser?"

"Can't be. Herpes shows up in about a week. The father hasn't been with the child for two weeks."

"Okay, fine. Go ahead and admit the kid and I'll send a couple of officers by in the morning."

"The morning? You can't do anything more tonight?" I wanted to reach through the phone, grab this fellow by the collar, and shake some sense into him. How could a person whose job was supposed to involve helping people become so jaded to the horror of child abuse?

"Can't see how I can do anything more 'til the morning," he responded. "Did you get the guy's name, the one you think might be responsible?"

"No. Should I?"

"Couldn't hurt. Have a nurse or someone call me the mom's address, and the guy's name if you get it."

After arranging for the child's admission, I returned to the victims of the crime. Mr. Gordon held Amelia tightly and hummed a lullaby.

"What's the name of your wife's boyfriend?" I asked.

Mr. Gordon's face flushed and he spat a tobacco stain onto the cubicle's floor. "Jerome Peterson. He's an ex-con. Probably a drug addict. The police coming here or going out there?"

I donned my most reassuring smile. "We'll be admitting Amelia to the hospital. The police will wait until tomorrow, so that you and Amelia can have a quiet night's sleep."

Amelia clutched her father tightly. "I don't wanna go back."

He returned the hug, his voice quavering. "I'll take care of that man. Daddy promises."

A nurse guided the Gordons to a pediatric room upstairs, and I made sure the nurse called Henson with Peterson's info. I supposed the wheels of justice turned slowly, yet hopefully swiftly enough to prevent Amelia from going back into Peterson's clutches.

About four in the morning the patient flow slowed, providing an opportunity to call up old records on Jerome Peterson. It took an hour for the records to be found, a relatively slim manila folder with four E.R. visits over the past couple of years. On three of them, Peterson presented seeking narcotics for his back pain. The fourth was about eight months ago … for Herpes.

I had just closed the folder and put it back in the basket to be refiled in medical records when I heard the overhead speaker announce, "James Gordon, please report to the pediatric nurse station."

I called up to the station and the nurse who answered said she'd just come back from rounds and Mr. Gordon wasn't in the room with his daughter.

"You mean he abandoned his daughter? That doesn't sound like him. I mean, I hardly know him, but he seemed stuck to her like glue."

"Well, he's come unstuck. Maybe he's in the snack bar."

I remembered how he had promised to get his revenge on Peterson and felt a knot tighten in my midsection. "How long has he been gone?"

"Could've been a couple of hours."

One of the E.R. nurses interrupted the conversation by banging on my window, signaling for me to come quickly. I followed her into the trauma cubicle where the paramedics had just unloaded a bloody-bandaged patient onto our stretcher.

"Someone took a baseball bat to him," the paramedic told me as he read off the notes on his clipboard. "Multiple head injuries, face smashed. Probably flail chest, fractured arms. He's a mess."

The nurses stripped off the victim's clothes and started IVs. I called out orders for x-rays, blood work, catheters, and lines, while I examined his many injuries. He was unconscious, but had stable pulse and blood pressure. Blood seeped out of both ears. Large raccoon eyes suggested a skull fracture. Busted teeth, exposed bones, shattered pelvis, bloody urine; whoever had taken out his frustrations on this guy had meant to leave his mark.

"What's his name?" I asked, palpating along the chest wall, counting broken ribs.

The paramedic read off his record, "Jerome Peterson."

My stethoscope clattered against the stretcher as I stepped back to take another look at Mr. Peterson. His face was a swollen meaty mess, but his youth offered hope, with both his lungs and heart working fine.

"Should I call the helicopter?" the head nurse asked.

I knew she should. If Mr. Peterson didn't get shipped to a neurosurgeon promptly, his brain would be mush. If he did get shipped, he might recover. Eventually.

I looked at the helpless man. Splints held his broken arms. Oxygen flowed into the tube I had stuck down his throat. IV tubes brought fluids in. Other tubes brought out urine and sucked blood from his chest cage. I hesitated a moment, wondering if this fellow deserved all of society's efforts to save him.

"Yes, call for the helicopter," I said.

When I stepped out of the cubicle I found a policeman waiting. I read his nametag. "Bill." I guess a beat-up addict was more important to the police than the child he had abused.

"Can I talk to him?"

"Nah, he's unconscious. Depends on how much brain damage if he even survives. The helicopter should be here in a couple of minutes. What happened?"

Bill checked his notes. "Dispatch got a call from a woman to come to her home. When we showed up there was a hell of a fight going on. Well, almost over. Some gorilla was standing over Peterson here, beating the hell out of him."

"What happened to the other man?"

"He wouldn't stop. When the officers tried to grab him he turned on them. One of them shot him dead." The policeman checked his notes again. "Ex-husband of the woman who'd placed the call. Guy named James Gordon."

I thought about Peterson, about how, if he recovered, he might go back in the home with Amelia and her mother, or maybe on to some other helpless child. Wandering to the nurses' workstation, I palmed a bottle of potassium additive. When no one was looking, I mainlined Mr. Peterson. The good thing about a potassium bolus is that its 100% immediately and reliably deadly. I felt nearly certain no one would ever know what I'd done. Once a person's dead, their cells break down and potassium is everywhere. Besides, the forensic pathologist would have enough obvious causes of death to consider before looking for a murdering physician.

Nurses and technicians rushed in at the call of the alarms. I led them through a short code, and after a few minutes declared Mr. Peterson dead.

Bill had snuck inside the curtain to watch. "Didn't make it, huh?"

I shrugged. "Some people are meant to die."

Child Abuse, Herpes, and Physician Morality

Many times, nurses and technicians I work with have complimented me on my calm nature. I'm as unperturbed by treating a patient with a gunshot wound to the chest, as I am by a child seizing, a schizophrenic shouting obscenities, or a sudden cardiac arrest. I recognize the need to captain the ship, assess the situation scientifically, make quick and appropriate decisions, and quietly orchestrate the treatment plan. Child abuse, though, still claws my gut. Even mild abuse, such as when a parent swats a child for not sitting still in front of me, earns the parent my admonishment. Severe abuse, as in this case, or intentional burning, or choking, or shaken baby syndrome, has caused me to leave the room for ten minutes to calm my temper.

In the 1980s, the time setting of this story, child abuse didn't receive as much urgency as it does now. This story is based on a true case of a child being brought in to my emergency room with genital herpes. My call to the child welfare person brought even less response than what is portrayed in this story ... the child was sent home and follow up occurred several days later. Nowadays the police and child protective service representatives would have come to the E.R. promptly, and the perpetrator arrested by the next day. The rest of the story, about the father beating up the sexual abuser, being killed, and then my response with the potassium are all fictitious.

Of the dozens of venereal diseases I see, herpes genitalis ranks fourth in frequency, behind chlamydia, gonorrhea, and trichomonas. Single or double doses of medications will cure the first three, but because Herpes is a viral infection, once infected, the victim can only control the infection's symptoms, which will flare up on occasions of stress. As in this story, herpes presents with painful white ulcers about 2 mm across, grouped in clusters, each surrounded by red halos. The initial episode erupts roughly a week after exposure, and, if untreated, may last two to three weeks. Medications introduced in the 1980s can shorten the duration of the ulcers and even prevent outbreaks if taken regularly.

I would never, ever, purposely take a patient's life, no matter how horrid they had been. If, for example, a mass murderer, shot by police, or an attempted suicide bomber who survived, came to my

E.R., I would do everything in my power to treat them with the same respect and diligence as if they were my brother. I have seen the results when physicians did not keep this high moral standard, for example, saying "Oh, it's just another drunk," and it turned out the drunk had hit his head and wasn't responding because of the subdural hematoma. A physician's morality, his constant devotion to doing good, must always be prominent in his mind.

Brave Heart

I read the chief complaint from the chart I had just picked up. "Possible broken rib." This should be an easy one, I thought. A brief history, an x-ray, a rib belt, some pain pills, maybe a work note, and I'd have the patient on his way.

Bringing the chart into the cubicle I held out my hand. "I'm Doctor Grant Saunders, nice to meet you."

Brad Peters' handshake was firm and friendly.

"How you doin' Doc? Sorry to bother you, but the company insisted I get this checked out. I slipped off the back of the truck pullin' out a load of bread. I must have hit the truck rail pretty hard."

Mr. Peters' chest supported huge muscles on a giant's frame. At thirty-one-years-old, he could have played Hercules at the local playhouse. I felt the telltale step off of a broken rib as I gently rubbed his bruise.

"Any other medical history?" I asked, filling out his chart. "Heart problems, diabetes, asthma?"

"Nah, Doc. Never been sick a day in my life."

I returned his cheerful smile. Brad Peters had a likeable aura, a friendly fellow who enjoyed the honest pleasures of life. In my emergency department I spent much of my time treating the sallow, depressed, and chronically ill. Mr. Peters brought a ray of sunshine to my windowless workday.

"Married? Smoker?"

"Wife and two little 'uns. Never been a smoker though."

"The nurse will take you to x-ray in a few minutes, Mr. Peters. Would you like something for pain first?"

Mr. Peters laughed. "Nah, but thanks anyway. Just patch me up and let me get back to work."

"X-ray first. It won't take long."

In thirty minutes I saw that Mr. Peters was back on his stretcher, so I headed over to the viewing station. One glance at Mr. Peters' x-rays squeezed my breath away.

When I returned to his cubicle he greeted me with his big toothy grin. "What's the verdict, Doc? Broken rib or only a bruise?"

I settled into a chair next to his stretcher, looking into his eyes, trying to see if God had left some sign on this Golden Boy's face of the challenge He had cast upon him.

"There is a broken rib, Brad. But there's something more. Have you been feeling well lately?"

Peters looked puzzled a moment, and then the boyish smile returned. "Now that you mention it, I have been tirin' out for a couple of weeks. Too much pizza, my wife says."

"There's something wrong with your x-ray," I told him. "There are shadows along the hilum that shouldn't be there."

"Hilum?"

"The place where the breathing tubes separate from your windpipe. I'm going to order some blood work and a CAT scan. This will take about an hour. Can I get you anything else right now? Coffee?"

"Nah. Do what ya' gotta do, Doc. I'm just fine."

The radiologist called me an hour later with the results of the CAT. Mr. Peters' tumor not only encircled both bronchial tubes, but also had invaded the sack surrounding the heart. Surgery would be out of the question. His blood counts confirmed my guess of cancer induced anemia, explaining his recent fatigue.

How do you tell a young working man that his chest is full of cancer? I wanted to do something special for Mr. Peters, maybe take him to the conference room, or down to the coffee shop to discuss this over java. With a full twenty-patient E.R. there just wasn't the time. Even for this, there just wasn't the time.

In a few minutes I was back on the chair next to him. "I have the results of your CAT scan," I said. "It's bad news, I'm afraid."

"I figured somethin' was up, Doc. Go ahead."

"You have lymphoma. It's not the worst of the cancers, by any means; there are a lot of treatments available, especially radiation and some types of chemotherapies. But you're in for a rough time for at least several months. Maybe years."

The smile never left his face. He hadn't the bravado of the eighteen-year-old. He had, instead, an inner strength one rarely finds, a brave heart. Good. He would need it.

"Well, when do we start?" he asked, already geared up for the fight. Perhaps he thought this was like any other obstacle thrown in his path. His confidence, strength, and moral certitude had always been enough to overcome any obstacle. Those qualities might pull him through this as well.

"This is Friday afternoon. It's not going to make much of a difference if you wait another couple of days. If I arrange an appointment with the oncologist on Monday morning, could you get there? His office is in the building next door."

"Monday will be fine, Doc. I'll let them know at work. Gotta coach my kid's ball team tomorrow. Wouldn't want to miss that."

I called the oncologist, and he agreed to see Mr. Peters on Monday. I finished up the chart and handed it off to the nurse, including instructions for a rib belt and pain pills.

I went back to work, but Brad Peters remained on my mind. Where was the justice in this? People who smoked and over ate and whined about minor aches and pains lived until old age, yet this young fellow might not see Christmas.

When my relief came I told him the story of Brad Peters and his bravery.

He nodded and said, "Life doesn't play fair, Grant. Someday we'll each have to face our own lymphoma or similar crisis. Maybe that's why there are Brad Peters in this world, to show us a role model."

"I don't know if I could be that brave," I said.

He shrugged. "You are who you are, Grant. Meanwhile, our lives go on. Go home and enjoy your time off. You never know what tomorrow will bring."

Cancer

Cancer is caused by a normal cell in our bodies going rogue. Normal cells follow certain rules: they look like their type (liver cell for example), they stay in the place they're formed, they only reproduce to make exactly similar cells when there is a need for more of them, and they produce only the hormones or enzymes delegated to their tasks. In cancer, a DNA mutation causes an override of one or more of these functions. If the cell loses the function to stay in its place, it wanders through the body and sets up a new colony somewhere else, called a metastasis. If the cell loses its ability to not reproduce unless needed, it copies itself frequently, creating more and more cancer cells. Any type of cell can turn cancerous.

The three standard treatments for cancer include surgery, radiation, and chemotherapy. Surgery succeeds in cases where the cancer is well contained, that is, small, localized, and without metastasis. This is typically true of some skin cancers, colon polyps, small breast lumps, and early prostate disease. Occasionally, lung segments and certain brain cancers may qualify as well. Radiation shrinks cancer, so, for example, when a bulky tumor presses on the brain, radiation will relieve the symptoms and make surgery easier. Radiation also can be used near the area of a cancer in the hope of killing cells that have just started to metastasize, such as in melanoma. Chemotherapy kills cells dividing rapidly. Since this typifies some types of cancer, chemotherapy is particularly useful in killing certain cancers such as leukemia and lymphoma, both of whose cells divide very rapidly. However, chemotherapy also kills normal cells undergoing replenishment, typically hair cells and bone marrow (blood producing) cells, resulting in baldness and anemia.

Within our immune system runs lines of filters known as our lymph, a system of vessels and nodes, whose roles are to filter body fluids and capture and kill foreign substances, such as viruses or strange chemicals. When a lymph cell turns cancerous, it creates the cancer called lymphoma, of which there are two types: Hodgkin and non-Hodgkin, though differentiation has little impact on the disease, treatment, or patient's survival. An aggressive cancer, without chemotherapy, a patient may die within months of the diagnosis. Fortunately, with radiation shrinking the cancer and chemotherapy aggressively targeting this tumor, lymphoma and its cousin leukemia (cancer of the blood cells) often can be cured – or at least reduced to nondetectable levels, which we refer to as being in remission.

New cancer medications being developed target genetic markers specific to the cancer cells, thus killing only cancer cells and not any normal cells. Initial studies report extraordinary success. Although we'll never live in a "cancer-free" world, future medicine will develop more treatments, and perhaps even more cures for those who are stricken.

By the Numbers

Jennifer watched Dr. Mathews hold his stethoscope against Mrs. Hairston's back, the doctor's silver hair falling in front of his eyes. He straightened up slowly, unhooking the earpieces to allow the instrument to hang around his neck. He read his orders out loud as he wrote them on the chart in his crisp penmanship.

"One point five Proventil nebulizer, forty of Lasix, 125 of Solumedrol, and two liters nasal oh-two. Chest x-ray, CBC, and a chem panel." He turned his back on the two women and took the chart with him to the workstation.

Jennifer hooked the clear plastic tube to the oxygen outlet and fed the line into Mrs. Hairston's nose. The elderly woman gave her a smile of appreciation and pointed over to the doctor. "I thought they retired him."

The nurse glanced over at the doctor hunched at his desk, writing on a chart. Sixty-seven years of worry lines overlaid drooping bushy gray eyebrows, a perpetual frown showing on pinched-in lips. "Nope. I guess he'll be here 'til he dies. Medicine is his life."

Mrs. Hairston sniffed. "He always seems so calculating, like treating me is getting in the way of his numbers."

"Not at all, ma'am. He loves what he does. That's just his way." Holding the reservoir up to the light, Jennifer carefully poured in one milliliter of the breathing medicine. Hooking the chamber onto the mask, she set it onto Mrs. Hairston's face. After pushing the attached oxygen flow up to high, she stepped back to be sure the vaporized medication was working properly.

When she returned to the desk she sat watching Dr. Mathews write. When he felt her stare he looked up. "What?"

"Nothing."

"No, what?"

Jennifer shrugged. "Just something Mrs. Hairston said. You know, you don't always come across as very friendly. Would it kill you to smile every now and then?"

He set his pen down carefully. "Medicine isn't about smiling, Jennifer. It's about making the patients better." He pointed across the room at the monitor. "Mrs. Hairston's pulse ox shows 90%. When she reaches 95% we'll be able to send her home."

He took off his glasses, scrubbing them on his jacket before putting them back on his nose. "Numbers, Jennifer, it's all about numbers. At ninety-five per cent, Mrs. Hairston will be fine. Health and illness, life or death ... everything can be quantified. The balance might depend on a single digit; a blood pressure drop of ten points, a minute without oxygen. Pay attention to the numbers and the patient will be fine. Miss something, well ..."

"Come on now, Dr. Mathews. Medicine isn't like that. A lot of times you can't tell what's going on. Like a kid with a fever. You can't rely on just numbers. You gotta use judgment."

She watched him run his hand through his hair, pausing halfway to scratch his scalp. "I'm been a doctor for coming on forty years. I've made a few mistakes in my time, sometimes serious ones. But one lesson I've learned from those mistakes is to trust the facts. If a child's got a fever, that kid's getting a CBC, chest x-ray, urinalysis, blood cultures, and a spinal tap."

"Yeah, I know. You do more spinal taps than all the other doctors put together."

His deep brown eyes stared at her unblinkingly. "And you think that's wrong?"

She hesitated. "I don't know."

"Let me tell you, Jennifer. I've never missed a case of meningitis. Never. If I have to do ten thousand normal spinal taps to catch the one occult meningitis, then I'll do all ten thousand and one. That's why I work in this small town E.R. you know – plenty of time to get all the information and make appropriate decisions."

The emergency radio crackled. "Hey, Jennifer, you there?"

Jennifer pushed down on the transmit button. "I hear you, Brandon. What've you got?"

"Car wreck on Highway twenty! Three victims. We got the driver of car one; probable broken hip. ETA twenty. Sharon's at the scene in unit two for the other car. We called in the unit with the jaws from across the county."

"What about the helicopter?" Dr. Mathews asked.

"Not running today. Too windy."

Jennifer surveyed the unit, the six empty stretchers and Mrs. Hairston at the end. The space was good, she just needed help. She told the secretary to page the nursing supervisor. Fran called right back and said she'd be there in twenty minutes.

A young woman holding her low belly came in from the waiting room. Jennifer took her by the hand and led her into the private examining room down the hallway, picking up a blank chart on the way. She shut the door, instructing the patient to sit on the stretcher. The girl appeared to be in pain, an anxious look on her face and both hands pushing in at her pelvis.

"What's your name, dear?"

"My friends call me Bev. Oh, you want my full name, don't you? Here, I have my driver's license and insurance card. Uhh." She had let go of her belly to pull the cards from her purse, when, with a grimace, she dropped the two cards onto the floor and grasped the area again. Jennifer picked them up and clipped them onto the chart. She noted the girl was eighteen.

Filling out Beverley's name and birthdate on her form, she asked, "What's wrong, Bev?"

The girl took a few deep breaths, her cheeks deeply flushed. "I'm so embarrassed."

"Something to do with a fella?" Jennifer asked.

Beverly lowered herself to lie flat on the stretcher. "Yes. We only had sex once. But then I heard from another girl that he had VD. Now it's my monthly, and it's the worse cramping I've ever had."

"That sure can hurt," Jennifer said, placing a comforting hand on Beverly's shoulder. "How long has it been hurting?"

"Started about four hours ago, I guess." Beverly looked up with a half grin. "At least with my IUD I don't have to worry about pregnancy!"

Jennifer handed her a gown. "We're expecting to get busy real soon. Let me help you get undressed." Each garment Beverley took off Jennifer carefully folded and placed neatly onto a stack on the counter. She noted the panties had a large blood spot. Jennifer then helped her patient into the gown and tied the back.

She watched Beverly lie back on the stretcher, curling into a ball and holding her belly. Covering her with a sheet, Jennifer attached the blood pressure cuff and obtained a set of vital signs which she wrote onto the appropriate slots on the chart. Removing the cuff, she cleaned a spot on Beverly's inner elbow and placed a small IV. The blood flowed into a collection of small tubes before Jennifer capped it off.

"I'll try to hurry up Dr. Mathews and see if I can get him in here before the ambulances arrive," she said.

Back at the desk, Jennifer gave Dr. Mathews her report. "Eighteen-year-old with low belly pain for four hours. Says it began with her period. She had sex with a boy who might have had VD."

"Numbers, Jennifer. What are her vitals?"

She read from where she'd written them on the chart. "Temp 100. Pulse one ten. B.P. ninety over sixty. You think you can get in there before the trauma arrives?"

Dr. Mathews rubbed his forehead. "Probably not. Those numbers are a little weak. Better give her a liter bolus and run her I.V. at 300. Let's get a CBC, CMP, thyroid panel, serum lactate, serum preg, urinalysis, and urine drug screen."

Jennifer recorded the orders as he gave them. "She's got an IUD, Dr. Mathews. You want to skip the pregnancy test?"

He cocked back his head to look down at her through his gold-rimmed reading glasses. "No. A pregnancy test is part of the complete workup."

Jennifer made out the lab slips and attached them around the blood tubes with a rubber band, putting them in the "Out" box. Stepping over to the supply cabinet, she pulled out a plastic bag of saline and the associated tubing. She flushed the saline down the line, ready to return to Beverly's room with the bottle.

The ambulance sirens blasted from around the corner and Jennifer glanced at her watch, "Shit. It's only been twelve minutes."

She hung the just prepared I.V. line on a hook over stretcher three, and turned to watch Brandon and his partner roll a leg-splinted patient towards her. She helped them transfer the young fellow from their gurney onto the E.R. stretcher.

"Twenty-six-year-old male driver involved in a two car head-on collision," Brandon reported. "Angled and shortened left leg, probably broken femur or hip. Better check the chest too; steering column bent."

"Vital signs?" Jennifer asked as she inserted an I.V. into the fellow's right arm. She attached the fluids she had prepared into the line.

"Pulse ninety-six, blood pressure one sixty over ninety-four. He seems pretty stable."

"What's his name?" Dr. Mathews asked, looking at the rhythm shown on the ambulance's monitor.

"Uh ... Johnson, I think."

"Mr. Johnson? I'm Doctor Mathews. Can you hear me?"

The patient struggled against the restraints as he tried to see the physician.

"The name's Bob Jones, you idiots. And I'm in a lot of fucking pain."

"Alcohol on board," Jennifer said, wrinkling her nose and waving her hand in front of her face.

Dr. Mathews listened to Mr. Jones's lungs and heart with his stethoscope. As he pushed on the man's chest, Mr. Jones groaned. Jennifer placed an inflatable cuff around the patient's arm and turned on the automatic blood pressure machine.

A second ambulance roared up to the E.R. entrance. Sharon Stone and her partner rushed in with the accident's second victim, an elderly woman.

"*Jesus!*" Jennifer thought. "*She looks awful.*"

"Bella Murdock," Sharon called, following Jennifer to stretcher five. "Seventy-four-year-old passenger, unrestrained. Flail chest, tachy at 150, zippo blood pressure. She's got some major bleeding in her scalp and her belly's puffing up. Three failed attempts at a line."

Jennifer rushed to set up the oxygen, monitor leads, and attempt an I.V. She shouted to the secretary, "Call a code!"

Red splotches accented the bone whiteness of Bella Murdock's skin. Even before she had been pummeled, the old lady had been frail. Now with the jagged end of a broken humerus sticking out of her arm and blood running out of scalp bandages, she looked corpselike. Her right chest was caved in. A bluish discoloration of her belly suggested accumulated blood. *Probably tore her aorta,* Jennifer thought.

"Get a chest tube, stat," Dr. Mathews ordered. He grabbed some equipment from a nearby cart and guided a breathing tube through Mrs. Murdock's mouth and down her trachea.

"Vital signs?" he shouted.

Jennifer glanced at the monitor. "Pulse one-fifty. Machine can't find a B.P."

As she attached equipment, Jennifer called out orders. "Brandon, get the chest tube tray off the top shelf there. No. Next one over to the right. Grab those bottles under the sink. Sharon, pull down a suture tray. Yeah! Thanks." Jennifer pumped up the sphygmomanometer's cuff, listening intently as the needle plummeted to zero again. "Confirmed, no blood pressure," she reported. "Should we do CPR?"

Dr. Mathews shook his head. "Her body won't tolerate it. Start Dopamine at five mikes. Get her pressure up to eighty."

As Jennifer was pulling the dopamine bag and tubing out of the cabinet, Fran came into the E.R., took them from her, and began preparing the line.

Dr. Mathews slit open a hole between Mrs. Murdock's ribs and pushed in a tube. A gush of blood poured out the tube's end and onto the floor. Brandon grabbed some towels and threw them onto the sticky puddle. Jennifer hooked up the tube's bleeding end to the suction bottles.

"Still can't get an I.V.," Fran called out.

"Get me a subclavian set," Dr. Mathews ordered. Jennifer rushed to the cabinet and grabbed another tray wrapped in blue cloth. Dr. Mathews painted Mrs. Murdock's left chest wall with orange Betadine, then nimbly placed a large plastic catheter under her collarbone, adding another porcupine quill to her body.

"Blood coming from the Foley," the head nurse announced. Jennifer looked down to where Fran and Sharon had been inserting a catheter into Mrs. Murdock's bladder. Instead of yellow urine, the attached bag was filling with blood.

"Christ! This lady's a disaster."

Sirens signaled the arrival of a third ambulance.

"Must be Mr. Murdock," Sharon said. "They were cutting the car apart to get him out when we left."

Before stepping out of the curtained enclosure, Jennifer looked at Mrs. Murdock, her bloody broken body an exhibit of tubes and machine attachments.

Just outside the curtain she watched the third ambulance crew bring in Mr. Murdock, air splints on his left arm and leg. A too-big white plastic collar kept his neck in line with his chest.

"Stretcher two!" She preceded them to grab the monitor leads.

"Emile Murdock," the paramedic told her. "Seventy-six-years-old, restrained driver in a head-on collision. Passenger side took most of the blow. B.P. 170 over ninety. Pulse eighty-five. Minor cuts. Looks like he's got a broken wrist and maybe ankle. He keeps asking about his wife. She's here, right?"

Jennifer ignored the question, quickly moving the monitor lines from the ambulance's portable defibrillator to her overhead machine. She checked the I.V. line that the paramedic had started and began gently prodding Mr. Murdock's body. "Where are you hurting?" she asked.

He looked up with tear-filled eyes. "Bella? Is she here? Is she going to be all right?"

"The doctor is with your wife now," Jennifer assured him.

"Bella?" he shouted. "Can you hear me?"

"I need to know if you're hurt," Jennifer said. "Did you hit your head? Were you knocked out? Does it hurt when I push here?" After her quick exam Jennifer jotted orders on the chart.

Dr. Mathews came into the curtained cubicle, pulling off blood-stained gloves. "You're Mr. Murdock?"

"Yes sir. Are you the doctor taking care of my wife?"

Dr. Mathews nodded. He turned to Jennifer, "What have you found?"

"Broken left wrist, possible neck, chest, and left ankle injuries."

"Have you collected blood yet?"

Jennifer held up a baggie with a half-dozen blood tubes, each with a different color stopper. "The paramedics got it in the field. Are these orders okay?"

Dr. Mathews scanned the list she'd written and said, "Add an EKG and a pelvis x-ray.

"Is she going to die?" Mr. Murdock asked. "Bella and I celebrated our fifty-third wedding anniversary last week, Doctor. If she dies please let me go, too."

Dr. Mathews stood still for a moment, his head cocked. "So you think death might be better than a life of pain?"

Jennifer stared at him, watching him turn and stride out of the stretcher's curtains.

"Hey, Doc," Mr. Jones called out. "What about my shot?"

Dr. Mathews called back to Jennifer, "Thirty of Toradol IM for Mr. Jones." She heard him tell the secretary, "Please page the surgeon and the orthopedist on call."

Mr. Murdock signaled to Jennifer and she walked up next to him.

"Is that the man who hit us?" he whispered, pointing to Mr. Jones' stretcher hidden by the curtain. She nodded.

"It sounds like he's in pain."

Jennifer wanted to make a smart-aleck comment, but just shrugged.

The alarms went off in stretcher five. Jennifer rushed across the room and inside the curtain. Fran was handing Dr. Mathews two hand-size paddles attached to a defibrillator machine.

"Charge to three hundred," he ordered. Jennifer watched Fran push the charge button. The machine whined. The screen numbers zipped up to three hundred. *Ding.*

Dr. Mathews held the paddles hard against Bella's chest. "All clear!" Pushing a button on each paddle he completed the circuit through her body, causing her arms and legs to reach up for her soul as it departed for heaven.

"Flatline," Jennifer reported.

"One milligram of Atropine. Two of Epinephrine. Fifty milliequivalents of sodium bicarb." Dr. Mathews spat out orders, each number precisely measured in the battle of life and death. Jennifer helped record the details as well as helping Fran administer medications *ad nauseum.*

After half an hour she slipped out, preparing another breathing treatment for Mrs. Hairston.

"That woman ain't gonna make it," Mrs. Hairston stated.

Jennifer shrugged. "Dr. Mathews is doing his best."

"Dr. Numbers? That's what people call him, ya know. He's so busy asking about numbers, he doesn't see what's important in life. When I asked him about his kids, he told me he hasn't seen any of them in ten years."

Jennifer shook her finger in the older woman's face. "Don't you go talking Dr. Mathews down. He's a very good doctor. Just … just different, that's all. He cares very much about his patients. He takes his job seriously. That's all."

When she brought Mr. Jones his medicine, the fellow cursed her. "Been half an hour since Doc said I could have it. What the fuck took you so long?"

"I've been trying to bring back to life the woman you killed."

He glared at her and she returned the favor, until finally he averted his eyes.

Jennifer got back to the desk in time to take a call from the orthopedist. She told him about Mr. Jones's broken hip and sore chest, and Mr. Murdock's broken wrist and ankle. She handed the phone to the secretary who took down the doctor's orders. When the secretary hung up Jennifer reminded her to call the surgeon again.

Fifty minutes into the resuscitation Dr. Mathews stepped back and asked Jennifer to recap.

She read from her notes. "Seventeen epinephrine, three atropine, two bicarb, one calcium, one magnesium, dopamine at 30 mikes, four pints of blood, and shocked six times." She looked up at him, observing the frustration on his face. She wondered if he thought Mrs. Murdock's death could have been prevented, as if he hadn't done everything humanly possible. She had worked two other codes with him over the past three years. After each one he had gone into the private doctor's room and mourned.

She touched his shoulder. "Nobody could have saved her, Dr. Mathews. The numbers were stacked against you."

He looked to Fran and asked, "How about more blood?" She shook her head. There was no more available. He glanced at the clock. "Eleven fifteen."

Jennifer filled in the numbers on the "Time of death" slot.

Dr. Mathews reached up and gently closed Mrs. Murdock's eyelids and pulled the sheet over her face. He shuffled across the ward to stretcher number two.

Jennifer followed him in and stood on one side.

The old man hesitated, his eyes fixed on Dr. Mathews's face. "My wife?"

Dr. Mathews shook his head slowly.

Mr. Murdock's eyes puffed up as he let out an anguished moan. Turning to her colleague, Jennifer saw Dr. Mathews tremble, and then stand petrified, his only motion the opening and closing of his fists. Mr. Murdock wailed.

She led Dr. Mathews out of the enclosure and to his desk. "Perhaps a tranquilizer for Mr. Murdock?" Jennifer suggested.

Dr. Mathews shook his head. "No, let him grieve."

The orthopedist came down and Jennifer showed him the x-rays. The bone doctor arranged admissions for both Mr. Jones and Mr. Murdock, and left. Fran left with Mrs. Murdock, heading to the morgue. Jennifer went to work putting the emergency department back in order. When the surgeon finally called back, she told him about the two admissions, and he promised he'd check them both out right away. Mrs. Hairston finished her breathing treatments and Jennifer checked her out of the unit, cleaning up her stretcher as well.

Once everything was put away, Jennifer settled onto a stool and watched Dr. Mathews writing his long records.

"I guess Mrs. Murdock's number was up?"

Dr. Mathews stopped writing to look at her. She had hoped her witticism would bring a smile, but he looked sadder than ever. "We're all nothing but numbers, Jennifer. Vital signs; pulse, blood pressure, temperature, these are just the beginning. We routinely measure the amount of sodium ions in a drop of blood, the strength of the thyroid hormone keeping us active, even the force of each heartbeat pushing through our system."

"Mrs. Murdock was a crushed animal, Dr. Mathews. You couldn't save her life by adjusting her numbers."

He let his head droop into his hands. Jennifer stood, resisting her temptation to hug him, instead just laying her hand on his shoulder. He looked up at her with a forced smile.

"One, Jennifer. When all is said and done, that's the number that counts. Mrs. Murdock had the one life. And I couldn't save it."

"No one could have. This wasn't because of your error. You didn't miscalculate. Everything was as much by the book as I've ever seen a code run."

Dr. Mathews raised his hand, setting it on top of hers on his shoulder. "I hold life and death in my hands. Every number is important."

Picking the top page off from a stack of papers from the desk, he said, "Look here. Mrs. Murdock's white blood cell count was thirty-two. It tells us what was happening to her body. Look at this CPK. Eight-hundred and sixty five. That's all crushed muscle."

He shifted to the next one. "Here's a positive pregnancy test. You know what it takes to have a positive pregnancy test? A minimum of a five-day-old fetus."

Jennifer snatched it from his hands. "Positive?" She looked at the patient's name. "Good God. It's Beverly."

"Who?"

"The girl in the private GYN room. Remember?"

His face turned ashen.

Dr. Mathews took the report back from her. "It says her HCG is 4378. That puts her at about four weeks' gestation. That pelvic pain could have been a ruptured ectopic pregnancy. She could bleed to death. Has she been getting the I.V. fluids?"

Jennifer shook her head. "Her fluids never got started, Dr. Mathews. I completely forgot about her."

The two rushed around the corner to the closed examining room. Jennifer beat him by one step and flung open the door. Beverly lay with unseeing eyes, a dried river of blood draining down the side of the stretcher into a pool on the floor.

"Call a code!" Jennifer yelled to the secretary and rushed back past Dr. Mathews to grab an I.V. set-up. She pulled the crash cart with one hand, dragging tubing in the other, and clenching the saline canister in her teeth. In a flurry of activity she tried to do everything at once; attach the monitor, start the I.V., and begin CPR. She looked up and saw Dr. Mathews standing paralyzed.

Jennifer stood six inches from his face.

"Dr. Mathews," she yelled. "Snap out of it!" He didn't respond, just stared at her in bewilderment. Jennifer slapped him.

He blinked and his focus returned. Racing to the cart he grabbed the intubation equipment and had Beverly tubed just as Fran and the aide rushed in. For almost two hours the medical staff sweated under Dr. Mathews' orders. Beverly never regained a pulse. She needed blood, and all that the hospital had stocked had been used up on Mrs. Murdock.

After exhaustion of the team members forced Dr. Mathews to call a halt, Jenifer saw a chilling freeze settle onto his face.

"Dr. Mathews?"

He turned to her, but his eyes were unseeing.

"Dr. Mathews? Are you okay?"

He shook his head. Gently putting both hands on her shoulders, he pulled her to him in a tight hug. She reached around and held him, patting him gently on the back.

"This was the one, Jenny," he whispered. "This was the last one."

Jennifer had thought her three years had toughened her enough to accept undeserving death. Now, as the tears poured down her face, she knew she'd never be tough enough. "I'm so sorry, SO sorry. It's all my fault. She wouldn't be dead if I had started that I.V., or if I had checked on her earlier."

She could barely hear his reply. "Not your fault. An eighteen-year-old, IUD or not, you – you have to play the numbers. The odds are strong you're dealing with a ruptured ectopic pregnancy. This is what we get for not adding it all up."

He pushed away from her and trudged slowly into his doctor's lounge. Jennifer hesitated and then followed. She knocked, and when he didn't answer she peeked in. Her heart stopped at seeing a gun in his hand.

"Dr. Mathews? What are you doing?"

He kept staring at his weapon. "You ever hear of Russian Roulette, Jennifer? It's sort of a gambling game. You see, you mix five blank cartridges and one live one together, then place them in random order in the gun. You were right. I do make mistakes. I do mess up the numbers. So every time I've lost a patient, when it was my fault, I've let the numbers determine my punishment."

He toyed with the gun, shifting it back and forth between his hands. Grasping it firmly in his right hand, he held the barrel to his right ear. "It works like this; you hold it to your head ..."

"Don't do this," Jennifer whispered, taking a tentative step towards him. She stopped abruptly as he pulled back on the trigger. It clicked. She felt her stomach plummet to her shoes.

Standing still she held out her hand. "It's over. You're innocent. Give me the gun."

He shook his head. "You're not keeping count, Jennifer. That one was for Mrs. Murdock – this time for Beverly."

The blast echoed in the small room.

Ectopic Pregnancy and Death in the E.R.

Ectopic pregnancy occurs when the fertilized egg implants in the fallopian tube instead of the uterus. This generally occurs in a woman who has had venereal disease resulting in scars in the tube, and also has a high association with IUD use. As the fetus grows, the tube, unlike the uterus, cannot expand to sustain it, so the tube ruptures, spilling blood into the woman's belly as well as out of the uterus. The woman can bleed to death fairly quickly.

When I started emergency medicine in the late 1970s, we didn't have a test to determine the pregnancy level (now called the Beta HCG), or even a quick pregnancy test available. Many of the smaller hospitals where I worked didn't have an ultrasound to determine if a pregnancy was ectopic or intrauterine, or if they did, they limited technician availability to 9 – 5. With modern American medicine, these cases can be easily diagnosed, though if the physician doesn't consider the possibility and run a pregnancy test, the ectopic pregnancy diagnosis can still be missed, with deadly results.

Dealing with people suffering every hour, day, week, and month for years, a physician must maintain a careful balance between too much emotional involvement and being jaded. The good doctor must always be able to sympathize with the pain and the circumstances that brought the patient into their current predicament, yet not personalize the patient's suffering, indeed, not accept blame when outcomes are not ideal.

We fight against death in our workplace. When a ninety-year-old cancer-riddled severely-demented skeleton of a woman is brought in by her family, and that family wants "everything done," it's still our duty to do "everything." I'll intubate, do CPR, give fluids and medicines, and perhaps my efforts will prolong the patient's heartbeat for another few hours of hospitalization. Sometimes not, and I have to declare the patient dead. These kinds of deaths can be a blessing, and in general cause little sense of failure.

I remember one time a fellow came in from an airplane crash. He was talking on arrival with stable vital signs. I ordered proper resuscitation procedures, and he seemed to be stable for a bit. The moment the helicopter arrived to transport him to a major *trauma center, the patient abruptly died. He had sustained too much internal injury to be saved.*

Perhaps the hardest to take is when a patient is sent home and then brought back dead. My first shift as an E.R. doctor I had such an event. A couple of snowbirds came down from the north to South Texas, and the woman brought in her husband due to heart irregularities. I obtained an EKG which showed frequent PVCs, basically an irritable heart, but no signs of insufficient blood supply that might mean a heart attack. During history, the fellow admitted to drinking over a dozen cups of coffee a day. We had no cardiologist or cardiac care center in those days, and so I advised the patient to cut down on his coffee. That night he died in his camper. As you can imagine, I felt terrible, though I knew the outcome would have been the same even had I admitted the patient to the hospital. I asked the grieving widow if there was anything I could do for her. With tear-streaked face she shook her head and said, "Not unless you can bring my husband back."

In any case, I certainly wouldn't shoot myself over a failed resuscitation or medical error. Doctors are only human, after all. All humans make mistakes, and patients are going to die. We just have to continue to try to do our best.

Rebecca

Rebecca suffered from poor impulse control. In other words, she was a criminal. For the past few months she'd not been making her usual frequent E.R. visits, instead serving a three-month incarceration for stealing her neighbor's car to run a drug deal. Now she was back. The other E.R. doctors grumbled about having to see her, cursing her drug-seeking manipulations.

But I liked Rebecca. I enjoyed her clever stories, her cheerful attitude, and her positive view of her strange life choices. Just after midnight, one Friday night, she showed me a scar on her left shoulder. "Malignant melanoma," she reported. "The dermatologist took off the mole last week."

I was stunned. One of the most vicious of cancers, diagnosis with malignant melanoma offers a life expectancy of two months. She showed me where to feel the swollen lymph nodes in her neck, though on my exam I wasn't convinced. She told me further surgery was scheduled for next Monday and asked my opinion of one of our local plastic surgeons.

I told her I liked and trusted him. For the next fifteen minutes we talked, exploring her knowledge of melanoma and her reactions to the disease. She told me her boyfriend had died from melanoma the previous year. She vividly described his last few weeks, the emaciation, the plunge into illness, and then death.

I asked if she liked sunbathing, and she broke out her wide Irish smile. "Red hair," she said, pointing to her flames. "I should a known better."

I couldn't help but admire her bravery. Though I doubted if she had much pain at the moment, I acquiesced to her request for a narcotic injection and prescription.

Was I fooled? Did she really have the disease, or did I fall for a clever story? Perhaps it was nothing more than a weird dark fantasy or bizarre drug-seeking hoax.

The value of the lesson was not lost. It had been years since I had been to the dermatologist. In a week I was in his office. I'm happy to report there are no new scars on me, no swollen lymph nodes.

Any day now I'll find Rebecca back in the emergency department seeking pain medications. I pray she is not stricken with that terrible disease. Instead, I look forward to seeing her impish smile, hearing her clever story, and, perhaps, learning another lesson.

Malignant Melanomas and Opioid Addiction

Although skin is the most common body organ to have cancer, of the three types of skin cancer, two grow slowly enough to usually be cured. These two types, squamous cell and basal cell, come from the two skin levels, surface cells and the base cells, respectfully. However, the third cell in skin makes the color pigment that determines our natural skin tones, and these are called melanin cells. Unlike the surface and base cells, when the melanin cell turns cancerous, called melanoma, it grows quickly and metastasizes early. As mentioned in the story, even with aggressive chemotherapy, the life expectancy of someone diagnosed with metastatic malignant melanoma is about six months.

Two main factors influence a person's risks for developing skin cancer: genetics and sun exposure. The cells from light colored skin have little natural sun protection, UV radiation damaging the DNA and converting some cells into cancer. Other factors, such as medicines and radiation exposure, may play a part. I personally have yearly dermatology appointments, just a look over to be sure.

When a drug addict comes to the E.R. seeking pain medicines, it's because they truly are in pain. It's important to be sympathetic, but also important to not give pain meds just for non-terminal chronic pain. Each exposure to an opioid creates more endorphin breakdown enzymes in the brain, requiring larger and larger doses to achieve the same pain relief, and an ever-greater withdrawal syndrome. Limiting pain medicine prescriptions for only those in acute pain prevents participation in this addiction cycle. Patients who undergo narcotic withdrawal will suffer pain and associated syndromes, but they won't die. It takes about a week to overcome the withdrawal. The addiction will always be there.

The Sacrifice

The shrill call of the phone shattered my war-torn nightmare. Images of wounded soldiers disappeared as I reached out from the warm comforter for the offending instrument. Eight years of interrupted sleep had trained me to snap awake as I read two a.m. off the bedside clock.

"Tell them you'll see them in the morning," my wife murmured, pulling a pillow over her head.

"Dr. Schwartz here," I said into the phone. Mrs. Parker, our small county hospital's night nurse, told me that Mrs. Cramer was in labor, already dilated to four centimeters.

"You be careful," she directed. "Roads are full of ice patches, and you're half the medical staff this county's got!"

"Thanks Mother Hen."

She chuckled. "It seems to me this baby's pretty big. You want me to call in Betty?"

"Let me check her first. Have the delivery room ready to go and a cup of hot fresh coffee."

"I'd never forget your coffee, Doctor Schwartz."

As I dressed I thought about Mrs. Parker's remark that my father and I were the only doctors in the county. After my stint in Nam, I'd returned to my hometown determined to be a country doctor like my dad. Yet times and attitudes were changing. In many ways it was better, a wider array of medications, more lab tests, and better equipment. Heck, the new x-ray machine in the hospital had an automatic developer; I no longer had to deal with dipping the sheets into those vats of chemicals. On the other hand, people expected more. The old adage, "Take two aspirin and call me in the morning," no longer satisfied. This working all day and being available all night couldn't keep up.

Snow flurries danced in the headlights of my brand new '76 Chevy like tracer shots from a machine gun. I hit a patch of ice turning onto Main and nearly spun into the curb. As I righted the car I thought about Mrs. Cramer. Over the past four years I had delivered her twice, two fine baby boys of eight and nine pounds. This time I had promised her a girl.

As I pulled into the hospital parking lot, a piece of ice broke off an overhead tree limb and crashed onto my windshield. I reflexively slammed on the brakes, causing the car to skid, sliding into the brick wall. My head slammed against the window with a crack.

"Major! We need you over here! Kid's shot in the neck."

Good Lord, I can't save this boy. I'll never be able to stop all these arteries spouting blood.

"Over here! Jumped on a grenade to save his buddies. His guts are nothing but spaghetti sauce."

Oh my God! How can this boy still be alive? I should put him out of his misery with a massive morphine overdose.

"Major, over here! This one's stepped on a booby trap. Both of his legs gotta come off."

No! No! Let me be!

I awoke with a start, the engine still running. I shut it off, pulled my gloves back on, and hustled into the hospital. Mrs. Parker met me at the door with steaming coffee. She wore her starched white uniform, complete with six-inch hat, her sixty-year-old face lined with crow's feet and heavy scowl.

"Good Lord, Doctor Schwartz. What happened to you?"

"What?"

She reached up and touched my temple, causing me to wince. Her hand came away bloody.

"Missed the parking spot," I said, sitting in the chair she indicated and submitting to her cleaning and bandage.

"Can't have you bleeding in front of the patients. There, you look half presentable. You okay to do this, or you want me to call your dad?"

I snorted. "We'll have this baby in the nursery long before he could get here. You have everything ready?"

"Yes, Doctor. Mrs. Cramer's in the labor room, and I have the delivery room ready, oxytocin drawn up. You sure you don't want Betty in case you decide to section her?"

A wave of nausea swept through me. For a moment I saw two Mrs. Parkers staring at me.

Stretcher after stretcher, dozens of wounded wait on me, counting on me to sew them back together, to save their lives.

"Doctor? Doctor Schwartz? You sure you're okay? You're looking awfully green."

I shook my head, as much to dispel the cobwebs as to deny any illness. "I'm fine. Let's get going."

On reaching the obstetrical area I greeted George Cramer in the waiting room. He had stepped out of the labor room for a smoke. At six-foot-four, his three-hundred pounds seemed only slightly pudgy.

"You get in a bar fight, Doc?" he asked.

I smiled sternly. "Slipped on the ice. It's nothing. Let's go check the patient." He followed me to his wife's bedside where I leaned over to lightly brush Mary Cramer's hair in greeting. Beads of sweat soaked those locks.

Putting on a rubber glove, I checked her progress. Eight centimeters out of the needed ten. The baby's head had dropped to engage in the pelvis. We were near the point where a C-section would be impossible.

Mrs. Parker handed me the special obstetrical stethoscope which I fitted onto my ears, guiding its long silver nose onto the mother's belly. I counted fetal heartbeats as I watched fifteen seconds sweep along my watch. Calculating a pulse of one hundred and sixty I smiled, glad we had a strong baby.

"She's gonna be a big one, ain't she, Doc?" George asked in his nasal tones.

"Takes after her dad," I said. He guffawed and took hold of his wife's hand.

I felt around the pelvic opening. Mrs. Cramer had delivered two large babies, but maybe I shouldn't take chances.

"How about we go for that c-section like we discussed last week?" I ventured.

George and Mary looked at each other, love and concern flashing in that glance.

"Do you really gotta cut out the baby, Doctor?" Mary asked. "I think I can push her. I'm pretty strong."

George held up his hand to silence her. "The doc's gotta make the choice, Mary. If he says cut, then you gotta go under the knife."

Going with the c-section would be safer, but not easy to do in the middle of the night in this understaffed hospital. I reassessed Mary's pelvis. Probably all would be fine.

Smiling reassuringly, I said, "We'll give it a try from below. You delivered some big babies before." I turned back and said to Mrs. Parker, "Take Mrs. Cramer back to the delivery room. I'm going to scrub."

"Yes, Doctor."

Mrs. Parker put Mary on the table as I transformed into surgeon; gown, cap, mask, paper shoe covers, eye shield, and rubber gloves. Not a bit of the real Doctor Schwartz contacted the room's pristine air. Mary's exposed labia puffed, bulging from the pressure of the baby's head. I turned away a moment, and when I turned back I saw a fountain of blood.

"Doctor Schwartz, I can't keep up his blood pressure."

He's bleeding to death right before my eyes ... I can't save this life. Please, God, don't let another one die in my hands. Don't do this to me!!!

"Doctor, your clothes are completely soaked with blood."

Blood! Blood everywhere! I can't stand it!

"Doctor Schwartz? Doctor Schwartz, are you okay?"

Mrs. Parker looked at me with concern, still holding the bottle of bright orange Betadine she had just poured over Mary's skin.

"Is something wrong, Doctor?" she insisted when I didn't respond.

I shook my head. "No, of course not. I was thinking of something else. Sorry. Hand me the long needle and I'll numb her up from the inside."

Mrs. Parker passed me the instrument and I tried to place the needle along the pelvic ridges, hoping to find just the right landmarks to insert the numbing medicine. The baby's head was engaged too tightly to reach them.

"Get me some fetal heart tones, please."

I waited as Mrs. Parker listened with the special stethoscope. I was worried that the dilation hadn't progressed past eight centimeters.

"Doctor, I'm having trouble locating the fetal heart tones."

I cursed to myself, wishing our administrator had honored my request for a fetal monitor. He had refused, claiming it was too expensive for as few deliveries as we did in this little county hospital.

"Try again," I said. "The baby's dropped so the heart tones will be found lower than you're used to."

Mrs. Parker readjusted the scope and looked at her watch. "One hundred," she reported.

The baby's pulse had fallen, probably because her head was being squeezed against her mother's unyielding bones.

"I'm going to try a little friendly persuasion here. Bring me those Piper forceps that we fit around the baby's head. They're in the second left drawer over there."

George noted the tenseness in my voice. "Anything wrong, Doc?"

I looked him directly in the eyes. "The baby is not coming down like she should. I'm going to try pulling her out."

As I watched Mrs. Parker shuffle through the instrument drawer I reached over the top of the drapes to feel Mrs. Cramer's contractions. They were hard; very hard. I watched her expression as she panted, her face sweaty and pale. Leaving my left hand on top, I checked inside her again with my right. Still eight centimeters, but wet. When I pulled out my hand it was covered with blood. A trickle of red flowed to the floor.

"You can't leave Major Schwartz. The chopper's just landed with six more casualties. Look, they're wheeling them in now."

I've been up for days. I can't stick my hands into another bloody human cavity. But if I don't, they'll die. They'll all die.

I snapped back to the sound of Mrs. Parker's voice. She held up a celluloid wrapped package. "I can't find Pipers, Doctor Schwartz. Can you use these Kielland's?"

"I guess I have no choice. Lay them on my tray. Try those heart tones again."

It took her a valuable minute before she reported, "Eighty."

I turned to the father. "In all honesty, George, we may be having problems. Would you like to step out to the waiting room?"

"Gosh, Doc, I'd rather stay. What's going on?"

"The baby is stuck. I'm going to try to ease her out with these big clamps you see here."

"What if you can't get the baby out?" he asked.

I gently spread the labia for a better look. The baby's scalp remained too high, and her skin looked too dark. Blood clots were flowing around the baby's head, pooling inside the mother and creating puddles on the floor.

"There's no choice, George. The baby needs to come out now, or she'll die. Mrs. Parker," I commanded. "Measure Mrs. Cramer's blood pressure and pulse."

"Eighty over forty," she said, "with pulse of one hundred and fifty." Her experienced eyes showed the anxiety we both felt.

"I suppose an emergency c-section is out of the question. Is there anyone to give anesthesia in house?" I asked.

She shook her head. "Betty's a half hour away at best, longer in this weather."

Blood poured out of the birth canal.

Major, we've got two fellows fading fast. This one's got a chest wound. That one's got shrapnel in his belly. Which one do you want to try and save?

And which one will I condemn to certain death?

Stomach acid bubbled into my throat. Mary whimpered a moment, and fell silent.

"Mary? Mary? Doc, I think Mary's fainted," George said. "What's happening?" He looked wide-eyed back and forth from me to his wife, shaking her head and calling in her ears. "Wake up, Mary. For God's sake, wake up."

"Mrs. Parker, run those I.V. fluids wide open. How quick can you run to the blood bank and get me two units of A positive?"

"It needs to be warmed first, Doctor Schwartz. I'm certain the blood bank won't have anything ready."

"You sure you don't want to wait outside, George?"

"I ain't leaving my Mary! Is she gonna die? Please, Doc. Please save my Mary. I can't live without her!" He smothered her with kisses, shaking her gently and crying. "Mary, Mary. Oh Mother of God, please wake up!"

"Just don't look this way, George." I grabbed the scalpel from the table and made a large episiotomy. Sweeping out a large handful of blood clots, I placed the Kielland forceps around the baby's large head.

"I can't find a blood pressure or a pulse," Mrs. Parker reported, her hands trembling.

"Get the ambu-bag and get some air in her lungs," I ordered.

Mr. Cramer knelt at his wife's head, gently stoking her hair and praying.

"Major, give it up."

No, I can still save him. I can do it! Keep cutting, keep stitching, keep working. Please, don't say he's dead. Don't say he's dead."

"Major Schwartz. It's not any good. You've got to stop. There are others that need your help."

I applied pressure across my end of the forceps, squeezing down on the baby's head. Leaning back, I braced my legs against the delivery table and pulled as hard as I could. She came down only a centimeter and stopped. I pulled again. No change. Wrenching out the forceps, I reached inside to feel for the problem. Behind the huge head the shoulders were locked against mother's bones like an anchor.

I tried to pull out the bottom arm, but it just wouldn't budge. A river of blood flowed into my lap and onto the floor. I pushed the baby's upper arm across her chest hoping to slip it out. That didn't work either. I reached in and hooked the upper clavicle. Pulling outward I felt it snap in two. I repeated the maneuver for the second shoulder.

"Mary, oh, Mary! Don't die, Mary. I love you, Baby." Mr. Cramer cried at the head of the table. Mrs. Parker was pumping oxygen into her mouth with a rubber bag.

I reattached the forceps and pulled again. The baby just was not going to budge. Her head was blue, complete loss of oxygen from either premature placental separation or prolonged cord compression.

I despaired of saving either mother or child. Cutting open Mary's belly now would only kill her and deliver the fetus dead. If I didn't sacrifice the baby, two young boys would be motherless.

After removing the forceps, I reached inside the uterus with my scalpel. I began sawing at the baby's arm. New blood, this time a dark purple strain, joined the red ocean at my feet. With a snap of bone, I severed the arm. I paused just a moment, offering a silent prayer for the soul of the sacrificial lamb. The baby's other arm suffered the same fate. It took only seconds for the two.

Rehooking the forceps, I finally succeeded in delivered the fetus. It had been a girl. The arms followed and the placenta too, complete premature separation. The kid hadn't had a chance. A tidal wave of blood announced the clearing of the cavity.

Bayoneted babies. Napalmed babies. Dismembered babies. Hellfire inspired images danced around me in red gory glory.

I realized I had passed out momentarily. I checked Mary and saw that the bleeding was slowing. "Blood pressure, Mrs. Parker," I demanded.

"Eighty. Recheck coming. Now one hundred over sixty."

Mrs. Cramer moaned.

"She's waking up," George's voice cracked with relief. "Thank you God. Thank you Doctor Schwartz."

The bleeding from the vagina slowed to a mere trickle as I threw some stitches into the episiotomy. I finished quickly and lay a drape across her opening. Standing, I came behind George and gently lay my hand on his shoulders. Mary looked up at me.

"My baby?" she asked.

I shook my head. "I'm deeply sorry, Mary. She didn't make it."

Her face screwed up with agony as her tears ran down her cheeks. "Poor little thing," she moaned.

I stepped back and George turned to me briefly. "Thanks for all you did, Doc."

I nodded. "You're welcome, George. I'm sorry about your loss. I'll be in during lunch to check on Mary."

I turned to Mrs. Parker. "I'll write the orders and a note before heading out. Make sure Mrs. Cramer stays at bed rest. I'm going to order a couple of units of blood I'd like you to start right away."

"Yes, Doctor Schwartz," she said, in her normal nursing voice.

As I walked down the hallway to the parking lot, I wondered now odd it seemed to carry on as if nothing unusual had just happened. I had just dismembered a baby, sacrificing one human life to save another. I had returned to my hometown thinking I'd left behind life-deciding choices. Yet they wouldn't leave me. Instead I kept adding more terrifying images to the nightmares that would forever haunt my dreams.

PTSD and Obstetrics

Post Traumatic Stress Disorder can affect anyone exposed to a severely stressful situation. Certainly many of the soldiers returning from Viet Nam fell victim with a combination of symptoms, such as depression, flashbacks, and anxiety. Trigger events, such as the sight of blood, are typical of the cases. Cure requires counseling, positive feedback mechanisms, and the occasional short-term drug program. Those suffering from PTSD suffer a high rate of suicide.

We all react to emergencies in different ways. With my forty-years as an E.R. doctor, I've seen a lot of weird human events, many of them bloody, and quite a few deaths. Yet I generally don't find my job stressful. In all fairness, I should report I've never been in a war zone.

Rural medicine in the 1970s operated under a different set of rules. People expected illness rather than health. If the baby died, well, these things happened. The doctor knew what was best for the patient and felt no need to explain the choices.

I've delivered about 200 babies in my career, mostly in the early years while a family practice resident. Usually delivering a baby is easy, after all, God made the process natural for the species to evolve. However, I found that a delivery almost never went smoothly. From inadequate pelvis, as in this case, to a cord around the neck, to a breech delivery, to heart decelerations, to premature placental separation, it's amazing how many things can go wrong!

This is a horrifying tale, of course. My medical school obstetrics training occurred in 1978, the time setting of this story. The style described here remains true to the techniques of the time. Although breaking collarbones was a tried and true delivery technique, I never heard of it going as far as this barbaric event.

Chamber of Salvation

Shattering sirens announce the arrival of a new victim to my Cathedral of Salvation. Foreheads anointed with the holy water of fear propel the stretcher with tonight's prostrate offering. The gurney bounces over the portico, a crimson trail marking passage from outside evils into magical monastery.

"Trauma room," Julie, my archangel, directs. Thrusting her fingers into the ceremonial adornments, she pulls the latex tantalizingly tight. She slips into our torture chamber just ahead of the bloody mummy. Dressed in multi-colored nightmare, my tribe of fellow tormenters tumbles in, brandishing needles designed for the most intimate invasions. Boisterous monitors solicit the silent specimen's secrets.

I hastily primp my holy habit, inserting enchanted surgical digits into resilient rubber. I conceal my countenance behind crystalline, a sophisticated shield through which I eyeball the fellow laid out in death's cradle. Tonight's special course features a teenager – fifteen – sixteen at most, baby hair on chin. What devilish disaster has brought this cherub to suffer indignities at the hands of the willing?

"Albert Jones, gunshot wound to left chest," a panting rescuer announces.

My boy's been struck down by that perpetrator of penetration, a forty-five caliber condiment. "No blood pressure, pulse of one ninety," a minion announces. Atropos stands ready to cut life's thread.

I glance at the scarlet path, a Hansel and Gretel trail leading to a modern witch's hut. Back at Albert, a peculiar paleness bleaches his dusky darkness. My struggling stallion has seeped away his fluids, a porous carcass with an empty pump.

"Pour in the fluids," I order.

I lever the laryngoscope, its eerie luminescence lighting rings of time travel, a tawdry tunnel to vocal cord pearly gates. Guiding a gilded, I attach the tube for determined sailboat breezes.

"Absent breath sounds on the right," Julie calls. Participants in a secret code, our language confuses all but the deeply initiated. Our boy's down one lung. Another Hermes arrow will join the red, yellow, and clear.

I stage my assault on that most precious of cages. Splash orange. Needle skin. Slice with knife. Thrust the tube, a bayonet as ballistic as any shimmering saber. Sting! Slash! Stab!

Lava spouts in fire-hydrant release, an eruption greater than this experienced assaulter of leaking corpses has ever seen before. Asclepius paints the devil's profile on my gown. Julie glances at the portrait, and smiles wickedly behind her mask.

Whooo. The gleaming automaton hums a new tune, a lighter lullaby of renewed life, the return of the ghost. Ah, wandering spirit, what did you see on that short journey? Will you be able to tell us about God?

"Ventilating," Julie reports the obvious, for each moment must be recorded for posterity. Cringing in a corner, our scribe certifies "one soul sustained."

"Blood pressure?" We diligently document details. All the teeth must be crossed. All the eyes must be opened.

Julie's blue bonnet bobs, studying the sphygmomanometer's twitches. I wonder, how many lives has she saved? If honorariums were granted for each, like a soldier in war, how many medals would decorate her ample chest? Day after day she raises the dead, or leaves behind haunts.

"110 over 80."

Zeus' choir belts Hallelujah. This time we flipped heads. Soon our surgeon will slice and dice, suturing seams on the renewed renegade.

Two days later I venture into another world, one where a haven of angels glide on quiet quests. In these halls of heroism, life and death struggle as gravely as in my workshop. Here, though, the contest is prolonged and quiet; chess instead of rugby.

The artisans startle at my arrival. I'm not a stranger in a strange land, for I've visited this Vatican before – when summoned. Then I came as priest of last hope; chanting conjurations, prescribing pharmaceuticals and prophylactics ... and deliberating finalities. I've earned the respect due a doctor of death.

"Aren't you a little out of your path?" The guardian goads.

"Albert Jones," I murmur. "Gunshot wound."

A smile steals across faithful features. "Oh, of course. I'll make the introductions."

She leads me to a capacious cubicle, a prison cell where the last walk has come to so many. Albert sits, watching TV. Broad bandages crisscross his compromised torso, brazen clamps containing life forces. Instead of the rag doll I'd know, my boy looks strong, as if he'd merely bandaged a sore spot.

"Albert." My guide greets genteelly, but the study stays stationary.

"Albert." She commands, a stout summons.

Again the fellow fakes deafness, defiance his one remaining dignity.

I study my companion, watching her lips curl. "Albert," she murmurs, "if you give me a hard time, you will get it back tenfold."

He doesn't turn from the TV. "What do you want?"

"This is Dr. Roth. He saved your life."

Albert turns, and I gaze upon a mouth still swollen from my recent assault. We exchange stares for five seconds, reading each other's lives. He returns retention to the TV.

I stand studying my survivor, a commercial's silly patter adding a human tone to the medical machines' machinations. Had he tarried but five minutes, my work would have been in vain. Had not Julie discovered the limping lobe, he'd be a chilling corpse. Could Albert even imagine how he'd danced with Death?

The silence stretches, until my handmaiden barks. "Albert."

Albert finally deigns to answer, his tone defiant. "So what?" he quietly queries. "It's his job."

The nurse readies her retort, but I arrest her arm. Leaning close I whisper, "Let him be. The ceremonial offering was accepted. This time the gods spared the sacrificial lamb."

Trauma

    Perhaps a fast pace multi-person response with desperate interventions that save lives are the images most Americans have when they think of the emergency room. Certainly, these cases make up a portion of the E.R. work lives, albeit a small portion. In some major trauma centers gunshot wounds come in daily, maybe even several a day. Mostly, though, these are uncommon adrenalin rushes in a day made up of patients with sprained ankles or abdominal pains.

    Today's trauma centers do save lives. Amazing interventions by highly trained personnel coordinating teamwork results in tremendously successful resuscitation rates. All E.R. doctors and nurses recertify in Advanced Trauma Life Support techniques every few years. I love cases like this, making split-second decisions and committing to penetrating tubes. When I'm in the middle of a code it's like being in the zone in a sports game, all concentration focuses on saving that life.

    I hope you enjoyed the metaphors here, the E.R. as the underworld and the ICU as heaven. The alliteration technique adds to the mood and cadence, a fast-paced story to show a fast-paced lifestyle. The ending, with Albert's entitlement attitude, actually happened to me. It's important to be humbled every now and then, and be reminded I do my work for my own love of it, not for the patient's gratitude.

The Overdose

I studied Cheryl Stevens as she lay on the stretcher beyond the sliding glass door. She rested comfortably, her bronzed hair neatly brushed above a carefully made-up face. Lipstick ran in perfect lines, mascara accented her long-lashed lids. Only crow's feet around the eyes gave away her late-forties age. Wires ran from the monitors on her chest, arm, and finger to the scope in the corner. Vital sign readings were displayed there, as well as on a central monitoring station outside the locked door.

"Sixty beats a minute," Rosie, the desk clerk noted. "Not as upset as our typical suicidal patient, huh Greg?"

"Did she come in with her make-up like this?" I asked.

"Yeah, but she had to reapply it after we gave her activated charcoal. That stuff makes a mess of everything."

I reviewed the chart Rosie handed me, the brief description of Dr. Morgan's treatments and the lab tests ordered, though the test results hadn't returned yet. A one-line suicide note read, "The world will be better off without me." Dr. Morgan handled the medical part. It was my job to handle the psychological.

Passing in, I gently slid the glass door closed. I stood a moment, watching her quiet, easy breathing. "Mrs. Stevens?" I spoke softly to judge the depth of her trance. Immediately her eyes flickered, then snapped opened, dazzling blue opals evaluating me.

"Cheryl Stevens? I'm Greg Phillips, the counselor tonight."

"Nice to meet you, Greg. Please call me Cheryl." She brought her hand out from under the sheets for a gentle squeeze of my hand. It's unusual for a patient to want to call me by first name, a warning of too easy familiarity.

"I understand you took some pills tonight?"

Mrs. Stevens nodded. "I couldn't stand living with Robert another minute. Please, don't let him back here. No telling what he's liable to say or do. Best just send him home."

"Robert? You mean your husband?"

She nodded emphatically, raising her eyebrows in a little girl pleading look, her lips in pout. "Robert's been very erratic lately. One minute he tells me he loves me, the next he's threatening to divorce me. You best put me in the hospital to protect me.

Otherwise I'll probably end up taking an overdose again. You must promise to keep him away."

I nodded. "We can certainly keep him away from you for now, if that's what you prefer. Tell me what happened tonight."

I watched Mrs. Stevens' expression, her eyes closed, her brow pursed in thought.

"Promise you won't tell anyone, Greg?"

"I can't make that promise."

She shrugged. "I guess I have to trust you. Robert and I have been married for thirty years. At first we were very much in love, I worked while he attended law school, and then he took care of me as his career blossomed. We never had time for children ... at least, that's what he kept saying. I'm sure it's a story you've heard a hundred times. Husband is off at work; wife is home bored. I suppose I've been depressed for a long time. Tonight I prepared a delicious meal: prime rib, cooked just the way he likes it, asparagus au gratin, twice baked potatoes ... the works. Robert called at the last minute saying he had to go to some meeting. I ... I just couldn't take it anymore. My doctor had prescribed some nerve pills for me. I took them all."

I glanced at the chart. It listed an empty bottle of Xanax found at the scene, sixty pills, filled four days before. "So you tried to kill yourself?"

"Yes. That's what I just said."

"And how do you feel now? Do you still feel like hurting yourself?"

"You send me out and I'll do it again, Greg." Mrs. Stevens put her chin up, a defiant gesture that surprised me. Most people who perform situational-overdose gestures like this usually say they're sorry and won't do it again.

"Did you call for help or did someone find you?" I asked.

"I woke up when the rescue squad started to roll me onto their stretcher. I guess Robert finally came home and found me."

I nodded, putting a note on the chart. Clearly she expected to be found. This "suicide attempt" continued to have a strange feel to it. "Please tell me more about why you wanted to kill yourself, Mrs. Stevens. Was it just because your husband was late for dinner?"

"I can't stand living like this, the constant worries, the mental stress, the fear. You can't imagine what it's like. Robert has to have everything perfect. If the laundry isn't stacked neatly in the drawers, exactly as he wants it, he loses control. If dinner isn't served precisely on time, he screams. Last week I slightly overcooked the steak and he threw his fork into the wall. Oh, it's fine if he's late or forgets to put something away. But everyday, in every little way, he insists that I have to be just so perfect.

"I try so hard to please him, but I'm just never good enough. 'That dress doesn't work on you,' he'll say. He never takes me out for a little romance anymore. And even when he has to take me to some company function, he'll tell me exactly what I can say and who I can talk with.

"And jealous? Oh my God. Yesterday the mailman came to the door to get me to sign for a package, and Robert acted like I was trying to seduce the chump. You should have seen Bruce ... that's the mailman, you should have seen Bruce turn white and run down the sidewalk when Robert came at him.

"My life has become a living hell. Tonight I couldn't stand it anymore and I emptied the bottle."

"You took sixty tablets of Xanax tonight?" I asked.

She shook her head. "Not all sixty. I might have taken a few over the last day or two."

"Fifty?"

"Well, no. I flushed some down the toilet."

"So, how many do you think you took?"

"I don't know!" she cried. "Leave me alone, Greg. I don't want to talk about it." She turned away from me.

After a moment I asked, "Twenty? Mrs. Stevens, do you think you took twenty tablets?"

With her back towards me she murmured, "Yeah. Maybe twenty. Or fifteen. Maybe only a dozen."

That's still a lot of Xanax. "When did you take them? It's three A.M. now."

She rustled under the sheet, finally turning back to me. "I'm not sure. Maybe nine o'clock after I cleaned up the kitchen."

Six hours ago? The Xanax had already run its course. "Did you take anything else? Tylenol? Other pills or drugs? Alcohol?"

She shook her head. "Just the Xanax." She pulled her arm out from under the sheet to pat her hair straight and I saw the band aid over where the nurse had drawn blood. I noted that there weren't any "track marks" on her arms, that is, no sign that she injected herself with drugs. I'd know soon enough if anything else showed in her system when the drug screen results returned.

"Do you have any other medical problems?" I asked.

"Yes, Greg. I suffer from migraine headaches."

"Migraines? What do you take for them?"

"I have Percocet at home. I took one tonight. When they're real bad I come to the E.R. for a shot. I've had to do that more often lately."

I noted the history of migraines on her chart, and told Mrs. Stevens that I'd be back after awhile. Leaving the cubicle, I slid the glass door closed, and turned back to the nursing station. "What do you think, Rosie?"

The clerk shrugged, her magenta scrubs adding a bright sense of surreal to the psych unit.

"Doesn't seem very suicidal to me. Did she tell you not to let her husband come back? He's waiting in the Quiet Room."

"Yes, she told me. I'll go talk with him there."

I found Mr. Stevens picking at some food while reading the Wall Street Journal. He stood when I came in, displaying his tailored business suit, sporting a red tie hung with a perfect Prince Edward's knot. With his gray tinged hair and artificial tan I placed him at a handsome fifty, maybe a few years older. I held out my hand.

"Mr. Stevens? I'm Greg Phillips, the counselor taking care of your wife."

He grasped my hand in both of his, a strong controlling grip.

"Dr. Phillips, thank you for coming to talk with me. Is Cheryl going to be all right? When can I see her?"

I succeeded in freeing my hand and directed him to sit back down. I settled into another chair at the table, placing Mrs. Stevens' clipboard beside me.

"Your wife is doing well right now. Her vital signs are stable and we're fairly confident she'll have no long term ill effects from this."

"Thank heavens," he cried. "Thank you for saving her life, Doctor. When can I go back to be with her?"

"Dr. Morgan took care of the medical part. I'm just a counselor, not a doctor."

He nodded, then indicated his pie. "Excuse my eating. I missed dinner, so on the way out the door, following the rescue squad, I grabbed something."

"Don't worry about it." I picked up the chart again, ready to take notes. "What happened tonight?"

Mr. Stevens' long legs brought him to a quick stand. He began pacing.

"Mr. Phillips, I don't know what to tell you. Cheryl's been very wound up lately. She keeps pleading with me to stay with her. I've been very busy at work, and she keeps calling me and checking up on me. She's developed an obsession with keeping the kitchen spotless. If I touch anything she goes crazy. She's a great cook, in fact, she had a home dinner planned for tonight. She always thinks everything has to be so perfect. She'll wash her hands several times a day. If her makeup isn't just the way she wants it, she'll cold cream it out and start all over.

"Trying to get her out of the house is almost impossible. When we do go out, she's absolutely paranoid of saying the wrong thing to the wrong person. She's constantly asking me what can she say and who should she talk to.

"Yesterday something very strange happened. The mailman came to the door to have her sign for a package, and she tried to seduce him. You should have seen him blanch, then rocket down that sidewalk.

"Tell me, counselor. Is she having a nervous breakdown? Good Lord. How stupid a question is that? Of course she's having a nervous breakdown. She took a bottle of pills tonight after all. I should have seen it coming. The signs were all there."

He wrung his hands a moment, then made fists and lowered himself carefully into the chair. His version of their interactions didn't surprise me. I supposed the truth to be somewhere in the middle.

"Tell me the circumstances of how you found Mrs. Stevens tonight, please."

His mouth twisted just a moment, then smoothed again in his chiseled handsome face.

"As I said, she had planned on us having dinner tonight ... some idea she came up with without telling me. When I had to stay late at work, I called to let her know and she blew her top. I guess I was a little ticked off at her, so after my meeting I just stayed out a little. Went to a lounge for a drink. When I got home I took a shower in the downstairs bathroom, then flicked through the T.V. for a couple of minutes. Checking on the weather report and the overseas financial news."

He paused a moment, shaking his head. "I can't believe I wasted all that time while she was comatose from an overdose upstairs. What if she had died due to my fiddling around? I'd never have forgiven myself. What would the police have thought?"

"So, what time did you finally find Mrs. Stevens?" I paged through the sheets on the chart while I waited for his answer until I found the EMS rescue sheet. There I read, "911 call received 0120."

"Hmm," Mr. Stevens muttered. "I guess about midnight. No, later than that. I watched the end of the game before retiring, so it must have been a little after one o'clock. When I went upstairs I didn't think anything was wrong at first. Cheryl looked natural, lying under the covers. It took me a few minutes to notice the empty pill bottle. Then I tried to arouse her, and when I couldn't, I called 911."

I waited patiently while Mr. Stevens took out a handkerchief and dabbed at his eyes. Both he and his wife knew how to add the dramatic touches.

I asked, "When you had your argument on the phone, did you have any idea she might be thinking of hurting herself?"

Mr. Stevens rose again, this time walking to the bookshelf and picking up a knickknack he fingered absently. He had his back to me when he answered. "Cheryl told me that she was getting one of her headaches and was going straight to bed. That would have been around six o'clock. I have no idea when she took the pills."

"Do you think she expected you to find her? I mean, normally after such an argument would you have gone straight home to check on her?"

Mr. Stevens turned back to face me. "Maybe so. Sometimes she pulls stunts to try to manipulate me. I hope I'm not sounding cynical if I wonder if this was another one of those. These pills she took, Xanax, are they likely to be fatal?"

I hesitated, then shook my head. "Usually not, unless mixed with other sedatives like alcohol. But even so, a suicide gesture should never be considered trivial. People who may be acting out often accidentally succeed. This certainly is a serious call for help."

Mr. Stevens shook his head, his mouth a grim line. "Cheryl is very bright, Mr. Phillips. I'm sure she knew exactly what she was doing. Well, since she's going to be okay, I would appreciate you letting me back to talk with her."

"She's not quite ready for visitors, I'm afraid."

Mr. Stevens strode across the room to stand a few inches directly in front of me. "Imagine how you would feel if you thought your wife had attempted suicide. Besides the personal devastation, the blow to my reputation could be incredible. I can't remember when I've been this upset. I'm so disgruntled that I broke my diet, grabbing something from the kitchen on the way out. I guess this is from the fancy dinner Cheryl cooked tonight."

I made a few notes in my chart, writing that Mr. Stevens seemed as concerned about his reputation and his diet as about his wife's suicide gesture. "Mr. Stevens, has your wife ever attempted suicide before? No? Has she seemed particularly depressed lately, crying a lot, not sleeping well, losing weight." This time he nodded vigorously.

"Yes, Mr. Phillips. She has been crying a lot lately, and not sleeping well. Perhaps I should have expected her to do something desperate."

"To your knowledge has she been hearing voices or seeing things other people don't see?"

He shook his head. "She's not crazy, if that's what you mean. She just got a little upset tonight and took some pills." He seemed to be getting agitated. "Look, if she's doing so well, why can't I see her?"

I stood too. "I'll go check on her and send word. I'll let Mrs. Stevens know that you're here and concerned. I anticipate that she's going to be admitted, probably in isolation for tonight. She suggested that you might want to go home."

I noticed that his face looked flush and he seemed to be breathing hard.

"Mr. Stevens, perhaps it would be best if you went for some coffee. Do you have a friend or relative you can call?"

He sat down on the chair. "I'll be okay. Too much excitement." He took out something small from an inside coat pocket, but then glanced up at me, and replaced it. I wasn't sure, but it looked like a small pill bottle.

I reached the door, then turned to ask one last question. "By the way, Mr. Stevens, what's your mailman's name?"

"The mailman? How should I know? Do you know your mailman's name?"

Back in the psych unit I found Rosie watching Mrs. Stevens through the glass door.

"How's she doing?"

Rosie nodded. "Just fine. Sitting up reading a magazine. Fixed her make-up again. She doesn't act like someone who's hell-bent on suicide. What do you think? Just a lover's spat?"

"Rosie, I want you to have security keep an eye on Mr. Stevens. He's not to come back here. Also have someone tell him that his wife is doing fine but still can't have visitors."

I flipped through Mrs. Stevens' lab test results. Blood counts were normal, urine clear, heavy metal screen negative. I paused over the drug screen.

"Did you see this, Rosie?" I asked, showing her the paper.

"Yeah, negatives except positive for opiates. Didn't she say she took Percocet?"

"It's like the Sherlock Holmes mystery, don't you think? The strange thing that the dog did in the night?"

"What did the dog do?"

"Nothing."

"I don't get it."

"Neither did Watson, my dear Rosie."

I went back in with Mrs. Stevens. "How are you feeling, Mrs. Stevens?"

"Did you talk with my husband, Greg?" she asked, a hint of a smile turning up at the corners.

I nodded. "Yes. He's very concerned for you. He'd like to see you."

Her smile vanished. "Oh of course he would. He needs to be sure his little possession is in perfect shape. You promised you wouldn't let him come back here. Am I safe? Why doesn't he just go home?"

"Are you concerned for your safety, Mrs. Stevens? Has Mr. Stevens hit you or threatened to strike you?" Physical abuse would change this picture.

She shook her head no.

"You're quite safe, Mrs. Stevens. There are two locked doors between him and you as well as security guards. There may be alternatives to your being admitted. If you're not still suicidal perhaps you could stay with a relative?"

Mrs. Stevens' perfect composure cracked for just a moment with wide-eyed anxiety. "I'm still suicidal, Greg. I think it would be a good idea to admit me to the hospital, don't you agree?"

I nodded. "I suppose that's the safest option. Are you hungry? What time did you last eat?"

"Lunch time I guess. I cooked dinner for Robert, but when he told me he wasn't coming home I lost my appetite. I became so upset that I developed one of my headaches. Well, you know the rest. I went upstairs and downed those pills."

"That's when you wrote the suicide note?" I asked Cheryl.

She nodded. "I'm a woman of few words."

"You put all the food away before you went to bed?"

"Of course. I told you, Robert insists on a clean kitchen. Besides, he never eats late at night. Too concerned about having a perfect body. Can we talk about something else?"

I nodded. "Do you have any idea why Mr. Stevens didn't come home?"

"Well, he SAID he was at a meeting. He's always going to meetings."

"Did he tell you when to expect him home, when you could expect him to find you overdosed and rescue you?"

She glared at me and turned away. "I don't feel like talking to you anymore, Greg. You're a bore."

"I apologize. Let's change the subject. What's your mailman's name?"

"Bruce Krueger. Bruce doesn't wear a wedding ring. Maybe that's why Robert blew a fuse."

"Were you purposely trying to make Robert jealous by flirting with the mailman?"

She glared at me again, and I thought she might shut me off once more. Instead she spit on the floor. "Yes, damn it, I was. I may be over forty, but I'm still attractive to men. You know what they say about the goose and the gander, don't you Greg?"

"You mean that Mr. Stevens is having an affair?"

For a moment she stared at me defiantly, then she dropped her gaze and nodded. "Twenty-four years of marriage, and I've been as faithful as Odysseus' wife. I want Robert to consider what it would be like to lose me. He needs to value me, damn it!"

I left quietly, leaving her to her tears. Outside Rosie had been watching us on the monitor.

"One thing I always admire about you, Greg," Rosie said, "is your devotion to your patients. You're determined to find out why she did this, aren't you? Other counselors would just admit her and let the inpatient folks tease it out."

I nodded. "Every case is like a detective mystery, Rosie. These things never are as simple as they seem. Go ahead and get the psychiatrist on the phone." I waited while she dialed the number. I turned when I heard the door open behind me. Bill Reeves, the security guard, was signaling for me.

"Hey Greg. You know that guy you wanted me to watch, Mr. Stevens?"

My pulse jumped as I asked, "What happened?"

"He collapsed in the waiting room. They're coding him on stretcher six."

"What?" I raced past him and around to the trauma center. A crowd of people were working on Mr. Stevens. His heart kept jumping out of rhythm, requiring shock.

"What's going on, Dr. Morgan?" I called to my friend who was running the code.

"Don't know. He grabbed his chest and collapsed. Must have had a bad heart. He had a bottle of nitroglycerin tabs in his pocket. Funny though."

"What?"

"Well, he's not acting like a typical MI. His complex is very strange looking. Could have a bundle branch block I guess. ALL CLEAR! SHOCK!" he called out.

I ran back to the crisis area.

"Cheryl!"

She looked alarmed. "Oh my God, he didn't collapse already did he?"

I stepped back. "What made you ask that?"

Mrs. Stevens tried to smooth her expression. "You're coming in to tell me Robert's sick, right? Through the glass door I saw you run out of here when that guard signaled you. And now you've run right back in here, so naturally I assumed something has happened to Robert. I know he has a bad heart after all."

"Okay. But what did you mean already?"

"I didn't say already, Greg."

"Yes, you did."

Suddenly it all came together for me.

"You poisoned him, didn't you?"

She looked frightened. "What do you mean? Of course not! He has a bad heart I told you."

"You staged this whole thing. You never took any pills. There weren't any in your system. You set up a poison meal for your husband, then staged this overdose so you'd be in the hospital when he died, giving you the perfect alibi. You didn't expect him to eat the poisoned dish you prepared until tomorrow."

She shook her head vigorously, but her eyes betrayed her.

"Mrs. Stevens, I know you did it. I'll insist they get an autopsy and they'll find the poison. You'll go to jail, maybe even the electric chair. Tell me NOW what you gave him and we can save his life."

Her face turned pasty white and her pulse shot up to a hundred and thirty on the monitor.

"Oh my God," she sobbed. "You don't know what it was like. He was supposedly going to meetings all the time. I couldn't be good enough for him, but he sure found a new young one that he thought was. I couldn't stand it!"

"Cheryl. Tell me what was the poison."

"Wintergreen. I baked wintergreen into his favorite apple pie. I read somewhere it will kill you quickly, and I figured with his heart history no one would suspect a thing."

I ran back to the trauma room.

Between breaths, I puffed out, "Dr. Morgan, it's wintergreen."

He stared at me for a moment, and then comprehension dawned. "Sodium Bicarb," he barked to the nurses. "Four amps. Stat!"

A stunned silence broken only by machine alarms enveloped the room. "Four amps?" someone asked.

"Yes," Dr. Morgan repeated. "Four amps and I mean 'Stat.'

Mainline them as fast as you can."

I don't claim to know medicine, but I trusted Dr. Morgan. So do his nurses. Four ampules of clear strong base joined the dozen drugs already in his body. Over the next several minutes Mr. Stevens' vital signs stabilized. He even opened his eyes for a moment and tried to talk. Dr. Morgan sedated him and transferred him to the I.C.U.

The police took Cheryl Stevens and the leftover apple pie. Bringing that food and eating it in the Quiet Room had saved Robert Stevens' life. It was a crazy idea of hers to prepare the poison in his favorite food, counting on him to not eat it until the next day. But then, I see all sorts of crazy people on my job.

Suicide Counseling

While this story belies the seriousness of this suicidal gesture, as Greg said, even gestures should be taken seriously. Risk factors for suicide include mental or mood disorders, depression, drug or alcohol abuse, impulsivity, and the use of antidepressants. The list of risk factors runs long and deep, including a family history of suicide, prior suicide attempts, anniversary grief events, and childhood abuse. Suicide occurs in all age groups except the very young, and in all socioeconomic brackets. Young minority men living in poverty and single older men are at particularly high risk.

Chronic pain, living in a stressful situation (such as bullying or abuse), financial, marital, or school difficulties all can put extra pressure on an individual considering suicide. Copycat behavior, that is, if someone's friend or relative committed suicide, can up the odds as well.

Certain signs indicate higher suicide risk. When the person talks of feeling helpless or hopeless, being burdened, or in unbearable pain, those are worrisome talks. People who isolate themselves, withdrawing from their usual activities, giving away prized possessions, or acquiring lethal vehicles, such as collecting pills or buying a gun, should be considered at high risk. A usually calm and happy person who demonstrates rage, anxiety, impulsiveness, or going from a deep depression to a sudden sense of peacefulness, may be on the verge of suicide.

You may ask someone if they're considering suicide, asking does not increase the likelihood of the person proceeding. If they say yes, or even if you just suspect there's danger, reach out to a professional. 1-800-273-5322 is a 24-hour help line, or, if the person specifically threatens suicide, call 911.

"You're Going to Die"

"Good afternoon. I'm Doctor Lewis."

"Arthur Miller." The middle-aged African-American shook my hand and pointed to the handsome young man next to him. "This is my son, Jason."

We shook hands and Jason stepped back, respectfully quiet.

When I asked why they were here, Arthur pointed to a bulge in his neck.

I reached to touch, but jerked back as it pulsed, a snake preparing to strike. I studied Mr. Miller's face, finding no premonition of his impending calamity.

"How long has this been here?" I asked.

"An hour. It's growing fast."

I glanced back at the serpent, watching it slither its way up his neck.

Jason asked, "What is it?"

I looked him over, wondering how to approach the topic of sudden death. Would he be strong enough to spend these last few minutes with his father?

I turned back to Arthur to explain. "There's a weakness called an aneurysm in your carotid, the main artery in your neck. When it bursts, you'll die."

A nurse responded to my call. "Set up two IVs," I ordered her. "Draw a surgical panel and page the vascular surgeon. Oh, and better get me an intubation tray."

"Wait!"

We froze at Arthur's command.

"You're saying I'm about to die?" he demanded.

I studied him, his lips clenched, his brow furrowed. My nod came slowly, my hand offered out gently.

He took that hand and pulled me down into a hug. His heartbeat pulsed hard against my chest, boom, boom, each beat another particle of sand falling from his life's nearly empty hourglass. He released, and I backed away.

His eyes pleaded for a reprieve that wasn't to come. "How long?"

"Soon. Very soon," I murmured.

We gazed into each other's eyes until Jason broke the silence. "What are his chances if you do everything you're about to start?"

I looked again at the viper, its pulsations edging a bit higher. "Even with everything in my power, even if everything worked perfectly, there isn't enough time to fix this."

Arthur settled back on his pillow, staring at the ceiling. "Please do nothing further. I'd like to spend my last minutes in contemplation."

The nurse looked to me, and I looked at Jason who bent close to his father. "Are you sure, Dad?"

The old man gave his son a loving smile. "Yes, Jake. It's been a good life." He turned to face me. "Dr. Lewis, could you perform this one last request for a condemned man? Please, allow me to die in peace."

I looked again at Jason. He nodded and smiled, a small glimmer, clouded over by tears. "Please, Dr. Lewis."

I knew no matter what I did, the outcome would be the same. I took Arthur's hand in both of mine. "I'll do my best. Allow the nurse to start an IV and we'll hold off on everything else."

Arthur nodded.

"What about the vascular surgeon you mentioned?" Jason asked. "Can he help?"

"If he's available, we'll get his opinion."

"What was that about a tubing tray?" from Jason again.

I watched the snake bite off another millimeter of Arthur's neck. "When this bursts your father will suffocate unless I've already placed a tube down his throat."

"Would it save his life?"

I shook my head and turned to my patient. "It might save your heart and lungs, but not your brain. All blood supply to and from your head will be shut off."

Arthur spoke up from his hush. "No intubation. I want what any man desires; that my passing be peaceful."

The nurse started the I.V. and bowed out gracefully. The patriarch settled back onto his deathbed. His son reached down and helped tuck him in. I watched the serpent slide upward, straining to find that weak point, the spot where the artery would burst. He couldn't be stopped. Not in time.

"I'd like to stay," I offered.

Arthur smiled. "Thank you Dr. Lewis. I'll appreciate your company."

The beeps and echoes of the emergency room pervaded the deathwatch as Arthur lay with eyes closed.

Jason's voice came quietly. "What are you thinking about, Dad?"

"I'm reminiscing. Had my share of troubles and triumphs. It's been scary at times, but now that I'm facing death, I'm not frightened."

The two gazed into each other's eyes. Jason bent down, and they hugged. A few more pebbles dribbled from that dwindling hourglass. They resumed positions, the father, now laid in funeral shard, stared at the ceiling. His son stood against the wall, watching.

"I'd recommend some morphine," I suggested.

Arthur didn't move, so I looked to Jason for guidance.

"Is it going to hurt?"

"It will be terrifying."

Arthur grunted and I stepped out to tell the nurse. In moments we were back, she holding the treasured dose securely.

"The vascular surgeon is tied up in surgery," she reported.

Arthur's neck began ballooning.

"Any last words?" I asked.

He shook his head. His son turned to face the wall, respectful to the end.

The asp bit. The vessel burst. The nurse pushed in the morphine.

His neck swelled shut. He choked to death.

So quick. So inevitable.

So terrifying.

"It's over," I said quietly.

Jason twisted to take one last look at his father's now bloated head. "Good-bye Dad. I love you."

The nurse covered Arthur and left. Jason took a few deep breaths and turned to me, his eyes calm.

"Thank you Dr. Lewis. Thank you for letting him pass in peace."

I came around the stretcher and we hugged.

Inevitable Death

The event inspiring this story happened about ten years ago—the only time I've seen a carotid artery aneurysm. Once the aneurysm starts, death can't be prevented. Aneurysms can occur in any large or medium-size artery, commonly in the aorta where the problem can usually be diagnosed and treated before it bursts. However, if the aorta ruptures, the patient will bleed to death in less than a minute. If an artery in the brain bursts, the patient suffers a severe stroke. I had a colleague whose patient presented with a bulge on the wrist. The physician thought it was a cyst and put a needle into it, causing a massive bleed that nearly cost the patient his life.

Other diseases can present with a patient fully alert but with death inevitable, such as complete body burns, massive internal injury like from an airplane crash (one of my patients), or a big pulmonary embolus (blood clot to the lungs). There's always an ethical dilemma of how to relate the news to the patient. I usually tell them that their condition is quite serious, but there's always hope. Yes, people always need hope. When I leave for work each day, I tell my girlfriend "I'm off to save lives, stamp out disease, and bring hope to the huddled masses." Perhaps a bit melodramatic, yet still true.

The Corpse Who Wasn't Dead

"Heh, heh, heh!" I immediately looked up from my chart when I heard the characteristic eerie-toned laugh. When I stood, Dr. Byrd grabbed me around the middle in a long-armed hug. "Well, hey there, Doc Boy," he said.

I hugged back, enjoying the eighty-year-old's warmth. When he stepped away I gave him the onceover and realized he wasn't looking well. Bags hung heavy beneath his bloodshot eyes and his clothes draped in wrinkles. "Are you losing weight?" I asked.

He turned, staring at an old mercury sphygmomanometer some nurse had left on the bench, and from there he focused on a jar of little glass thermometers soaking in rubbing alcohol. One final spot caught his attention, the rack of patients' charts. Each one held the story of life's struggle against death, a battle we physicians could do surprisingly little to effect. Dr. Byrd seemed to be drinking all this in, studying the story of his profession as if he might never see it again.

He gave me a signal, and I followed him to the private dictation room behind the nurses' station. After we were seated, he said, "The truth is – I've got stomach cancer. Mets all over. Bill Lewis gives me two months."

I took his hands in mine. "I'm so sorry, Dr. Byrd."

He managed a smile. "Yeah, well, I always hoped I'd kick the bucket in bed with a mistress. Maybe I still will!" He raised an iodine-stained coat sleeve to wipe at his eyes.

"I guess I'm ready," he said. "It's been a good life. My kids are grandparents now, and with Miriam three years gone, life is lonely. Only one last loose end. Doc Boy, I need you to do something for me."

Images of the many times I'd turned to him for advice flashed before my eyes. When I'd hung up my shingle eight years before, he'd led me through all the important hurdles: introducing me to the other facility doctors, the area pharmacists, and the important hospital personnel. During the subsequent years, he'd often been there to help me out on a tough case or cheer me up when a special patient passed. I owed him bigtime.

"Anything, Dr. Byrd. You just name it and if it's in my power I'll do my best."

"Good. I'm going to hold you to that. I want you to take over my job as medical examiner."

I felt my smile melt away. "Medical examiner? I've never done anything like that. I'm just a G. P. – a family doc. You know, kids with fever, health physicals, old people with hypertension. I haven't done an autopsy since medical school."

"Ah, it's right up your alley. You say you provide 'cradle-to-grave care,' don't cha? Well here's the grave part. And it's pretty grave! Heh heh heh. The county needs a medical examiner, and you know it's got to be easy work if an old man like me can do it. It's interesting and educational too."

I felt my reluctance melting away. The truth was, I used to enjoy going to autopsies during my training years. "I guess I can give it a try. Are you going to teach me the ropes?"

"If I had the chance you know I would." Dr. Byrd pulled at his loosely hanging shirt. "But I figure I'm a little too crabby for that. Heh heh heh." He handed over a slip of paper. "Here's the number for Dr. Wenger, the regional medical examiner. Call her tomorrow and set up an appointment. She'll bring you up to speed."

The next Saturday found me at the end of a hundred-mile trip to the regional medical examiner center in the big city. The building boasted a modern look, all glass and brick, with large oak trees shading a small parking lot. On one side, a driveway held a three-bay loading dock, one of which had a hearse backed in.

I stepped through the glass doors into a different world. Shivering at the thirty-degree temperature drop, I wished I'd brought a jacket. The reception office had an unattended desk holding a bell. After bopping it for a ring, I gave the room a gander, noticing the apparently unused plastic furniture, white chairs and black coffee table. A fake palm in one corner did nothing to filter out the formaldehyde smell, an aroma that brought back those medical school images again. What the hell was I getting myself into, anyway?

In a few minutes, a comely, tall woman in a mildly tattered coat stepped in from the back door and extended her hand. She had "Dr. Wenger, MD" stenciled above a pen-filled pocket.

"Dr. Hooper?" she asked.

"Yep, that's me." I admitted.

She placed her hands akimbo and cocked her head. I could tell she was sizing me up. "So you want to learn how to be a medical examiner?"

I wasn't sure if it was a warning or a dare. "Gotta admit, two weeks ago if someone'd suggested I'd be here now I'd've laughed. Still not sure dealing with dead bodies is for me."

Her smile twisted into a peculiar smirk. "Oh, you'll love it. You can work on your own pace because, after all, the dead never mind waiting. Heh heh heh."

I stepped back, mouth agape. Her laugh sounded so much like old Dr. Byrd's it was spooky. What I had figured was a unique characteristic now took on a morbid overtone. Now I knew I'd forever associate that sound with death.

Dr. Wenger took me on a tour of the building, showing me the forty-drawer morgue, autopsy rooms, file rooms, and several offices. We ended in a small conference room where she directed me to a seat and lowered the lights. What followed was the most bizarre slide show imaginable, corpses featured in all kinds of situations. One image I'll never forget showed a meat thermometer protruding from someone's belly.

"Stick it in the liver," Dr. Wenger advised. "You can estimate how long the body's been dead by seeing how much the core has cooled."

The next day I signed in at the county court house, received a badge, and became the official county medical examiner. My duties required me to certify any death occurring in the county that couldn't be certified by the patient's private doctor. Over the next few months I was called to certify a death every week or two.

My first case was a sixty-two-year-old found dead in his semi-tractor trailer. Mr. Braxton, a long-distance trucker out of Oregon, ended up having a lonely death a thousand miles from home. At sixty-four-years-old, a lifetime of sitting behind the wheel and living on coffee, donuts, and cigarettes had finally caught up with him. It took about half-an-hour for me to reach his wife back home. When I told her what had happened she burst into tears.

"This was going to be his last trip," she said between sobs. "He'd planned on retiring and staying home, planting a garden, and teaching his grandson how to fish."

As the months rolled by several curious cases rolled through. One evening I spent three hours studying an incredibly deformed stillborn. Another day I had to use a gas mask in order to be able to examine a woman who had been dead a week. She'd been found when the neighbors called the police to check out the smell. In one sad case a fellow shot himself in the head while having an argument with his girlfriend over the phone. Later that day I had to treat the girlfriend for emotional shock.

Perhaps the most bizarre case was the man who wasn't dead. I first heard about him one day when I received a call from Mrs. Flowers of the new Keystone Funeral Home.

"Dr. Hooper? Are you the local medical examiner?"

"Yes. How can I help you, Mrs. Flowers?"

"I need you to sign a medical examiner's death certificate on Mr. Leroy Hairston."

I pulled out a notepad to take down the details. "Have you had his body moved to the morgue?"

"Well, no."

"Over at your funeral home, then."

"Actually we buried Mr. Hairston."

My pen clattered to the floor. "Surely you didn't bury Mr. Hairston without a death certificate?"

Mrs. Flowers' explanation rushed out like the worms from a freshly unearthed corpse. "It was just a simple mix up. The family called us to pick him up, and they were eager to get the funeral done before grandma had to go back into the hospital. So we just embalmed him that afternoon and buried him the same evening. That was last month – on the seventeenth. So now we need a death certificate. I'm sure you understand."

I slapped my hand to my forehead. "Really? Dead a month without a death certificate? Well, I'll see what I can do. Who was the investigating officer?"

The *hmm* and *haw* coming over the phone told me the bad news. Keystone Funeral Home had buried a man who wasn't legally dead.

After hanging up on Mrs. Flowers, I picked up the phone and punched in the numbers for the regional center. I tried to imagine Dr. Wegner's face when I opened with, "What am I going to do with the corpse who isn't dead?"

After I explained the case, she laughed that hideous laugh of hers.

"Heh heh heh. Don't worry, Dr. Hooper. We take care of problems like this all the time. Stick around in the business of death for a couple of years and you'll see a world of strange."

She arranged for the exhumation of the body, the police report, and the death certification – all part of her routine duties apparently. Over the next few days I kept thinking about that strange laugh of hers, that haunting, creepy sound, laughing about exhuming a month-old body. I suppose working with corpses over the years might warp anyone's sense of humor.

A year passed, and one day I was at the morgue after being told a new corpse needed my attention.

"The rescue squad said someone sliced open his belly with a meat cleaver," the nurse said as the guard pulled the body out of the freezer.

"Some sort of gang killing," the guard suggested.

We positioned the victim on the table and unzipped the black plastic shroud covering him. He had been a fat fellow in his mid-thirties -- now yellow adipose tissue decorated bowels flopping around on the outside.

With a single glance I nodded sagely. "I know why they killed him."

"Why?" the nurse asked.

"They were afraid he'd talk to the police. You know, spill his guts. Heh heh heh."

The two others looked at me strangely.

"What? Don't you think that's funny?" I demanded.

"Your laugh … it reminds me of something weird," the nurse said.

I looked between them. "Yeah? What?"

The guard and nurse glanced at each other.

"A bit like …" the nurse started.

The guard finished for her. "… A death rattle."

Forensics

When I was a medical student, JCAHO (the Joint Commission on the Accreditation of Hospitals Organization) agency insisted hospitals perform a certain percentage of autopsies, and the residents had contests to see which team could obtain the most. When a patient died, the attending physician, usually a third-year internal medicine resident, was responsible for obtaining the family's permission. Most families were reluctant, and often the resident would try to persuade them by claiming that there would be great informational value obtained.

As part of my training I had to sit in on a few autopsies. I remember one where the pathology resident cut open the corpse's belly and found a pool of white foam. I asked him what he had found, and he told me the foam meant the patient had died from acute rupture of the pancreas. When I next asked if the doctors treating the man had known, the resident checked the diagnosis on the chart. "Nope," he said, thus proving the value of an autopsy.

In the days before CAT scans and rapid test results, autopsies truly provided educational opportunities. Nowadays, autopsies are rarely performed. State law requires an autopsy for any SIDS death, any death where the patient did not have a private physician willing to sign the death certificate, and any death due to violence or under suspicious circumstances. Otherwise, families who request one on their relative must pay in advance.

As described in this story, I became a medical examiner for the state of Virginia. The story above pretty well describes my experiences, which were, as I said, interesting and educational. When I was sworn in as an M.E., I received a real honest-to-God police badge. This allowed me to go into crime scenes as an M.E. to poke around. I never actually had the opportunity, though it would have been fun. In any case, I still have the badge – a wonderful souvenir!

The Crying Baby

"They're bringing in a four-month-old ejected from a car rollover!"

The nurse who had received the report brought me the sheet where she'd recorded the sparse details. Her neat cursive writing seemed better suited for a love letter than this ominous message.

"Single vehicle accident. Rolled off road, difficult extraction. Three victims. Unrestrained baby ejected through side window. Estimated time until arrival, six minutes."

We gathered in the trauma room to prepare for their arrival. Sharon, the head nurse, prepared two IV lines. The secretary paged the needed technicians.

In eighteen years of practicing emergency medicine, I could count the number of serious baby trauma cases I'd handled on one hand. Treating babies required trained precision skills, weight-based medication dosages, and special miniaturized instruments. Most of all, I had to master my anxiety of dealing with a new, innocent life in jeopardy.

My team was good, all experienced E.R. nurses and technicians. I watched Sharon bring out the pediatric resuscitation equipment. Sharon loved children. When the pediatric cardiologist visited from the medical center, she volunteered to accompany him on rounds. Her eyes widened, anticipation battling anxiety.

The ambulance crew burst through the electric doors, a wailing infant bundled in the arms of Hamp, the paramedic. He carefully placed him on our trauma warmer. In the green roll-up splint the infant looked pitifully small. Dried blood crusted his right cheek and a blue goose-egg decorated his forehead. He tried to look around, struggling to wave his arms and kick his feet.

I unwrapped him carefully. A little sand washed out easily from his right eye. Listening to his lungs, heart, and belly, I informed the group that all sounded fine. As the baby continued to wail, I found no problems with his collarbones, hips, or pelvis, though road burn tattooed his left arm and thigh.

The nurses hooked up monitor leads, showing a pulse of one hundred and sixty, slightly high for the infant. Sharon slipped an IV line into the clean right arm, providing the phlebotomist with blood samples for the tests I ordered. The x-ray technician maneuvered her heavy machine to shoot films of the infant's neck and body.

"There's got to be something wrong," Sharon insisted.

I trusted her instincts with infants, but so far, except for the arm scrape, cut on his cheek, and the bump on his noggin, everything seemed fine. After the x-ray reports and lab tests came back normal, I had the secretary call the surgeon.

Sharon sat in the big rocker, holding the screaming child, singing to him gently. Bob, the male aide, brought a pacifier, but the baby refused to take it.

"What about a CAT scan of the head and belly?" Sharon suggested.

I hesitated. Those were expensive tests, as well as heavy dosages of radiation.

"I don't know, Sharon," I said. "His belly is soft and he looks pretty good."

She looked steadily into my eyes. "There must be something making him cry like this. We have to keep looking."

I ordered the tests.

"Surgeon's on the phone," the secretary reported.

We all liked Dr. Dobbs, today's on-call surgeon. At sixty-seven-years-old and with a huge potbelly, he moved slowly. His puffy hands were gentle.

After I explained the situation he replied simply, "I'll be there."

The baby's mother was a shapely sixteen-year-old blue-eyed blonde, pretty enough to be a model if she lost twenty pounds. She'd been on the passenger side, the side that had been downward. The right side of her face was a bloody shredded mess, her cheek skin open with purplish serrations. I gently dabbed at her injuries with some saline soaked gauze.

We could hear her baby wailing. "Please, Doctor. Please tell me my baby is going to be okay."

I stopped my cleaning. "He looks okay and his blood tests and x-rays are normal. I've got a surgeon coming in to check him over."

Tears ran down her cheeks, creating blue mascara rivers down her cheeks.

"Your cuts aren't very deep," I told her. "I'm going to call the plastic surgeon to have a look."

I next checked on the father, curled up on stretcher five. He was a tall African-American seventeen-year-old. Someone had placed a plastic collar around his neck.

"Are you hurt?" I asked.

He looked up from his tear soaked hands.

"I'm broken, man," he said. "You seen what I done to my wife's face? And my baby? How is he?"

I tried to reassure him as I did a quick assessment and ordered neck films.

Dr. Dobbs arrived, looked at the x-rays, and then lumbered over to the x-ray department where the baby was in the scanner. A half hour later I joined them in the trauma room where Sharon again rocked the infant.

"He'll only stop crying for a few seconds at a time," Sharon told me. "I just know we're missing something."

"The scans all look okay," Dr. Dobbs said, "except for a piece of glass in the cut on his cheek."

I stepped out while Dr. Dobbs prepared to probe the child's cheek cut. The wailing ceased abruptly. I ran back to the trauma room to find Dr. Dobbs holding up the splinter of glass in his forceps, a wide smile across his face. The baby sucked peacefully on the pacifier.

"All along it was the piece of glass in his cheek that was irritating the baby," Sharon said.

The plastic surgeon assessed that the mother's wounds would heal with hardly a scar, and the police decided not to ticket the father.

Dr. Dobbs sat down with me, sipping a cup of coffee. "It's not every day I can cure a baby by removing a glass sliver. Looks like a happy ending all around."

"They should have been wearing seatbelts. That baby could easily have had his gourd squashed, the mother could have lost her eye, and the father could have broken his neck. I don't mean to cast negativity in the air, but luck can only take you so far."

The big surgeon drained what was left of his coffee and pushed up to his feet. Looking down at me he shrugged. "I've seen a lot of good luck and a lot of bad luck in my days, Guy. There's no justifying who gets what. Let's be grateful for their sakes, and pray for the ones not so lucky."

Car Accidents

When I started working as an E.R. doctor, in the late 1970s, hardly anyone wore a seatbelt and many people drove drunk. In the big open spaces of South Texas, a car going ninety with an unbelted drunk driver would smash into a deer crossing the road, throwing the fellow forward through the windshield, shedding his face, snapping his neck, and sometimes crushing him under the car. Changes in social morés and protective legislation have dramatically changed the frequency and severity of these outcomes.

I've heard people grouse about our "Big Brother" state. Motorcyclists who prefer the feel of riding without a helmet say they're only going to hurt themselves. Tell that to the hospital administrator who has to pick up the quarter million-dollar bill for the two month ICU treatment, and then the county government that ends up paying another quarter million in rehabilitation costs and long term disability care. We, as taxpayers, must pick up these tabs, so I urge all my readers to promote safe driving habits: don't drive intoxicated and always wear a seatbelt.

This story comes from that time period, say the mid-1980s, when I worked in small town E.R.s. When a major trauma came in, we did our best, trying to stabilize the patient, and then would try to find a higher care hospital to accept our problems: sometimes we could, sometimes we couldn't. In the late 1980s state governments set up designated area trauma centers, level 4 for smaller E.R.s without trauma service, those with a designated surgeon on call rated level 3, and those fully equipped level 2, which is the type in which I've worked the past thirty years or so. If a bad accident occurs, the EMS can bypass small hospitals to take the patient to a level 2 center or call for a helicopter to land in a nearby field, for a trip to a level 1, usually a university teaching hospital. The delay in initiation of care is almost always outweighed by the better care received.

There used to be a term called "The Golden Hour," referring to the first hour of a trauma when the chances of recovery are the best. I haven't seen that term used in quite a while, as almost all trauma patients are seen and treated promptly. In the 1980s the American College of Surgery developed a protocol called "Advanced Trauma Life Support," and all E.R. doctors have to keep *up their ATLS certification in order to work in a trauma center. I'm personally skilled in intubating, placing chest tubes, and placing needed lines. These are the exciting aspects of emergency medicine, though now they come into use more commonly in gunshot wounds rather than car accidents. I suppose that's a step in the right direction.*

The Old Biloxian

"When I t'was a boy, I worked in them canneries. You ever seen pictures of the point back then, Doc?"

I glanced up at Emile Babinski's face. At eighty-four, his bushy eyebrows shaded alert eyes. Sun marks polka dotted his arms and face, the latter holding an intent smile. I turned back to my work, repairing the six-inch skin rip he'd made in his leg when he'd tripped this morning in his bedroom.

"I've seen some of those postcards," I told him. "Piles of oyster shells made mountains in the gulf. You must have been a youngster."

I dabbed the raw skin gently with saline-soaked gauze, using a long-handled cotton-tip to work out a small particle of dirt. The edge of a glass table had jabbed into the muscle, whose red fibers bulged at the rip. Wheals of xylocaine pushed up the skin as I carefully numbed along the cut's edge.

His voice came back dreamily, telling the story as if it'd happened last week rather than six decades ago. "Came straight off the boat and set workin' ever' day, sunup to sundown. We'd pull them oyster bags off the boats, sling 'em over our backs, and drag 'em up to the shellers. Six days a week."

"Did you know anyone here when you came over?"

He grunted affirmation. "My uncle and a brother. Later dee whole family came over. Only here two years when I met my belle, Maricelle."

He lifted his head, and asked me, "You married, Doc?"

"Divorced."

"Ah, shame that. No blessin' like a perfect marriage. Sweetness and light, them's the words to describe my Marci. Her smile would knock rainclouds right out of the sky. Cooked like a chef, loved like an angel."

I finished the first run of sutures, the muscle tucked back under the cross-stitched inner tissue. Next came a few snares in the fat and then to finish up with nylon loops along the skin. I took a pause to wash the wound with more saline.

"How long were you married?"

He sighed. "The good Lord took her on beck to his heaven a year ago, jist a week shy of our sixty-sixth. You took care of her. Don't remember, huh?"

I paused in my work to look up at him. I had thought he'd looked familiar. Pushing hard into my memory I tried to pull up an image. Maricelle Babinski. Didn't ring a bell. I see so many patients, the details of individual cases tend to fade. "What was wrong with her?"

"Stroke. Seemed ta be recoverin' when you admitted her, but a few hours later said her head was a killin' her and that was it. 'Em strokes kill you. Read up on 'em. First heart attacks, second cancer, then comes strokes."

I finished my repair work, taking a moment to admire the evenly placed sutures. Although it's the inside that counts, patients judge the quality of the work by the appearance of the top sutures. I'm an artist.

After tidying up my workspace, I gave Mr. Babinski a wave. "The nurse will be in to apply ointment and a bandage. I'll be back after your lab results return. Should have you out of here in an hour or so."

Back at my station I pulled up Maricelle's chart. Eleven months before she'd come in at two in the morning with classic stroke symptoms: trouble speaking, one-sided facial weakness, and a stumbling walk. We'd put her through the stroke protocol, and with a negative CAT scan of her brain, I'd arranged for admission. Brent, the neuro nurse specialist, had come in from home and taken over.

Reading my notes brought back the memories. I'd laughed at Brent's appearance, he worked so hard all day, and then getting up in the middle of the night on call, he was unshaven, shirt buttoned unevenly, and clearly half asleep.

Paging through the records I found where Brent had authorized the infusion of the clot buster drug, TPA. Our hospital was the first one in the state to be certified as a stroke center, and the neuro group prided themselves on using this "stroke reversing drug." Despite the statistics in favor of its use, I remained skeptical, for it only improved survival by a few percentage, and that was almost balanced out by the increase in brain bleeds it created. It wasn't supposed to be given to patients over seventy-two-years-old. Maricelle had been seventy-nine.

I turned to the nursing notes. The neuro unit nurse had documented Maricelle's condition as improving, with return of her speech and normalization of her facial features. Return of neuro function was another contraindication to the use of TPA. I flipped over to the form for cause of death and read what I'd feared. "Intracerebral bleed." Mrs. Babinski had been improving until the TPA Brent had ordered killed her.

I closed the chart and sat back, thinking about Brent, and about the neuro service. He was a good man, but here he'd made a mistake, and his mistake had turned deadly. If I reported this, it would cause a lot of problems for both Brent and for the service.

I reviewed Emile's lab tests. All were in order and he was ready for discharge. I filled out the paperwork and went in to see him.

"All okay, Doc?"

I settled into a chair and placed my hand on his. "Mr. Babinski, about your wife. You said she seemed to be improving?"

"Yep. Nurse said maybe she'd get to come on home in a day or so. Guess God had other plans."

I studied his peaceful face, a man who'd worked hard all his life, asking nothing more in return but a fair shake. A technician's mistake had taken away the love of his life, and unless I told him, he'd never know. Certainly he deserved to be told. He'd been betrayed and then misled.

But what would be the advantage of telling him? He'd have to grieve all over again, with a much more bitter context, blaming humans instead of accepting God's will.

I gripped his hand gently. "Right. Well, all is good on your tests and your leg should heal up with just a bit of a scar. Stitches come out in two weeks. For that, you can come back here or see your local doctor."

He squeezed back. "Thanks Doc. I always tell ever'one, Memorial's the best hospital around. You can trust you'll get the best care, that's for sure."

I nodded and walked away.

TPA for Strokes

As Mr. Babinski found on his research, strokes are the third most common cause of death in the United States. If the patient doesn't die, strokes can cause significant disability, often making the person too physically disabled to work, and sometimes unable to speak or take care of their own basic needs. TPA, developed to break up blockages causing heart attacks, breaks up clots in the brain vessels just as well, actually reversing the stroke.

Although studies show statistical advantages to using TPA, one must remember that all strokes, even severe ones, will show improvement over time. TPA can actually make the situation much worse by turning a "dry" stroke into a "wet" one, with bleeding in the brain causing worse damage, as in this fictional case. There's an old saying, "Give someone a hammer and everything looks like a nail." TPA is the big hammer against the nail of a stroke. Over time these issues have caused more hesitancy for TPA use, and the restrictions are closely monitored, with more patients excluded than before, although the time period after onset to still receive the drug has been lengthened.

When I was in medical school, one of my lecturers told the class, "Someday you'll kill someone." Physicians are only human, and, like all humans, we make mistakes, both of omission and commission. Heaven knows I've made my share, although as far as I know none of mine resulted in a patient's death. We try to be careful about intervening, even when it seems that the patients expect us to "Do something!" that might help rather than do nothing. This is why so many kids with colds get antibiotics. Other examples abound, such as our vigorous treatment of our patients' blood pressure, with some of the medication side effects creating ever more difficulties. As another example, one of many, back surgery does help some people, but often does not help, even resulting in more pain.

It's important to remember that when we were sworn in as physicians, we took the Hippocratic oath. In it he said, "First do no harm."

New Year's Eve Celebration

It was the end of my shift, 7 p.m. on New Year's Eve. I had a party to go to, planning on rushing home for a quick change of clothes. As I pulled out of the hospital parking lot I spotted a familiar shape limping along the side of the road. I'd just treated Julie from injuries sustained in a drunken brawl. She'd broken her fibula, the smaller of the two bones in her lower leg, painful, but not serious – treatable with a splint for a couple of weeks. There she was, trudging along like Festus, swinging her bad leg out with every step. I was tempted to ignore her, after all, I can't be responsible for everyone's problems. But, gosh, it was barely above freezing, and she didn't even have a jacket.

I pulled up next to her and rolled down my window. "Need a ride?"

She flashed me a broken tooth smile and climbed into the passenger seat. "Thanks Dr. Lewis."

Once back on the highway, I asked "Where you going, Julie?"

"Walmart in Biloxi, if it's not too much trouble."

I glanced at the car's clock, accepting that I'd be late to my party. "That's a dozen miles. You were planning on walking all that way with a broken leg?"

She shrugged. "Don't have a choice."

"And you live near there?"

"In the woods. Got a tent."

As we drove through the holiday traffic I asked about her life, how she had ended up homeless, and about her family. She related one sad event after another: son in prison, another one dead, her trailer destroyed in a fire, her clothing stolen. By the looks of her stringy gray hair and wrinkled face, I had pegged her to be in her sixties. I'd overestimated by twenty years.

When we reached the parking lot she began to climb out and I stopped her with a touch. Pulling out my wallet I handed her a twenty.

She shook her head. "I can't take your money."

"Go buy yourself a jacket."

She hesitated, staring at the money, and then at me. Taking the bill, she gave me another of those cute crooked smiles and kissed my cheek. "Thanks, Dr. Lewis. You're a sweetheart."

"Happy Holidays," I said.

I sat in the car for a few minutes more, watching her hobble towards Walmart. When she reached the door she hesitated, then turned away, continuing down the sidewalk. A few doors down she entered the liquor store.

"Happy Holidays," I murmured again, and drove off towards my own party.

Poverty

Poverty is a leading cause of early death. Lack of access to health care due to distance, costs, and stigma, mean chronic diseases worsen for lack of treatment and acute illnesses may not receive necessary treatment. Free clinics rarely have the staffing or supplies to provide for the many needy, and so they end up in the county emergency rooms. A patient's blood pressure pill prescription might cost only $10, but if he can't get to a doctor to get the prescription, it might as well be a million bucks.

America's Medicaid program provides some free medical access to those who qualify. It's certainly better than nothing, though reimbursement levels run so low, many doctors shun it, and many needy poor don't qualify. Due to poor medical access, America ranks 35th out of 50 in infant mortality and 42nd in life expectancy. Our medical costs are twice as much per person as the next highest country. Clearly, though we spend a lot of money on medical care, we don't give good care for the money.

I don't have an answer to poverty. Socialized medicine provides care for everyone, but with governments handling the budget, they reduce reimbursements to providers and facilities resulting in limited medications, treatments, and quality. All we can do is open our hearts to those in need and be generous of our time and sympathy.

Heart Broken

"They strip you naked and keep these blasted examining rooms like igloos!" Carl groused. He looked over at his wife, wondering why her bare legs didn't have goose pimples below that tight black outfit. Why had she insisted on dressing up just to bring him to the E.R.? Ever since the nurse left, she'd kept looking out the curtain.

"Hey? You got a minute for me?" he demanded.

She turned to him, her eyes startled. "Sorry. What were you saying?"

Carl glared at her. "I said it's freezing in here. When is the doctor going to come in?"

"Oh, I'm sure it'll be just a few minutes." She came up and put her hand on his forehead. "How are you feeling?"

He studied her wrinkleless face, with its pencil perfect eyebrows and finely lined red lips. She sure knew how to look sexy. "Not too good, I can tell you that. That pill the nurse put under my tongue is giving me a terrible headache. I guess that's her plan, huh? Make my head hurt so much that I forget about my heartburn."

Sharon's attention had wandered to the cubicle's curtain again. "Hmm?"

He grabbed her arm, squeezing a bit too hard.

"Hey, let go," she whined.

"What the hell is so interesting out there, anyway? I'm dying here, and you're acting like you can't wait to go out on the town."

Sharon shook his arm off and walked across the room, settling into the cheap plastic chair. "Maybe you're right and all that's wrong is your fat stomach."

"I told you that cheese tasted funny," Carl grumbled. He shuffled the sheet again, trying to keep his feet warm. He'd always had cold feet, but ever since he turned fifty it was worse. Now why couldn't he at least have left his socks on? Why were all the nurses such battleaxes?

Carl looked up at a dark-haired man slipping in through the curtain. Dressed in a long white coat over green scrubs, his stethoscope swung as he walked. His name tag read "J. Santoni, M.D." Sicilian, Carl thought. Or perhaps Greek. Got those dark features that women seemed to love.

"Hello," the doctor said, granting Carl a brief smile. Checking the chart, he said, "You must be Mister Parker?"

"Yeah, that's me."

Dr. Santoni turned towards Sharon. "And you are?" he asked.

She came up and held out her hand. "I'm Carl's wife, Sharon. A pleasure to meet you, Doctor."

He took her hand and Carl watched their connection closely, counting seconds in his head. One, two, three, four. Too long. Damn the way men fell in love with her on first sight!

The doctor turned back to the chart, flipping through some pages. "Hmm."

"What?" Carl demanded. "What did you find?"

The doctor placed the chart on a small metal table and pulled out his pen. "When did you start having chest pain?"

"Right after dinner; Sharon here cooked up some veal parmesan. Always been one of my favorites." Carl watched him jot down notes.

"Have you had other symptoms? Sweating?"

Carl shrugged. "I like my dinners spicy; a couple of jalapenos on the side."

"Indigestion feeling?"

Carl turned to his wife. "See, I told you this was all nothing but a bout of gas. And you *insisted* we come to this damn E.R."

The doctor cleared his throat. "Actually, Mr. Parker, I'm afraid your condition is quite serious."

Sharon placed her hand gently on the doctor's wrist. "Oh! What is it, Doctor? What's happened to my husband?"

Dr. Santoni flashed a pink sheet of paper with wavy lines in front of Carl. "Your EKG shows you're having a heart attack."

Carl grimaced, grabbing at his chest and taking a deep breath. Could this be it? The big one? "No! No! This can't be happening to me!" He threw off the sheet and tried to swing his legs off the bed.

Dr. Santoni called out, "Nurse! I need some help in here."

Carl reached for the wires attached to his chest just as a nurse and two aides rushed in, the latter grabbing him by the arms. "Hey, leave me alone," Carl called out.

"Give him five milligrams of Ativan, stat!" Dr. Santoni ordered.

"You mean point five?" the nurse asked.

"No, five," the doctor repeated. "We need to keep Mr. Parker calm."

Carl struggled against the aides who forced him gently back onto the bed. "Please lie still," one of them said. "We're here to help you."

The nurse returned with a syringe, and Carl watched her inject a large vial of medicine into his IV. He felt drunk, collapsing into the mattress.

The doctor turned to the two aides and told them they could leave. To the nurse he said, "Please call the cardiologist and ask him to come right away. I'm afraid Mr. Parker's heart might give out at any minute."

"Yes, Doctor Santoni," the nurse said as she hurried out of the room.

Now there were only the three of them again. Carl watched Sharon walk up to the doctor, stand on tiptoe, and kiss his cheek. "That medicine you had me put into his food seems to have worked. But are you sure he's going to die, Joseph?"

"Don't call me that here," he hissed. He took a syringe out of his pocket and injected it into Carl's IV.

The last thing Carl heard was Dr. Santoni's deep voice. "Yes, I'm sure. And no one will suspect a thing."

Heart Attacks

Heart attacks rank as the number one cause of death in the United States. The most common symptoms of left sided chest pain may include radiation of the pain to the shoulder, back, or jaw. Indigestion, sweating, and nausea often accompany the symptoms, making the problem mistaken for a stomach issue. EKGs may not show the infarction early on or, if the heart damage doesn't include the surface of the heart where the electrical system runs, may not show the heart attack at all. Risk factors include obesity, lack of exercise, smoking, hypertension, diabetes, family history of heart disease, and high cholesterol.

When I started E.R. medicine, the standard treatment for patients having a heart attack amounted to bed rest and lidocaine. Over time we realized both treatments did more harm than good. We progressed to special cardiac units, and from those to clot breaker medications. Now we have specialized operating theatres where cardiologists snake catheters into the heart arteries to open up the clots and place stents. Amazing stuff!

In this story the man is poisoned and unless someone had enough suspicion to order an autopsy, the conniving couple would get away with murder. But does anyone ever do so? If the doctor and ex-wife later took their relationship public, suspicions might be raised and an autopsy ordered retroactively. Even if the body is cremated, blood samples are obtained from all cremations before the burning, and kept in safe storage just in case. Of course, there are medications that can't be detected, or, even if detected, could not prove they were used as murder devices. Certainly, stories exist of nurses who have killed many of their patients on purpose. It's a strange world.

Searching for Gildeen

I awoke from my nightmare soaked in sweat. The phone hadn't rung, yet I knew it was about to. I picked it up. "Hello Gildeen."

Gildeen started talking immediately, as if four years of silence had never been. "You've got to come right over, Marcus."

"Maybe I should at least get dressed?"

She laughed. My mind filled with the image of her crimson lips, dancing below those green diamond eyes. "Naked is fine with me."

The bedside clock read 3 a.m. I jumped in the shower.

Dawn was just breaking as I pulled up to Gildeen's secluded home. In the silver roadster's mirror, I smoothed a windblown hairlock back into place.

Gildeen slid open the door before I knocked. Nothing had changed; large plants covered much of the floor and crowded the wooden bookshelves and tables. "Strawberries?" she asked, holding up a plate with three bright specimens.

"Sure," I said, and reached for one.

My hand froze in mid-air.

"Maybe I shouldn't."

I looked again and saw that the plate contained only red pills.

Gildeen smiled, a wicked turn to the corners of her lips. "You always were the clever one, weren't you, Marcus? So, why haven't you sought my help with your nightmares?"

"How did you know about those?"

"You can't hide anything from me, Marcus. Have a seat." She pointed to the pentagram on the floor where we settled across from each other. From her neck she lifted her dark mahogany pendant, grasping its gold thread with two shiny red nails.

Four years ago those sequin-spangled nails were cat claws aimed at my face. She had jumped up screaming from a black symbol that I'd revealed with the Tarot cards. Had I seen her since? Trying to remember … nighttime, wasn't it?

As we sat cross-legged on the floor, the pendulum swinging before my eyes, the smells of her incense brought back séances of the past. Disharmonic chords pulsed through the darkened room.

Candles in the corners danced strange shadows. From the top of a bookshelf her dark tabby watched, its tail twitching.

Gildeen hadn't aged a day; her ivory skin glowed with mystic energy. A rare silver thread wove a statement through her red mane. A memory of the two us making love on the beach rose in my mind. Bouncing back to the present I sat still, watching the pendulum make curious patterns in the air.

"Large gray cat stalking you," Gildeen murmured.

I strained to hear her whispered voice. "Cat?"

Her eyes traced the dancing weight, brow wrinkled in concentration. "The red brings death."

I held my breath, but she said nothing more.

Gildeen reached out, her ring-bobbed fingers cuddling the pendulum, bringing it to her lips. She looked at me with her mischievous smile. "Learn anything?" she asked.

I shook my head. "Something about a cat, but I already knew that."

"That's all you remember?" Her tones rang with disappointment.

I stood and helped her up. "It was good to see you again, Gildeen."

She nodded, her face momentarily serious before breaking into her bewitching smile. "Why have you stayed away so long?"

"I meant to call. Things kept coming up."

Sadness darkened her features. "New lovers."

"They help me forget," I pleaded as she pushed me out the door.

The phone startled me out of a nightmare, the shattered images gone like rain down a gutter. "Hello, Gildeen," I said, knowing it was her even before she spoke. "Why must you wake me at three in the morning? Now I'll be exhausted for my ten o'clock appointment."

"I called to warn you not to go, Marcus. Danger is a panther in ambush."

"And if I don't go will I avoid the danger?"

I pictured her ruby lips pursing in concentration. "Maybe. I'll be right there."

I got up and rinsed, and when I came out she was waiting for me on the bed. She stretched naked across the sheets, her long flaming hair sweeping over her rosy breasts like surf. She stood leisurely, her red nipples shining like street lights. Her large tail swished out from behind her back, her motor roared, and she leaped at me, nails extended.

I became aware of the pendulum again, swinging in small circles in front of my face.

"What did you see?" Gildeen purred.

I closed my eyes to try to hold in the experience; so vivid, and yet already fading in memory's mists.

"Something about a large cat," I said. "Maybe a lion. Red. Something red I'm sure. Glancing at my watch, I read the time at nine twenty. "I've got to be going if I'm going to make my ten o'clock. I'm meeting Victor at the zoo."

"I'm coming with you," she cried.

Instantly we were strolling together down the pathway of large mammals. Gildeen broke into a dance on the sidewalk, in tune to the music always playing in her mind. About sixty yards ahead I spotted Victor standing next to the albino tiger cage.

"Hello, Victor." I called. "It's a lovely day for an outside reading."

"Ah, Marcus. I'm glad you've come. I see you have finally brought Gildeen with you. Four years, huh? I was wondering if I'd ever get to meet her."

I felt Gildeen pulling on my arm. "We've got to get out of here, Marcus. There's terrible danger."

I said to Victor, "Apparently she needs to go."

"You mustn't go," Victor said, as he swung open the cage. The tiger crouched, and pounced, its wheels squealing.

I awoke soaked in sweat. Why did I keep having these nightmares? And why was it always three a.m.? I sat on the corner of the bed and stared at the phone.

I picked it up and listened. Dial tone.

I placed it back down and picked it up again. Gildeen was on line. "Are you on your way yet?"

I shook my head, trying to clear it. "Where are we going?"

"To the library. I'll meet you there."

On my arrival I spotted Gildeen stroking one of the gray marble lions that flank the library's stone entry steps. "It's wonderful to see you again," I called up to her. "I wouldn't have thought it possible, but here you are, grown even more beautiful."

She smiled at me, a smile that shot yearning through my body. "You'll never forget me, will you, Darling?"

I stepped on the first level, just below her. "Forget you? I've been searching for you ever since you …"

"I what?"

I couldn't remember. I followed her finger as she pointed across the street. On the opposite curb stood Victor. He had Gildeen's pendulum in his hand, swinging it gently.

"Victor!" I called. "What are you doing here?"

He beckoned for me. I took one step down before feeling Gildeen's nails grasp my arm.

"Don't, Marcus," she pleaded. "You'll lose me forever!"

I pulled her with me, off the stairs and to the curb. Gildeen stood on the curb dancing, and when I glanced back I saw the two statues in front of the library coming to life. They stretched, looking at us with hunger in their eyes. "Come on, Gildeen," I screamed. "The street. We have to get across the street safely."

I ran, dragging her behind, and she stumbled halfway across, landing on her knees, scraping large red streaks, splattering blood. The library lights turned from green to red. As I watched in horror, both lions jumped from their perches, pouncing towards my precious love.

The pendulum swung slowly back and forth, making little circles in front of my face.

"What did you see?" he asked.

I squeezed my eyes, trying to remember.

"Lions, I think. And you were there."

"Who else?"

"Gildeen."

"And what did she look like?"

"She was wearing the same green dress she wore the last time I saw her."

"Look at the pendulum and remember."

We'd been out partying. It must have been three in the morning.

"Gildeen, you've had too much to drink," I said.

She laughed, flashing that magical smile of hers. "You love it when I'm drunk, 'cause I'm sexier."

Gildeen danced to the music in her mind. Suddenly she looked up at me, shaking off my grasp.

"Come on, I'll race you across the street."

I looked up at the traffic light and saw it turn red. "No, wait Gil ...."

"GO!" She shouted. She turned and jumped into the street, right in front of a speeding gray Jaguar. The roadster crushed her beneath its squealing wheels.

I screamed.

I looked up at Victor, who still held the pendulum in front of my face. Scanning his office, I recognized the certificates and leather couch. I knew I would never see Gildeen again. She had died four years ago in that accident.

"Why did you make me remember?" I asked, my tears streaming. "Why did you have to do that to me?"

"I'm sorry, Marcus. It was the only way."

That night for the first time in four years I had a dreamless sleep. I would have preferred the nightmares.

Post-Traumatic Stress Disorder

Because all humans deal with psychological issues, these disorders require strong consideration in my work as an emergency room physician. Depression and anxiety occur to some degree in almost everyone's life, frustration that we haven't achieved our life's goals, financial concerns, awareness of illness and disability, and interpersonal relationship failures. People don't take their medicines as a manifestation of passive/aggressive behavior. They ignore their pain or illnesses in a denial state or develop bizarre symptoms as a compensatory mechanism for psychological stress.

I sort psychological problems into three categories. The first, neuroses, affect a person's ability to cope with the world mostly through phobias. Many neuroses have childhood origins such as mental, sexual, or physical abuse. The stresses of poverty, deprivation, or a serious fright can set up these phobias, though some come naturally such as fear of heights or of snakes. Some neuroses, like PTSD, result from adult trauma. Although people rarely develop true amnesia, except under severe metabolic stress or brain damage, PTSD, as in this story, can result in suppression of memories. Although drugs, such as anti-anxiety and antidepressants, can be used for short term symptomatic relief, the best treatment, and only cure, requires counseling (as in this story).

The other two categories of psychological disorder are psychosis, such as schizophrenia and bipolar disease, and personality disorder, such as obsessive-compulsive disorders, narcissism, and borderline personality disorder. Affective disorders (psychoses) require lifelong medication, that is, they're treatable but not curable. Personality disorders are the hardest to treat, because, well, everyone has a personality that's part of who they are. Behavior modification techniques help, as do certain medications.

The Sore Toe

Sheila awoke to the nudge from her husband. Keeping her eyes closed, she murmured, "What is it, honey? You horny?"

She cracked open one eye, the glare from the bedside lamp making a halo around Riley's head. He was sitting up, squeezing his foot, and rocking.

"Wish I could, babe. But I'm hurtin' too much. Look at my toe, will ya? I think I got another of those staph infections." He held up his hand which still sported a scab from last month.

Sheila yawned. Leaning across him she retrieved her glasses and crawled down the bed to get closer to his foot. Although mildly swollen and red, the little toe didn't look too bad; it didn't have the white pus blister she had expected. She poked at it gently, and he winced. She poked again, and he jerked back.

"You want me to take you to the E.R.? What time is it anyway?" She focused on the clock. "Six already?"

Riley shook his head, rubbing his foot above the toe. "Nah, I don't want to spend all that money. All they'll do is poke it with a needle. You can do that."

"Honey, you can't even sit still for me to touch it. How do you expect to stand having me stick it? I think we should go to the E.R."

He held his hand up in front of her face. "It hurt like hell when the doctor stuck me – I guess that numbing doesn't work on me. I'll just grit my teeth. Besides, we sure can't afford another E.R. bill. Hey, it's just a toe. My dad used to pop these things on me when I was a kid. Took a straight pin and sterilized it with a match."

"I don't know …"

"Come on. If it doesn't work we can always go to the E.R. later."

Sheila watched him pout out his lower lip; he looked just like Petey when he did that. So cute! She shrugged. "I guess it's okay. We sure could afford to save the money. Have you called into work?"

He glanced at the clock and grimaced. "Maybe I can still make it if you can pop this right away, you think? If I call in now they'll think I'm just hung over from partying too hard."

Sheila swung her legs off the bed and made her way to the bathroom. Just at the door she turned and shook her finger at him. "You DID party too much. What time did you get in, anyway?"

"About one. Sorry I didn't call, babe. Man, you were totally zonked. I tried snuggling up, but you just turned away. Me and Joe had a great time though. Drank some beer, watched the late game. Those Saints are on a tear this year."

"You sure that's all you did? Sheila pursed her lips. "I don't like that Joe. He's too wild."

He gave her a wink. "I'm a big boy; I know how to take care of myself. Hey, hurry up, will ya? I wanta get this toe taken care of so I can try to get to work."

Sheila slipped into the bathroom to empty her bladder and wash her face. She squinted into the mirror as she cleaned her glasses; when she put them on again the squint turned into a frown. *Where did all those crowfeet come from? I'm only thirty-six, for God's sake.*

As she threw away her Kleenex something in the trash caught her eye. She pulled it out, a blood stained tissue. She left it on the counter as she headed into the closet where she changed into fresh panties and grabbed her bathrobe off the closet hook. Running a brush through her hair she picked up the tissue again, trying to figure out whether it was worth questioning Riley about it. *Probably nothing, a nosebleed or a minor scratch.* She dropped it back in the trash.

Coming out of the bathroom she found Riley curled up on the bed holding his toe and moaning.

"Hurts that bad, huh?"

He looked up with a sour grin. "I'm sure it'll be better when you let out the pus. Come on now."

"Okay, okay, I'll get a pin ready. But we're not doing it in our bed. Get your butt dressed and come out into the kitchen. I'll put on some coffee and some water for oatmeal." He started to object but she stared him down and left him hobbling towards the bathroom.

In the kitchen she put on a pot of water to prepare the oatmeal. She wished he wouldn't hang out with that Joe. They'd been high school buddies, but Joe had gone to prison for drugs. Sure, he was straight now, or so Riley said, but a single guy was always a source of trouble. They'd been getting together for several months now, including the last three weekends in a row – coming back real late each time. Still, Riley was a good breadwinner and a great father. He deserved a night off with his buddies.

She glanced at the kitchen clock. In another fifteen minutes it'd be time to wake the kids. *This better work, and better be quick. Too much to do today to have to take care of Riley too.*

Her husband shuffled in, settling into one kitchen chair and propping his foot up on another. She picked a safety pin and a cigarette lighter out of her widget drawer and blackened the pointed end. Using a paper towel she wiped off the ash.

"You ready?"

He grimaced. "As ready as I'll ever be."

Sheila adjusted her glasses and leaned over her husband's foot. The toe had swollen to nearly twice its normal size and had purple streaks around it. She hesitated.

"I don't like the looks of this at all, honey. I think maybe we should go to the E.R."

Riley shook his head. "No. Just poke it. Go ahead before I lose my nerve."

She saw his knuckles whiten as they tightened their grip on the chair leg. Hovering the pin over the toe's monstrous pad, she said, "Grit your teeth."

With a quick in and out she popped the toe, causing Riley to let out a curse. A drop of blood mixed in a slight yellowish fluid oozed out.

The sound of a child crying drifted down the hallway. "Petey's awake." She dropped the safety pin in a cup sitting on the dish board and hurried down the hallway. Their younger son was sitting up, looking confused and crying. She settled next to him, grabbed his blanket, and wrapped it around him.

"It's okay, everything's okay," she cooed, stroking the six-year-old's back through the blanket until his sobs relaxed into sniffles.

"Daddy said a bad word," he whined.

"Daddy's got a boo-boo, that's all. It'll be all right."

In the other bed Brandon sat up and stretched. "What? What happened? Is Petey okay?"

Sheila turned on the bedside lamp. "Yes, Sweetheart. He's fine. It's a little early, but since you're up, maybe you can help get Petey dressed and ready for school? That's what a good big brother would do."

Brandon sighed. "I'm only two years older than him. He can do it himself." He got up and kicked the bedpost. To the top of the post, he said, "He's such a baby."

Peter pushed away from her. "Am not!"

Sheila interrupted before the argument could get going. "You two get dressed while I go check on Daddy. I'm making oatmeal. There'll be an extra portion of brown sugar for two little boys, but only if both boys are dressed, hair brushed, and school books ready when they get to the table."

Brandon glared at his brother. "You better do what I say and get ready," he said.

Peter sat down on the floor with his thumb in his mouth. "Don't have ta."

Sheila grabbed his hand and pulled it out. "Stop sucking your thumb, Petey. You do what Brandon says about getting dressed this morning. Please help out Mommy, okay?"

She left them and paused in the hallway, undecided between going to her bedroom to get dressed, or returning to the kitchen to check on Riley. She decided she'd better do the checking first. Just as she got close to the kitchen door, she heard the bathroom water pipes knocking. She reversed course down the hallway and passed through their bedroom to find him sitting on the side of the tub, his feet hanging in.

"What are you doing, now?"

He didn't look up. "I'm soaking my foot."

"But I need to shower," she said, punching him in the back. "How am I going to get ready if you're in here taking up our bathroom?"

He jerked his foot out and reached over to adjust the temperature on the taps. "Sorry, babe. Maybe it's gout. I had an uncle who had gout and his pain always started in his foot."

Sheila bent down and kissed him on the cheek. "Well you just soak it then. I'm running a little early today, so I should have enough time to get ready for work after I drop the kids off at school. I don't have to be at work 'til ten today. You feel better?"

"Not really, but I gotta go to work. Don't we have some old Lortab or something?"

She hung her bathrobe on the closet hook and did a quick cleaning under her arms. Riley whistled and she turned, watching him ogle her nearly naked body. She gave her body a twist and wiggle. "You like?"

"Boy do I ever! How about a quickie before I head off to work?"

She gave him a wink. "Let's do it after I drop off the kids. That way I can be ... you know, less inhibited."

"Yummy!"

Sheila laughed, finished her quick toiletries, and hooked up a bra. From her drawer she pulled out a slipover dress, something easy to get on and off. She rummaged through the medicine cabinet and found the old bottle of Lortab. There were three left. Taking one out, she gave it to him and handed him the cup with a splash of water from the sink.

She stopped in the boys' room, broke up their fight, admonished them to hurry, and went on to the kitchen. In quick order, she fed the boys, pushed them out the door to the car, and dropped them off at school.

She drove carefully, but quickly, eager to get back to Riley. She felt so lucky to have a man like him. Her mind drifted to how much she loved him, what a great husband and father he was. When the kids were young he even changed their diapers ... how many men would do that? But it was the sex she loved the most. He was SO wonderful, and so eager to give as well as receive. Umm. Good thing she had her tubes tied after Petey or they'd have a house-full by now.

She checked her watch as she parked in the driveway. Just past seven; plenty of time for making love if they started right away. *Hope he's already naked in bed!*

She pulled her dress off as soon as she entered the living room and threw it on the couch. Rushing down the hallway she had her arms behind her back, grasping her bra hooks, when she pulled up abruptly. Riley wasn't in bed.

"Honey?" she called tentatively.

No answer.

"Baby? Riley?" She listened intently. Something? Yes, he was in the bathroom. She followed the sounds of his breathing, stopping abruptly as she reached its door. Riley lay collapsed on the floor, his feet propped up on the half-filled tub.

She grabbed the drinking cup from the sink and plunged it into the lukewarm water. Squatting over him she dripped it onto his face until he sputtered, his eyes jumping open, then shut, as the water splashed near them.

"Hey! You're drowning me!"

Sheila laughed. "Just a little water torture to get you going." She reached down and rubbed his crotch. "You ready for some fun, Big Boy?"

Riley smiled, but she saw it didn't have the expected enthusiasm. "Oh yeah, sure babe. Just give me a moment to get up." She reached for his hand but as soon as she grabbed it he jerked back. "Ouch!"

She watched him examine his hand and then hold it up to her. "Look," he said. "Look at my thumb." It looked like a grownup mimic of the toe – maybe not quite as swollen, but definitely nasty looking.

Her hand jumped over her mouth. "Oh my God, Riley. You got another one."

"Yeah, and they're both killing me. I think you better take me to the E.R."

Sheila stared at him. "Macho man is asking to go to the E.R.? You must be hurting bad."

He smiled weakly. "Hate to do it, babe. But pricking the toe didn't help. Get me some clothes and throw 'em out here, will ya? I don't want to get up more than I have to."

Sheila rummaged through his drawers and brought out matching shirt, slacks, and socks. Once again she wondered how men could be so blind to clothing combinations. On those rare days when she didn't pick out his clothing he'd come up with the strangest choices. She grabbed his bedroom slippers too.

She dropped his clothes on top of him and went back into the closet to pick out something for herself. She glanced longingly at the shower, but decided she'd better skip.

At the hospital Sheila told Riley to go on to the waiting room while she registered him. She stood in line at the triage window, and in a few minutes her turn came. The nurse seemed tired, maybe a bit frustrated – strange, since it was so early in the day.

"Are you here to see the doctor?" The nurse had short blonde hair, blue scrubs, and a dangling green ID badge with an outdated picture. It reminded Sheila of drivers' licenses, where everybody's picture was bad.

"No, I've brought in my husband, Riley Spraberry. He's in your computer."

Sheila waited while the nurse punched in numbers on her computer. "Birthdate February twelve?"

"Yes that's him. He's got a sore toe and a sore finger. I think they're infected." She watched the nurse type "sore toe and finger" on her computer.

"Have a seat in the waiting area," the nurse said. "We'll call you back in just a few."

"How long?" Sheila asked. "I'm supposed to be at work by ten."

The nurse's expression didn't offer much sympathy. "Emergencies have to come first. It won't be long."

Sheila sat down next to her husband. "How you doing, honey?"

"Look at this. He held up his hand, the redness now stretching across the palm. Sheila touched it gently.

"You think we'll be out of here in time for mom's birthday party?"

Sheila squinted at him. "What? What are you talking about?"

"You know," he insisted, "Mom's birthday party's today. Decorations and gifts."

"Your mother's birthday is in August, honey." She reached up and felt his forehead. It didn't feel hot. "You all right?"

Riley gave her a wan smile. "Guess I was confused. Getting a pounding headache."

The nurse called their names and brought them back to a small cubicle. It was similar to the one they'd been in six weeks ago, but this one had a sliding door, while the last one was just a curtain. Riley laid down on the stretcher and shut his eyes.

In a few minutes another nurse came in and talked to them briefly, rechecking Riley's temperature which still was normal, and glancing at his toe. She left with the words, "The doctor will be in shortly."

Sheila turned on the television, flipping to the morning news station. She kept checking her watch every few minutes, it seemed like the doctor would never come. She shook Riley, who opened his eyes and gave her a wan smile. "You okay?"

"Feel like crap."

She paced nervously, sat on the chair, got up and paced some more. When the doctor came in she felt tremendous relief. He was an older fellow, gray hair, with a reassuring smile. Even the picture on his nametag looked friendly. He switched off the television and started in with casual conversation. He had a warm, loving way of talking, and she could tell he cared. As she told her story, he jotted down notes on the chart.

When he started examining Riley's sores, a deep frown settled on his face. "What do you think, Doctor Merino? Is it that staph infection?"

He had his stethoscope plugged into his ears, its bell pressed firmly on her husband's chest. When he took it out of his ears he asked, "Have you ever had heart problems, Mr. Spraberry?"

"No, never. Always been healthy as a horse."

Sheila added, "Does a lot of sports; you know, pick-up basketball and church softball."

"Never been told you have a murmur, huh?" Doctor Merino thumbed through the chart. "Lortab?"

She tried to give a reassuring smile. "We had some left over from when he had staph last month. He's not a drug addict, if that's what you're thinking."

The doctor reached his hand out and placed it gently on her wrist. "Please understand I'm not accusing him. I just need information." He turned to Riley, staring into his face. "I'm just wondering if maybe you inject drugs?"

Sheila's eyes widened. "He'd never do that. We have two young boys, Doctor Merino. Six and eight. Riley's a good dad; works hard, plays with the boys, goes to church. We're good Christians, our whole family. I practically had to drag him to the E.R."

"And he's never had heart problems that you know of?"

She shook her head. "No! What are you thinking?"

She saw him hesitate and felt a shiver. Tragic images flashed through her brain. "Tell me the truth, Doctor Merino. It's just an infection, right?"

His eyebrow lifted and finally he gave the briefest of smiles. "We don't have a diagnosis yet. Riley, you said you have a headache?"

"Yeah. Like a jackhammer. Worse headache ever. You think you can give me something for pain?"

She watched the doctor studying her husband, who had closed his eyes again. She hated the implication that Riley was a drug addict. Surely it was just another staph infection. The doctor stepped to the door.

Turning to Sheila, he said, "I'm going to hold off giving pain medicine for now, at least until we have a better feel for what's going on. I'm ordering blood work and antibiotics. In a bit they'll take your husband to the CAT scanner. You can wait here." He slid the glass door closed behind him.

Over the next twenty minutes the nurse and a technician made several trips into the room, taking blood, starting an IV, rechecking vital signs, and hooking up a yellow fluid in a small bag to Riley's vein. The nurse said it was a powerful antibiotic. Once everything was going they rolled Riley on his stretcher away to the CAT scanner.

Sheila turned the television back on. Last time the doctor had been a brusque young woman; hadn't even waited for the numbing medicine to work before cutting into Riley's hand. But then, there weren't all these tests either. Just cut, wash out, and out the door. And Riley had been fine. She opened her checkbook and looked at the balance. Barely enough to pay the rent, and it was due in four days. How were they ever going to pay for a CAT scan? That's gotta cost a thousand dollars, easy.

It seemed like forever before they rolled Riley back. She could tell immediately something was wrong. He was sitting up staring, but didn't seem to see her.

"Riley? Riley, are you okay?"

He turned in her direction. "Sheila? Sheila? Where are you? I can't see you. I can't see anything."

Sheila ran out of the room, spotting Doctor Merino coming out of another room with a chart in his hand. "Doctor! Doctor, please! Riley's gone blind!"

The doctor's face turned ashen as he rushed past her into the room and up to Riley's bed.

"Mr. Spraberry, can you see me?" He waved his hand in front of Riley's face, then placed a finger right next to his eye. Riley didn't blink. The doctor took a medical flashlight from its hook on the wall and shone it into each of Riley's eyes. "You see the light?"

"No, Doc. I don't see nothing."

"What's going on?" Sheila demanded.

Doctor Merino grimaced. "I'll need to get a heart echo to confirm, but I think Riley's developed a heart valve infection. Once this type of infection sets in, it starts showering little packets of infection throughout the body. I'm going to go look at the CAT scan now, to see if it shows areas of infection in his brain."

"Oh my God." Sheila wrapped her arms around her chest and collapsed into the chair. "Is he going to be all right?"

Doctor Merino started to shake his head but stopped abruptly. He reached out and placed his hands on her shoulders. "I'll call the internist right away and we'll get Riley a room in the ICU. We'll do everything we can, but, as you can see, this is very serious."

Doctor Merino stepped out and within minutes the nurse and technician were back, bringing more antibiotics and drawing more blood. They rechecked his vital signs, and when Sheila asked, the nurse told her that Riley's pulse was too fast and his blood pressure was falling.

"Doctor Merino says Riley has a heart infection causing this," Sheila told her.

The nurse nodded. "Yes, he told me."

"Is this common?"

The nurse shook her head. "I've never seen it before. None of the other nurses here have either. We were all looking at the CAT scan."

"What could have caused this? Riley's only thirty-seven years old. He's never been sick in his life."

The nurse hesitated, a sour look on her face. "I shouldn't say."

"Please."

"Well. Doctor Merino says it's almost always caused by either someone who already has a damaged heart, or, more commonly, by someone injecting himself with a dirty needle, getting bacteria into his heart."

"What? No way! I know Riley! We've been married eight years … gone together for two before that. He's just not the type."

The nurse stared at her a moment, then slowly ran her finger along the top of Riley's exposed foot. "You see this run of dots here? These are called track marks. They're caused by self-injecting drugs."

Sheila felt her heart drop. "You mean … you mean Riley's been lying to me? When he's over at his friend's house, he's been injecting drugs? And his injection has caused him to go blind and maybe to die?"

The nurse stood with head drooped, unwilling to look Sheila in the eyes.

Sheila went up to her husband and shook him. He groaned. "You SON OF A BITCH! How DARE you leave me with all this? You better recover so I can kick your ass from here to St. Louis!"

Riley didn't respond.

Sheila pounded on his chest. The alarms went off.

"Good Lord, he's fibrillating!" the nurse shouted. She stuck her head out the door. "Call a code and get me some help!"

People rushed into the room, crowding Sheila into a corner. She watched in fascinated horror as Doctor Merino ordered a nurse to place paddles across Riley's chest and shock him. His body jumped in response to the jolt. The doctor placed a tube into Riley's throat, and reeled off orders. After a short eternity the atmosphere quieted, a machine breathing for him, the monitor giving off a steady run of beeps.

"We're moving Mr. Spraberry to the ICU now," Doctor Merino told her. "I'll come back in a few minutes and answer your questions."

They wheeled Riley out, everyone left, and Sheila stood quietly in the empty room. Trash from the code covered the floors and counters. She glanced at a red tool box, one drawer open showing short tubes, each one wrapped in sterilized paper. She picked one up and recognized it as the type of tube the doctor had put into her husband's throat.

She sat down on the chair and drooped her head into her hands. Yesterday the world had been normal. The kids were playing in the yard. Riley had mowed the grass. Sheila had done the laundry. Yesterday she was thinking about how they could maybe save a little money and buy a new washing machine. Yesterday she was a happily married wife and mother.

Life would never be the same. Even if Riley recovered, she could never trust him again. And if he didn't recover, what would she do then? How could she raise two little boys? *No! Don't think like that. What if he survived, brain damaged and blind?*

She began crying, holding herself tightly, rocking in the chair. When Doctor Merino came back in, she stood and opened her arms. He hugged her, patting her back gently. It reminded her of how she'd held Petey that morning, really, the same thing, patting the back until the cries subsided. She stepped away.

"Tell me the truth, Doctor Merino. What are Riley's chances of a complete recovery?"

He looked at her sadly. "You said you're a Christian, didn't you?"

She nodded.

"Then you best pray for a miracle."

Endocarditis (Heart Infection)

Like most of the stories in this anthology, this tale comes from a real case I treated in the emergency room. The patient deteriorated rapidly as the bacteria being pumped out from the infection in his heart traveled throughout his body. Fortunately, I recognized the problem and with prompt antibiotic treatments, he survived with a relatively good outcome.

Bacterial endocarditis means bacterial infection of the heart, specifically the inner lining of the heart muscle, though often involving one of the heart valves. Birth defects with heart abnormalities set up this kind of infection, as will heart surgery, or, as in this story, introduction of bacteria by IV drug use. Symptoms include fever, fatigue, and aching muscles, with signs of infection such as a heart murmur, small hemorrhages under the nails, and multiple abscesses in the extremities. People at higher risk are those who can't fight off infections, such as diabetics, cancer patients, and those with HIV.

Clearly, it's a very dangerous infection. What strikes me about this story is how quickly a life can turn from peaceful to tragic. Sheila, the patient's wife, has a normal middle-class life, counting on her husband to be her partner. His poor choice to inject drugs results in what amounts to the ruin of all of their lives. Tragedy can occur in medicine so easily, even when it's not the person's fault. Another lesson to count our blessings every day.

The Drug Raid

Linda Ann glanced up at the clock. Only three a.m. Pulling her large behind off the shaky metal stool, she stretched. "What we need around here is a little action."

"Now you hush your mouth, Linda Ann," another nurse admonished. "You know that's bad luck."

Linda Ann laughed. "In this sleepy little town? Nothing's ever gonna happen here." She swung around slowly, looking at the only two patients among the nine curtained cubicles. "Guess I'll go check on Mrs. Jones."

"Hey, since you're up, check on Barbie, too. If her headache's gone, let her call for her ride."

Linda Ann slipped into cubicle six and pulled the curtains closed. Checking the IV, she let her hand run gently along the bruises and skin tears left behind by an understaffed nursing home. Linda Ann hoped she'd be dead before she ended up in Whispering Pines.

She froze at the sounds of loud voices coming from outside the curtain. Peeking through a gap, she counted four men, dressed all in black even to the ski masks. They were waving guns. Linda Ann backed up against the one solid wall, hoping to melt right through it.

One of the men threw back the curtain and pointed his gun at her. "Get out here you."

Linda Ann paused; the man's stance looked familiar. "I said come out here." This time the man shouted. His voice sounded familiar too.

When she stepped out she glanced at the far end of the room where two of the attackers held the three other staff secure in a small bay. Linda Ann's gaze drifted to the counter. Not twelve feet away sat the red phone, the one hardwired to the police dispatcher. All she'd have to do was knock it off its perch and police would come investigate.

Her captor directed her to the drug dispensing machine.

"Open it up. Let's see what you got … you know; Demerol … and them Percocets."

Linda Ann bent to enter her code in the security lock when she stopped abruptly. "What did you say?" She turned and stared into the ski-masked face. He stared back.

"I wanta hear you talk again," she insisted, but the fellow remained silent. She walked up to him, studied his profile a moment more, and then lifted up the ski mask. "I thought I recognized that voice. Jerry P. Kelly, just what the hell do you think you're doing?"

The other attackers pulled off their masks, and Jerry patted down his hair with one hand. "Surprise! It's a drill."

Linda looked around the room, recognizing the four men that made up the security guard team here at Memorial Hospital. She shook her finger at one of them. "George Conrad, you should be ashamed of yourself!"

George gave her a little smile. "You shoulda seen your face. I thought you was gonna pee them pants." Jerry gave a small chuckle.

"Funny?" Linda Ann choked on her words. "You thought this was funny! Threatening someone with a loaded gun is your idea of a joke?"

"Ah, the guns ain't loaded. Show them George." Obediently George pointed his shotgun at the copying machine and let both barrels go click-click.

Linda Ann began to reach for the red phone but paused, and redirected to her purse. "Funny huh? Then you're going to love this." She unzipped a side pocket and pulled out a derringer, a tiny antique thing with a shiny barrel. She raised it slowly until it pointed straight at Jerry's head. "Mine's loaded to poppin' Mister Jerry P. Kelly. And I've got half a mind to shoot this off in self-defense."

Jerry backed up a step, but Linda Ann leisurely advanced, the gun held steady.

"I got plenty of witnesses who will testify that I was terrified out of my mind. Why, I'm certain no court in the world would convict me."

Jerry backed until he was flat against the glass wall.

Linda Ann came closer, bringing the gun to rest snugly against Jerry's left temple. She pushed in, just a touch, indenting the skin against the bone beneath.

"The more I think about it, the more I like this idea. You know, Jerry, I've never really liked you."

"Now wait a minute, Linda Ann. This wasn't anything personal. I thought we were all past that. This here ... this here is just about hospital safety. You know I'm the safety officer. You do know that, right?"

Linda Ann raised her other hand and slowly pulled back the hammer until it clicked into place. "I'll tell you what I know, Mr. Safety Officer, Sir. I know how you're always making comments about my legs in public. Yes sir, I've heard them. And I've seen you and your boys here pointing and laughing."

"No, No. That ain't right. We weren't laughing at your legs."

"Really? Then, what were you laughing at, Mr. Safety Officer, Sir? What is it about my rear view that you find so amusing?"

Jerry's sweat began to drip down the gun and onto her hand. She pushed a little harder.

"Linda Ann. Baby. This was only a joke."

"Don't you go calling me Baby. I never was your Baby and I never will be. Because this is the end of the road for you, Mr. Safety Man."

She pulled the trigger and the hammer flew closed. It clicked.

In the silence that followed, Linda Ann casually withdrew the gun and dropped it back into her purse. "Oh. I guess mine isn't loaded either. My mistake."

Jerry collapsed onto the floor in a faint. George came over and slapped him a couple of times until Jerry's eyes snapped open.

He sat against the counter and stared up at Linda Ann. "You think that was funny?"

Linda Ann nodded slightly. "I thought it was hilarious."

Violence in the E.R.

This actually happened in an E.R. where I worked – well, except for the part about the nurse with the gun. The safety officers ran this drill, scaring the be-jeezees out of the nurses and the E.R. doctor on duty (not me). I oversaw the quality assurance for the E.R. at the time and wrote up a nasty report about it. The nurses sued the hospital. The hospital paid them all off and fired them, including the other E.R. doctor and me. But not the safety officer, who stayed on duty for several years to follow.

However, real violence in the E.R. has become a worrisome issue. Most E.R.s now have locked entrances and video surveillance, and some have armed guards and metal detectors. Even so, emergency rooms are areas of high stress for patients, and a target for those with mental illness and drug abuse. Reports of gunshots and violence pop up in the medical literature all too frequently.

While it's a felony in Mississippi to assault a medical provider in the line of duty, at the time of this writing, the NRA is lobbying hard to allow concealed weapons to be allowed in all public areas, including hospital E.R.s. I don't mind taking care of patients who are the targets of gun violence ... I just don't want to be one!

Mississippi Farmer

"Good morning."

"Good mornin', ma'am. Welcome to my farm."

"Is this your farm, Sir?"

"Yes ma'am. My name's Elias Carter."

"Nice to meet you, Mr. Carter. My name is Beth. You were saying that this is your farm?"

"Shore 'nuf. Ain't a purtier spot in the whole planet. Why just bend down, ma'am. Draw up a handful of this good Mississippi dirt, thick and rich. I've been farmin' on these fine twenty acres my whole life. Jest like my pappy done for his life. And my grandpappy done before him. Look over there, ma'am. See that silo? My grandpappy built that silo in 1901."

"Do you live here alone, Mr. Carter?"

"No ma'am. My wife, Violet, she's up at the house. She's probably standin' in front of our little stove, frying pan sizzlin' with bacon. Can't you just smell it? Say, where're my manners? I imagine you're hungry, comin' all this way to see me. You want to mosey up to the house and I'll have Violet put a little somethin' together for us?"

"That's very kind of you, Mr. Carter. But I'm afraid I can only stay a minute. I just wanted to meet you."

"You gotta be goin' so soon?"

"I'm sorry, Mr. Carter. I'll be back tomorrow. I promise."

These young folks. They wander off so quickly. But I got plenty to do. Gotta repair that fence along the south pasture. Don't want Bessie to get out and wander off again. First though, 'magine I'll just relax on these here steps and watch the corn grow. Umm ... lovely day. Nice to rest the old bones for a spate. There's a hawk. Look at it swoop! That'll be one dead field mouse, shore enough.

"Mr. Carter?"

"Yes sir?"

"It's time to eat. Come on over to the table."

"Why, that's mighty kind of you, sir. What about Violet? Ain't she comin' to dinner?"

"I'll take her a plate. I promise. Here, don't forget your vitamins."

"You shore are good to an old man. Thank ye kindly."

Time to get up. Them sunbeams be kissin' them lacy drapes Violet likes so much. Gotta get up and milk old Bessie, go fire up the tractor, and plow a couple of acres for plantin'. 'Course, twenty acres don't make much harvest. Still, we make ends meet, don't we, Violet? Eh? What'd you say? Yeah, shore did. I wouldn't forget that. Now you don't go worryin' your little head about them bills. We'll be fine. Jest fine. As long as we got each other, we got everythin'.

"Good morning, Mr. Carter."

"Good morning, ma'am. Welcome to my farm."

"That's what you said yesterday."

"Ma'am?"

"It's Beth, Mr. Carter. I was here yesterday."

"Sorry, ma'am. You'll have to forgive an old man. I'm afeared my memory ain't what it used to be."

"That's okay, Mr. Carter. How are you feeling today?"

"Why kind of you to ask, ma'am. I'm fine, jest fine. And yourself?"

"Fine, too, thank you. Yesterday you were telling me about your farm."

"My farm? Yes ma'am. We have our good years and not so good uns. When the rain comes jest right, why, the beans and corn reach for God's heaven. It's quite a sight then, ma'am. Not like now. No ma'am. It's been cold and cloudy all day. Must be winter creepin' on, I reckon. I better see if Violet's got the tomatoes put up. You want a jar of home canned tomatoes?"

"No, thank you though. Point out some of the features of this farm for me, would you please Mr. Carter."

"Well now, up there, that's my home, with that little red brick chimney and the white picket fence. The creek must be back there, behind that ... thang over there. This here's the dirt road runs past our farm. Sometimes I jest sit here and watch the people passin' by."

"Do you like it here?"

"Shore do, ma'am ... lived here all my life. Sun just won't come out, today, that's all. Maybe storm headin' our way. Guess I better get up to the barn and tend to old Bessie. You want to come see old Bessie?"

"No, thank you though, Mr. Carter. I'll need to be going on. I still have a lot of other people to talk to today."

"My neighbors?"

"Yes, I guess you could call them that."

"Well, you be shore and give Miss Pritchet our regards. Violet's been meanin' to get down that way for quite a spell. She's got some fresh canned okra to share, I reckon."

I wonder if we'll get any snow this winter. I 'member back in '20, I was fourteen then. That were a winter! I 'member me and Pappy walkin' down to the creek and knockin' out chunks of ice tryin' to get at the crawdads. They was all froze solid. Grandpappy's toes all turned black on his right foot and began fallin' off. He planted them, sayin' they'd grow back, but they never did. We was livin' on hardtack. Momma worked some sewin' for some ears of corn.

Poor Momma, I remember when she died. Her feet got blue, then all red and puffy. Doctor said it was sugar, never did make no sense. Pappy was out workin' on the plow one summer day, grabbed his chest, and fell like a stone. Then it were up to me and Violet to look after the farm and we done it ever since. And right now I better go get that cow 'fore she has a fit.

"Good morning Mr. Carter."

"Good morning, ma'am. Welcome to my farm."

"You still feel that this is your farm, don't you."

"Yes, ma'am. I've been farmin' this land since I were knee high to the cow. You see them rows of corn over there? Back across the meadow I have a couple of acres of sorghum."

"Mr. Carter, do you recognize this fellow next to me?"

"Cain't say I do. How you do, young man?"

"Grandpa, it's me, Rusty. Don't you remember me, Grandpa?"

"Rusty? I've got a grandson named Rusty. How 'bout that?"

"Grandpa, that's me! I've grown up. Try to remember, Grandpa. You're not on your farm any more. You're in a nursing home. Please, Grandpa."

"I should climb up to the house and see if little Rusty is around. Violet's probably fixin' up a mess of cornbread. You all wanta come up for a spell?"

"Grandpa. Violet's dead. Grandma died six months ago. Please Grandpa. Try to remember. Try harder. Grandpa!"

"Mr. Jacobs, calm down. You're not going to help your grandfather by shouting at him."

"I'm sorry, Beth. Sorry. It just hurts me so much to see him like this."

"But you're happy, aren't you, Mr. Carter?"

"Happy? I suppose so. Cain't say I ever thought about it. Shore, I guess so. Jest relaxing on my farm. Digging in the good earth. Gonna go up to the house in a spell and have some vittles. You want something? Violet shore can cook up a nice mess of greens."

Dementia

This is the oldest short story in this book, written in 1977 when I was a third-year medical student. My first rotation brought me to the psychiatric unit and my first patient, an old farmer, with what we called "organic brain syndrome." He truly believed he still lived on his farm, pointing out the couch as his tractor and a photo on the wall as his distant farmhouse.

It's important to differentiate between delusion and dementia. A delusion is a firm, fixed, false belief. A husband and son brought in their family member to my clinic early in my career with concern for her mental health. I interviewed her for nearly fifteen minutes and found her completely oriented to self, place, and time, and able to carry on a totally rational conversation. When I turned to them with a shrug, they suggested I ask her about the Queen of England. Sure enough, the patient claimed to have daily conversations with the Queen, the Pope, and the president, all calling her for advice. I placed her on antipsychotics and they returned three weeks later reporting she'd been cured. Another time a nurse came out of a patient's room all giddy about the fabulous life the patient reported to her, being a counterintelligence agent for the CIA, traveling undercover every week to Russia, and having written a book about espionage. When I told her the patient was probably delusional, the nurse was crestfallen.

Dementia and delirium both manifest with delusions and/or hallucinations. Dementia is a permanent deterioration. We recognize Alzheimer's as the best known type of dementia, as well as the most common, accounting for about three quarters of the cases. In Alzheimer's, loss of cognitive abilities occurs from changes in brain tissue, though other causes, such as by mini-strokes or atrophy (wasting away with age), commonly cause dementia as well. These irreversible changes affect 25% of people over 85.

In contrast, temporary (and often reversible) delusions represent delirium, often from drugs (LSD, Ecstasy), alcohol withdrawal (the famous D.T.s), or, commonly, schizophrenia. Other causes include metabolic changes, such as low sodium levels, toxin exposures, or dehydration. Malnutrition, particularly protein loss or vitamin B deficiencies, can cause temporary or permanent delirium. Otherwise asymptomatic urine infections in elderly patients often present this way. I remember one case of a four-year-old girl whose doctor admitted her to the hospital with a tentative diagnosis of early-onset schizophrenia as she swore she was seeing ghosts. It turned out she had pneumonia, and curing the disease cured the delirium.

The moral of this story is that not all senility is Alzheimer's. Before labeling someone as having dementia, it's incumbent on the physician to be sure the patient doesn't have delirium and treat a reversible cause.

Christmas Eve in the E.R.

I pulled back the curtain to greet my first patient of this Christmas Eve night shift. Mr. Lubrick, a man near ninety, sat up on his stretcher, his swollen legs hanging to the floor. From the chart, I read the listed chief complaint of "Short of breath." He certainly looked it. Lack of oxygen had turned his fingernails blue. His chest struggled for air. I glanced at the monitor. His systolic blood pressure hung at over 200, his pulse at a too-rapid 130.

"Nice to meet you, Mr. Lubrick," I said, offering my hand. "I'm Dr. Klein, the emergency room doctor on duty tonight. You seem to be having trouble breathing."

His face held a quiet serenity, as if he had conquered more serious problems than not having air. I glanced at the monitor to check his latest vital signs. Even with tubes bringing oxygen into his nose, his saturation level hung at the ninety percent danger line. I usually recommended admission when the number dropped below ninety-four.

"I've been having problems." He paused between each few words to pant a few times. "Been a couple of days. I finally found a neighbor. She's watching my wife. Only for a few hours."

"Your wife is at home?"

I saw his face soften, the edges of his lips curling in smile. "Martha. Married sixty-seven years." He let out a sigh. "She's had it rough. Alzheimer's."

I knew Alzheimer's all too well. "Visiting nurses could be arranged."

"They come … for a few hours." His expression showed the frustration we all feel when dealing with bureaucracies. "Medicare don't pay much."

My stethoscope brought me the sounds of his struggling heart and wet lungs. My finger indented the edema in his legs at least an inch. "Have you ever been short of breath before? Are you on medications?"

"First doctor visit. In years."

I made notes on his chart, selecting tests and treatments. "Mr. Lubrick, it appears you're in heart failure. The nurses will be giving you medicines that will help your breathing while we're waiting for blood and x-ray results. Those will take a couple of hours, but I'll check on you before then."

He nodded slightly. "Sitter has ... 'till midnight."

I put down the chart. "You're quite ill, Mr. Lubrick. We'll talk about whether going home would be a good idea once I have your test results, okay?"

Mr. Lubrick reached out, resting his wrinkled hand on my arm. "Ill be going home tonight."

I dropped the chart off with the secretary and went on to see other patients. After about an hour I checked in. Mr. Lubrick relaxed against the back of the stretcher, no longer having to sit upright to breathe. Still, his number had only reached ninety-two.

"Feeling any better?" I asked.

He nodded. "A little. Thanks."

I looked at the Foley bag hung from his bed, expecting to see it bulging with yellow fluid. Instead it held a few ounces of cranberry sludge. I realized Mr. Lubrick's kidneys had shut down. Without his kidneys clearing the fluids from his body his lungs were drowning.

"Have you been noticing blood in the toilet after you urinate?"

My patient shrugged. "I thought it would go away."

"This could be your problem, sir. I'll know when your test results come back. We'll talk more then."

Once we had all of Mr. Lubrick's results, I brought his chart into my small office to review his case and study his x-rays. Besides the expected overload of fluid on his chest x-ray, other worrisome shadows appeared. Rifling through the laboratory results my heart felt heavy with confirmed suspicions.

I stopped just inside his curtain and studied his breathing patterns, his skin color, and his vital signs. Due to my treatments his breathing came easier, his skin had pinked some, and the oxygen level was up to ninety-four. Not normal, but improved. The Foley bag remained empty.

He looked up, his smile faltering at seeing my heavy expression. "It's bad news, isn't it?"

"Tell me about your wife," I suggested.

His gaze shifted away, focusing on places and scenes from long ago. "I met Martha our freshman year at the university. I'd just come home from the war, the big one you know. Using my GI bill for tuition to the university, standing in line at the cafeteria, looking forward to getting back into life. Martha stood in front of me, sporting a fur shawl. Cold outside, but it was warm in that crowded building. She turned to me, asking if I'd hold her place while she hung up the wrap. When she returned, we began talking, fell in love, and married within the month. Sixty-eight years, Dr. Klein, and never an argument. She's the icing that makes my cake sweet. She's the rose that excuses my thorns. She raised our three kids while I was out in the fields roughnecking and managed a home on a workingman's budget, squirreling away enough savings to put our three kids through college."

He raised a handkerchief to his face and coughed several times, taking away a blog of bloody bubbled phlegm. He tucked it away, pretending I hadn't seen it.

"There's no angel like my Martha. When she started losing her marbles, I hung true. Some people put their loved ones away, don't you know. Stick 'em in those foul nursing homes, full of roaches and rude aides. Not me. No sir. I promised Martha I'd be with her by her side twenty-four-seven. She was always there for me, and I'll be true too. You just give me some prescriptions, and I'll get 'em filled day after tomorrow. Pharmacies all closed tomorrow, I reckon, being Christmas."

I placed my foot up on his stretcher's rail, flashing him a sympathetic smile. I knew he was going to be a hard sell. "Mr. Lubrick, I'm afraid I have bad news. Your kidneys have shut down. It's essential that you be admitted to the hospital tonight."

He shook his head. "Sorry, Doctor Klein. I've gotta go home to Martha."

I reached forward and held his hand. "Please, sir. Your heart is on its last legs. Your potassium level is high enough to send your heart into fibrillation unless you undergo emergency dialysis tonight. You mustn't go home."

"And if I were to stay here?" He tilted his head slightly, watching my eyes.

"You'd certainly be better."

"It sounds like I'm going to die."

I bit my lip, weighing each word carefully. "I wish I could promise you everything will be all right, Mr. Lubrick. It's possible that your kidney damage is permanent and you'll need long term dialysis."

He raised a bushy eyebrow. "There's more?"

I took a deep breath. "Yes. Besides your heart and kidneys, there are some suspicious spots on your x-ray that are going to need a closer look."

"Spots? You mean cancer?"

I took a deep breath and met Mr. Lubrick's eye. "Blood in the urine can be associated with cancer, and so might the spots. Those are just maybes. There are several other possibilities. We'll know in a few days. For now, though, I'll need to arrange for your admission and dialysis."

Mr. Lubrick shook his head. "I appreciate your kind intentions, Dr. Klein. But I'm ready to go home now. I wanted to find out what was wrong and whether you could fix it. Now I know you can't." He placed his hand on my wrist. "I appreciate what you've done. I'm certainly better than when I came in."

"Mr. Lubrick, please," I pleaded. "The treatments I've given will only help for a few hours. If you go home now, your heart will likely fail before dawn."

He squeezed my hand gently. "That wouldn't be so terrible, Dr. Klien. At least I'd get to spend my last Christmas Eve with Martha."

"What if I arrange to bring her into the hospital as well?"

He shook his head.

I needed to try once more. "Mr. Lubrick, I understand how important your being home is to you. But if your wife's Alzheimer's is as bad as you say, will she even know you're there?"

His smile never faltered. "She won't know, but I will."

I stood back and watched him disconnect the leads attached to his chest. A nurse ran in as the alarms sounded.

"Please prepare for Mr. Lubrick's discharge," I directed. "He's going home."

"Home?" she asked in astonishment, looking from one of us to another.

He nodded at her and turned back to me. "I appreciate all you've done, Dr. Klein. Now it's time for me to return to Martha."

The nurse and I removed all the medical attachments and helped him dress.

He stood and stretched. "Can I get a taxi from the waiting room?"

"Just ask the security guard at the front door to call one for you."

He offered his hand. "Merry Christmas, Doctor Klein. I hope you have a restful shift."

I grasped his hand with both of mine. "May the angels of the season watch over you and your wife."

He flashed me one final smile and shuffled down the hallway.

I watched until the metal doors closed behind him.

Multi-organ Failure

Every organ in the body must work well for the body to function. Without any of them, the heart, lungs, liver, kidneys, bowels, or skin, the other organs will not be able to function. Without the brain, such as being in a coma or after a stroke, the body can continue, though not for long and not very well.

The kidneys filter a third of each heartbeat's fluid. With as little as 10% of our kidney function we can filter out the waste products, but once below that level, the system begins to fail. Hypertension and diabetes lead the list of causes of kidney failure in the United States. I explain to my patients that hypertension is like watering your garden. Called "The silent killer," at low levels your plants appreciate the moisture. Turn the pressure on the hose up, and the plants lose leaves and stems. Ratchet up to firehose strength, and the garden washes away. The same happens to the cells of the kidney. At normal blood pressure the heart gently nourishes the delicate cells. Even mildly elevated chronic hypertension kills the kidney, a few thousand cells at a time.

Once the kidney dies, fluids build up in the system overwhelming the heart's ability to pump. Because the heart can't pump enough fluids, those liquids build up in the lungs, and the patient drowns in his own secretions. The liver also becomes engorged and dysfunctional, and while it's less likely to actually shut down, if its function of making albumin becomes impaired, more fluid will leak into the legs.

The lesson to be remembered: keep your blood pressure under control.

Old Dog

I didn't even have to step through the doorway to make this diagnosis. Mr. Randolf sat upright on the stretcher, adding spit to a bag already holding half a quart. Only one condition caused this; a clogged esophagus. I watched his wife wipe his forehead with a moist cloth.

"You're supposed to chew well before swallowing," I admonished.

"But it was such a delicious steak." His eyebrows drooped as he sighed. "I thought it had melted in my mouth."

I visualized the steak stuck in Mr. Randolf's esophagus somewhere behind his breastbone. The longer it stayed there the worse his problems would get.

"You understand this may mean surgery?" I could see by their eyes they expected as much. "You've had this before?" I asked

He gave a half smile. "Five times; I've got strictures. Each time they've taken me to the O.R."

I filled out his chart as I asked him about his medical history. In the elderly, even minor surgery could be dangerous. He had his share of surgical risk factors, maybe a few more than usual: hypertension, heart bypass surgery, poorly controlled diabetes, foot amputation from poor circulation, minor strokes, and more. As I examined him I made small talk. He told me he used to own his own company, one of the local construction companies.

"I hated being put out to pasture. Felt I still had a few good years ahead of me, but with this new stuff – you know, computers and newfangled equipment … it all became too much trouble. Don't suppose you ever have to deal with that."

I laughed. "They're forcing computers on us here too. I've always handwritten my charts, and now I have to hunt and peck my way on the computer. And equipment?"

I leaned forward to confide, "The worst is when the nurses want me to use some of this stuff I never trained with; portable ultrasounds and whatnot. I'm too old a dog to learn those new tricks."

Mr. Randolf patted me on the arm. "You're what? Sixty?"

"Sixty-eight next month."

"Don't look it. In any case, I bet you know a thing or two these younger guys would never think of."

Mrs. Randolf reached up and stroked her husband's cheek. "I wish there was an alternative to surgery."

I rubbed my chin. "Well, now that you mention it, there is a drug we used to use in the old days, way back before we zipped everyone off to the O.R. at a moment's notice. You ever been tried on glucagon?"

They shook their heads.

"It's a natural body enzyme," I explained. "It relaxes the esophagus muscle and, in some cases, the food blockage passes without surgery. It doesn't work every time, but it's worth a try. I'll have the nurse bring the shot and check back with you in an hour or so."

After explaining what I wanted to the nurse, I went on to other patients. It had been a busy shift, and I was getting tired. Mr. Randolf may have thought I didn't look my age, but as the end of a twelve-hour shift approached, I sure felt every day of it. When it was time to check on him, I brought along a present – a cup of fresh ice water.

"How are you feeling?"

He pondered, feeling his chest. "Looser I think."

"You want to try to drink?"

The first sip stayed down. A minute later he tried again, and then a third time. One more sip and he belched. A huge smile stretched his face.

"So … better?" I asked.

He sucked the cup down and hurried over to the sink to refill it.

"Better slow down," I advised.

His wife grabbed him in a bear hug. Nuzzling against his chest, her voice came out muffled. "Thank you, Doctor."

Between slower sips, Mr. Randolf asked, "What was the name of that stuff the nurse gave me?"

"Glucagon." I wrote it on the back of one of my cards and handed it to Mrs. Randolf who placed it in her white pearl purse.

"How come no one ever suggested this drug before?" he asked.

I grasped his bony hand in my own. "Some of us old dogs still know a few tricks, huh?"

Esophageal Strictures

Just below our mouths in an area called the larynx, the esophagus separates from the trachea, the former for swallowing our nourishment and the latter for air. It generally takes only a few seconds for food to travel down the esophagus from the mouth to the stomach, aided by waves of peristalsis that push the food down. Food can get stuck there even in normal conditions if someone tries to swallow too big a food bolus, such as a large piece of steak.

The esophagus can become damaged from swallowing something that cuts it, or from toxins such as swallowing bleach, or from cancer, as a result of surgery, or, most commonly, from changes due to acid reflux. These areas of damage result in scars and the failure of the normal peristaltic waves. Food becomes stuck in these areas and the sufferer can't swallow anything, even their own spit.

When I started off in medicine, we used glucagon to relax the esophagus muscle, hoping that would work because the esophageal equipment available in the 1970s involved stiff metal tubes. I've also heard of folk remedies, such as swallowing meat tenderizer or baking soda, but I strongly recommend against doing either. Those types of chemicals will damage the esophageal tissues and won't help move the food bolus. Nowadays, with flexible optic instruments, the gastroenterologist can push the bolus down into the stomach in a few seconds. Usually this is performed in the operating room, particularly if the patient has medical risk factors. However, the procedure is so easy that sometimes the surgeon will set up his machine right in the E.R.

Over my forty-years of emergency medicine experiences, I've learned a lot of "old tricks" other E.R. doctors don't know. Sometimes they're even useful!

Roger's Back Pain

Before entering a patient's room, I often created a mental picture, based only on those three bits of information: the patient's name, age, and complaint. According to the chart, Roger Harris, age sixty-two, had back pain. I imagined a sedentary fellow, probably salt-and-peppered hair, who'd tried to lift the couch to get a pen that had rolled underneath. He had waited at home all day, maybe popping an ibuprofen or two, before giving in to his wife's pestering to get it checked out.

I stepped into the curtained cubicle, giving the couple a greeting and a quick survey. I hadn't been far off, a bit grayer on top than I'd imagined, and perhaps a bit pudgier. Roger flashed me a goofy smile. The stretcher was in the sitting position, and he'd placed the pillow behind his head instead of his back. Clearly he wasn't in excruciating pain.

"Good evening, I'm Dr. Phillips. You must be Roger Harris, and …"

Mrs. Harris extended a bent wrist which I gave a light squeeze. Under dyed red hair and heavy makeup, she'd clearly seen the better side of fifty several years ago. "A pleasure to meet you, Doctor Phillips. I'm Bobbie, Roger's wife." Pointing to my patient she announced, "Hubby, here, is having back pain."

I offered my hand to Roger, and he gave it a soft welcome.

"Good evening, Mr. Harris," I said. "Where does your back hurt?"

He leaned onto one arm, pushing up on his elbow to expose a generous backside. Running his finger along the left side of his lower back, he said, "Down here, Doc. I think I passed a kidney stone."

Reaching out I thumped the area where the kidney hides, at the bottom edge of the ribs. He didn't wince. Continuing my explorations, I skimmed along the ridges of his vertebral tails, all the way down to the coccyx. None seemed particularly tender. Just to their left side I ran my finger along the muscle next to the backbones, tense with resistance.

"Your muscles are in spasm," I said. "This is the sort of reaction we see when someone sprains their back. Do you remember lifting something heavy?"

Mrs. Harris laughed. "It CAIN'T be a muscle strain, Darlin'. This man," and here she pointed with exaggerated disdain. "THIS MAN sits in his easy chair every evening watching TV. The only exercise he gets is pushing buttons on the remote."

Which would explain his obesity. "Is that true, Mr. Harris?" I asked.

He shrugged. "Bobbie drags me out to all her openings and all the other art events she can find. Last night we were at Blasies."

"Really? The Christie show? I was there. I thought you two looked familiar."

Bobbie put her hand on my wrist. "You love art, Dr. Phillips?"

I gave a wan smile. "I should think so. I'm a bit of an artist myself. Oils mostly."

Mrs. Harris fumbled through her purse to pull out a card. I read, *"Grucet Gallery, Bobbie Stanton, Owner."* I'd been to the Grucet a couple of times; she carried quality work.

"You have photos of your creations?" she asked.

I pulled out my cell phone, bringing up photos of my paintings. "I'm just a hobbyist."

Putting on her reading glasses, she flipped through carefully, studying each one. She brought the phone over to her husband. "Look, Darlin'. Isn't this just MAR-ve-lous?" She stretched out the last word with her deep southern drawl, so much I could smell the honey in the air.

Roger studied it and gave a whistle. "You really do have talent, Doc. Are you showing anywhere?"

I felt my cheeks flush. "Oh come on, I'm not that good. But … I mean …" I couldn't suppress my smile. "I mean, if you really think …"

Bobbie handed back my phone. "Seriously, Dr. Phillips. You have some talent. Can you bring in a couple of pieces for us to look at some time next week? Maybe we can hang one or two."

"I'd be quite honored. Please, call me Kevin." I put the phone back in my pocket and began writing on Mr. Harris' chart. "So, are you saying you don't remember injuring it?"

Bobbie clucked her disapproval. "I just can't do a THING with him. Ask him what he does around the house." She shook her finger at Roger. "Go ahead, just ask him."

"You didn't lift something heavy? Maybe trip and strain yourself when you started to fall?"

They glanced at each other and I saw Roger blush. "You know last night … I mean, when you wanted to … you know … in bed."

She put her palm to her mouth. "Oh! Don't say it!" She turned to me, her smile sheepish. "I guess I do know how he strained his back."

"Yeah," Roger interjected. "It was Bobbie's turn on top, and I …"

"Shh!" she interjected.

There was something odd about her actions, something a little too exaggerated, her makeup a little too heavy, her voice a bit too falsetto. Once tuned in, I recognized all the signs. Face powder caked on to hide a five o'clock shadow. Her hair wasn't that red, she was wearing a wig. Her Adam's apple was too big for a woman, and her arm muscle fat too thin.

"So how long have you been together?" I asked.

"Seventeen years this next month." She stepped over and kissed Roger on the lips.

"That's quite successful for a couple of your type," I observed.

Bobbie's smile faltered as she realized I knew. She placed a hand delicately on my wrist.

"Does it bother you, Kevin?"

"No, not me. But here in this Southern town I wonder if you find the community accepting of your relationship?"

"We don't flaunt it, if that's what you mean," Bobbie replied. She looked lovingly into Roger's eyes.

He said, "We've found our little bit of happiness, though running a gallery isn't an easy way to make a living."

"It's not like San Francisco, that's for sure," she said.

He stroked her cheek, his eyes radiating his love. "That's where we met, you know. Bobbie was working in a gallery and I was up visiting an old friend. I brought her back here to live with me and we've never looked back."

Rubbing his flank, he said, "Now, about my back …"

"It's pretty typical for a muscle strain," I explained. "Local pain on the muscles next to the backbone with back spasms and no vertebral tenderness. Some people remember straining themselves, while others don't."

"It sure did hurt." He turned to his partner. "I figured it was a kidney stone. I had one once before."

"How can you be sure?" Bobbie insisted. "Don't you need to check his urine and get x-rays, Kevin?"

"Yes, those are the standard tests we run for this problem. The urine might show infection, or blood, indicating a kidney issue, and the x-ray occasionally shows a stone." I wrote the orders on his chart. "Meanwhile, do you need something for pain?"

Roger nodded. "It's still pretty sore."

I told him the nurse would bring him a shot and that I'd be back with them in an hour or so once I had the results. Before leaving I handed Roger a urinal and told them to call the nurses when he had a sample.

A bit later, I noticed the marker indicated Roger's x-ray was ready and I pulled it up on the screen to give it a quick glance. Normal backbones, no evidence of a kidney stone. The urine showed a smidgen of blood.

I returned to find Roger dozing, the pain medicine having done its job. I told Bobbie about the normal test results.

"Are you certain?" she asked, her brow wrinkled in doubt. "I've never SEEN Roger in so much pain."

I hesitated. Roger didn't appear to be the kind of patient who would complain vociferously over a minor pain. Still, he seemed comfortable enough when I had seen him initially, and certainly now. "There were a few red cells in the urine. Roger might be right, maybe he passed a kidney stone and has some residual soreness. I suppose we could do a CAT scan. Though if the stone has passed, the CAT won't show much." Shaking Roger awake, I asked, "How do you feel?"

"Much better, Doc. That shot you ordered did the trick."

"Bobbie and I were just talking about maybe ordering a CAT scan," I explained.

Roger struggled to keep his eyes open. "I don't think I need a CAT scan. I'm feeling okay now."

Bobbie started to object. "Now Darlin' ..."

He shushed her. "She watches over me like a mother hen."

"You're lucky to have someone who cares so much," I observed. They gripped each other's hands and beamed.

Roger closed his eyes and seemed to drift back to sleep as I rechecked his blood pressure. It read forty points elevated despite his sedation. "Does Roger take his pills every day?"

Bobbie's face showed her exasperation. "He's SUCH a macho guy, if I don't keep my eye on him every minute … well, you know men!"

I explained about the pain medicine and muscle relaxer I was going to prescribe. I also talked to her about the dangers of high blood pressure, and emphasized how important it was for Roger to take his medicines. I left them with instructions to wait for the nurse.

At my station I finished Roger's discharge instructions and went on to more patients. Even in the late evening hours our E.R. stayed busy. Tonight we had the usual mix of those who were more frightened than sick, those with chronic pains, and the occasional truly ill.

In order to get patients treated quickly I usually read my own x-rays as soon as they were shot instead of waiting the extra hour or two it took for the radiologist to get around to viewing and reporting on them. After thirty years as an E.R. doc, I'd gotten pretty good at it, rarely getting a report that I'd missing something. So when the radiologist called, my ears perked up. I knew there had to be a problem.

"Say Kevin, you remember a patient name of Roger Harris?"

"Of course. Nice fellow with low back pain." I pulled up the x-ray on the computer screen.

"I just wanted to be sure you'd noticed his aneurysm. We don't have any old films on him, so I can't say if it's new or not."

I changed the density on the x-ray and caught my breath. Subtle calcifications outlining a bulging aortic aneurysm jumped into view. It looked like one of those old inner tubes with a weak spot. If it burst Roger would bleed to death in under a minute. I realized his back pain might have been a warning sign, a herald small leak warning of a rupture to come.

After thanking the radiologist, I pulled up Roger's phone number from the computer data base and called. Bobbie answered.

"How's Roger feeling?" I asked.

"It's SO nice of you to check on him, Kevin. He was still pretty zonked from the shot, but I made him take a couple of the pain pills you prescribed and tucked him in. Thank you so much for taking care of him. You MUST be the very best doctor in the whole world! Oh my GOODNESS! And talented too! I've been calling all my friends and telling them about you and your paintings. We're going to have a special show! We'll do lunch and iron out the details, okay, Darlin'?"

"You're too kind." I traced the bulge on the x-ray again. Now that the radiologist had pointed it out, it glared at me like an angry abscess. Taking a deep breath, I said, "Bobbie, we've got a problem."

"A problem?" she asked with subdued voice. "What does that mean?"

"The x-rays we took, well, there's something on them. I need you to bring Roger back to the hospital. "

"You mean … like tomorrow morning?"

"No. I mean right now." I glanced at the clock. 11:10 p.m. "Could you make it by midnight?"

I could hear a twinge of panic in her voice. "What is it Kevin? Tell me the truth. Is it … cancer?"

"No, Bobbie. The radiologist saw something in the x-ray that bothers him."

"The radiologist?" Bobbie let out a snort. "Is that all? We trust you, Kevin, dear. You looked at the x-rays and said they were fine and that's good enough for us. Really, now. Roger's asleep. He's a heavy sleeper anyway, and with those pain pills it's going to take a bull moose to move THAT man! We'll come in the morning."

I studied the x-ray. The aneurysm was dangerously large, but maybe it wasn't the cause of his back pain. What if my first impression was right and Roger just had a back strain, or a passed kidney stone? The aneurysm could be old, months, maybe even years old. What if I made them come in to the hospital and the CAT scan showed nothing to worry about.

"Bobbie, to put my mind at ease please go check on Roger. Shake him awake and ask him how he's feeling. If he's doing fine, then it can wait until morning. Okay?"

I heard her cluck. "I just left him fifteen minutes ago and he was snoring. I hate to bother my honey when he needs his rest. But … if you say so. I'll be right back."

The phone clunked as she laid it down, and I listened to the clicks of her high heels fading down the hallway. As I was holding the phone a nurse came to my cubby, holding a chart. "Dr. Phillips, I need you in room seven." Behind her another voice popped up. "Room three wants more pain meds, and lab results are ready on eight."

I held up my hand. "I need a couple more minutes please." They glanced at each other, shrugged, and walked back to the nurses' area.

It seemed like fifteen minutes before Bobbie finally came back. "Kevin, are you still there?" She seemed breathless.

"What's up?"

"Oh my Goodness, you were so right! You must be psychic. Roger is writhing in pain and his face is blood red. But his feet are cold and he says they ache all the way up to his waist. What's going on?"

Coldness swept up from my feet as well, but went past my waist and settled in my chest.

"Listen Bobbie. I want you to hang up and call 911 right away. Tell them you've talked to me and you need a Code One run straight to the emergency room. Did you get that?"

The only answer she gave came out as grunts as she gasped for breath.

"Bobbie! Get a hold of yourself. Roger needs you!"

I heard her take a deep breathe. "Oh, oh. Yes, I can do this. I know I can. Okay. Now tell me again?"

"Hang up. Dial 911. Tell them Dr. Phillips said it was a Code One. You got it this time?"

"Yes. I … I think so. What is it Kevin? Please, for God's sake, tell me what's wrong with Roger."

"It'd take too long to explain. Just do what I said. Call 911. Tell them a Code One. Okay?"

She clicked off. As soon as I hung up all four nurses came up to the cubby door waving charts, calling out room numbers and needs. I waved them all away.

"All that's going to have to wait. I need the vascular surgeon, and I need him now!"

They looked at each other, seeing which one of them would volunteer as having a patient that needed a stat vascular surgeon. One turned and asked, "Who's the patient?"

"Roger Harris."

She scoffed. "The old queer?"

"You knew?"

"That they're gay? Obviously. What's up with old Roger?"

"Ruptured aortic aneurysm," I said. The nurses crowded around the screen and I ran my finger along the calcified circle. "The ambulance should be on its way."

In a few minutes the vascular surgeon answered my call. I heard laughter in the background … sounded like a party.

"Basham, I've got a fifty-nine-year-old fellow with a seven-centimeter aortic aneurysm I think is leaking. Can you get in right away?"

I could hear him chewing and swallowing before his reply. "You only think – you don't know? Is the guy stable enough for a CAT scan? What are the vital signs?"

I swished some of my ever-present coffee to wet my lips before answering. "Actually he's not here yet; the ambulance is bringing him in. Radiologist saw the large aneurysm on x-ray, and I called the guy at home. His wife says he's having severe back pain and his legs are cold."

I listened as he took another bite of food, a female voice talking to him in some foreign language near his ear. He answered her before replying to me.

"Damn. Okay, I guess I'll head over there. Give him a look over in the E.R. I'll be waiting up in the O.R. lounge."

"Thanks, Basham. I owe you one."

"If this is a false alarm I'm make you pay for this steak dinner I'm abandoning."

I was just hanging up when a nurse called out, "EMS on line two."

"Dr. Phillips? This is Paramedic Jones. We're bringing in a Roger Harris. His wife said you saw him earlier?"

"Yes! How's he doing?"

"Lots of back pain. Okay to give him some morphine?"

"What're his vitals?" I asked. "You know morphine can bottom out his blood pressure."

I heard Jones calling to his partner, the one in back actually taking care of the patient. I couldn't hear their words, the siren drowned out anything not shouted into the mike. In a minute he reported, "Pulse 140, B.P. sky high at 250/160."

I choked on my breath. His blood pressure had been a little bit up when I'd seen him, but that level was crazy. I realized it was probably caused by the aneurysm, the heart pumping as hard as it could to try to get blood moving past the aneurysm, trying to reach the kidneys. "Give him ten milligrams of morphine," I ordered, "and do you have anything else to bring that blood pressure down?"

"Hold on, I'll ask." I heard the two paramedics shouting to each other. To me Jones said, "We got Labetolol. You want that?"

"Definitely. Push 10 milligrams every two minutes until you get the diastolic below a hundred. And give Mr. Harris a sublingual nitroglycerin every two minutes as well. What's your ETA?"

"Fifteen."

I pictured Bobbie and Roger as I'd seen them a couple of hours ago, dependent on each other for so many years. I remembered the way she'd kissed him, how much he meant to her. "Is his wife riding with you?"

"Nah, she … he … well, it's coming in another car. That's a strange dude, I'm telling you that. Wouldn't leave with us 'cause she wanted to fix her wig and put on fresh make up."

I told the secretary to call the nursing supervisor and respiratory technicians to our code room. In the fifteen minutes until they arrived I glanced through the charts the nurses had gathered for my attention and made a few orders. One of the nurses would stay at the station and handle all the other patients while the rest helped out in the code. The four of us, plus the technicians, congregated into the special trauma room preparing for Roger's arrival. Mr. Harris would need our full attention.

The two paramedics stampeded through the doors towing Mr. Harris with his three IVs. A monitor sitting near his head reported his pulse with rapid beeps. Six of us grabbed the corners of his sheet for a rapid shift from their gurney onto our stretcher. He looked cadaverous, paled skin, sunken eyes, limp features. I placed my hand on his foot, finding it cold and pulseless. Once the nurses had the monitor hooked up I read his pulse at 130 and his blood pressure at seventy over zip.

"How much Labetolol did you give?" I demanded.

Jones bit his lip, his eyes glancing from the patient to the monitor and back. "Just followed your instructions. Ten milligrams every two minutes. Forty M.G.s in all. Last reading on our machine was 250/170."

Either his monitor was wrong or Mr. Harris was taking a rapid turn for the worse. "Pour in the fluids," I ordered. Pointing at one of the maroon-suited technicians, I yelled, "Get me some oh negative blood, stat." She ran out of the room on her mission.

"Call the O.R. and make sure the vascular surgeon is up there," I shouted. "Tell the O.R. we need a room right away. What's the repeat blood pressure?"

One of the nurses hooked up the cuff from the wall sphygmomanometer. Its needle fell smoothly along an arch back to zero. "Nothing," she reported.

"Initiate CPR. Get me a scalpel and a vascular clamp," I ordered. "Pour Betadine on his belly."

While two of the technicians performed chest compressions and respiratory aid, a nurse rummaged through our drawer of extra equipment. She held up three various-sized hemostats. "Something like this?"

"No." I reached in the drawer and began dumping the sterile wrapped packages on the floor in handfuls until I found what I wanted near the bottom. I held up an eighteen-inch vena cava clamp, its ten integrated teeth producing a solid six-inch bite. It was the biggest clamp I'd ever seen. "This! Where's that scalpel?"

Another nurse handed me a plastic handled knife and I hovered over Roger's belly, saying a tiny prayer to myself before making the cut.

"STOP!" Bobbie rushed into the room, pushing off the guard who was trying to hold her back. "KEVIN, what are you doing to my baby?"

I beckoned for Bobbie and she came up. I gave her a hug, my latex covered hands pulling her firmly against me. I pushed her away far enough to look into her eyes.

"Roger's aorta has ruptured. His only chance is for me to open his belly and clamp off the vessel or he'll bleed to death. I've got to do it right now."

She stared into my determined eyes. Hers were filled with tears. She nodded. Turning her back she said, "Do it."

I sliced through Roger's cold bloodless skin, separating the fat, cutting deep until I reached the firm connective tissue that separated the skin from the guts. Slicing it open, I found his bowels floating in a pool of blood. Moving the loops out of the way, I isolated the aorta and ran my fingers along it until I came upon the rip. A two-inch hole in the aorta was dribbling out blood with each weak heartbeat. I placed the clamp above the tear and locked the teeth in place.

"Continue CPR and hang a norepinephrine drip, wide open," I ordered. The technician rushed in with the blood, and the nurses hooked up two bags to the IVs, squeezing in with enveloped fists.

"Blood Pressure?" I asked, my eyes on the aorta, which had begun to quiver a bit, the heart finally having something to pump.

"Forty-five palpable."

"Vascular surgeon's in the O.R." the secretary reported.

"Let's move Mr. Harris up there now!" I ordered. "Move, move, move!"

The crowd left, wheeling Mr. Harris out the door and down the hallway to the O.R. I had expected Bobbie to follow him, but she stayed behind, standing in the corner, her face to the wall. I took off my bloody gloves and walked up to her, placing my hand gently on her shoulder. She turned, hesitated at seeing my blood-soaked apron, and then threw herself against me. Her tears ran down my shoulder as I patted her back, allowing her grief to play out.

When she was ready, she stepped back and settled on a stool, holding her hands over her face. When she removed them, her mascara ran streaks, like black blood dribbling from a ruptured vessel.

"What are his chances, Kevin?"

I shook my head. "His body's taken a hell of a blow. Without blood supply for so long there's no telling if his kidney or brain will recover, even if he comes off the operating table alive."

I felt like a heel. Sure, once the radiologist had pointed out the aneurysm, I'd done my best. But my missing that leaking aneurysm had most likely resulted in Roger's death. I stepped over and stood humbly before her, my hands held together. She looked up at me through drooped eyes, her age showing through cracked makeup.

"Bobbie, I can't tell you how sorry I am. If I had only seen that shadow on the x-ray none of this would have happened. You must think I'm the worst kind of rat."

She shook her head, picking up my hand and kissing it.

"No, Kevin. You truly are a hero."

Aortic Aneurysms

A ruptured aortic aneurysm is a rare but usually fatal condition. Atherosclerosis builds up plaques on the aorta, and with the pounding of high blood pressure, the walls around those plaques weaken. Prior to the invention of CAT scans, making the diagnosis involved picking up those subtle shadows on a plain x-ray film. The classic symptom is a description of a "ripping" feeling in the back, with resultant severe pain and hypertension until, as in Roger's case, the rupture drains the body's blood supply into the belly. The time between the ripping and the actual rupture can take only seconds, though sometimes hours can pass.

This story was based on a case I had one day, although mine involved a relatively young man. I was working in a small town E.R. that didn't have a CAT scanner. The nurses thought the patient was drug seeking, moaning in severe pain. I recognized the combination of symptoms and arranged for emergency transfer. We heard later my prompt response had saved his life. It's also based on a couple I met in the E.R. where the hubby presented with low back pain and I wondered, "what if?" That's how most of my stories develop.

For many years, the standard treatment for aortic aneurysms was to cut out the diseased part and sew in a Dacron graft. Nowadays the preferred procedure is to put in a "sleeve" to line the diseased part, a much less invasive and just as effective procedure ... that is, effective if the diagnosis is made on time!

The Headache

"Better put on your thinking cap for the next one."

"Hmm?" I asked.

Kris rolled her eyes as she tapped the chart against her arm, her mouth pursed in her "Another loser" expression. "The intelligence level is so low in there they'll drag you down with them."

I gave her a half grin. Kris was only thirty-something, but already jaded and disparaging. Still, when the tough ones came in, gunshot wounds, car roll-overs, or respiratory distress, she'd be the first in the room, eager to save a life. She could sometimes be less patient with our more routine patients. More than once, I'd stood at the nurses' station while she mimicked what she liked to call a "POS patient"– short for Piece of Shit – someone who, in her opinion, just clogged up our resources and wasted tax dollars.

"Why, Ms. Kris," she'd say, straining her voice in false falsetto. "Mah toddler vomited two times! I was afeared he was agonna die!"

I took the chart from her and scanned her notes: Pearle Hammond. Twenty-eight years old. Headache. Duration, three months.

"Three months?" The astonishment in my voice made Kris laugh.

"Typical POS. I'm sure they're just drug seeking. Out of their Percocets. How about you just kick them out? Tell them to go to a local doctor."

I flipped through the chart to the insurance information. Self-pay. They'd never get in to see a private physician. "We'll see. Maybe social services can help."

Kris snorted. "Right. Waste even more of the taxpayers' money. They're just migrants anyway."

"Why are they in room three?" I asked.

She leaned close and whispered, "Head lice." She turned her back on me and busied herself with some other chart. I left the station and headed down the hallway.

Room three was a closed "reverse airway" room, one in which the air was continuously sucked up and pumped outside. Originally a storage closet, it had been refitted when the government required rooms where we could put people with suspected contagious respiratory diseases such as pneumonia or tuberculosis. We used it for the noisy drunks or other less desirable cases, such as Pearle with her head lice.

I pushed open the door, doing a quick survey. Our isolation room only offered a small space to begin with. The stretcher took up most of the room, leaving the two family members squeezed in the corners.

"I'm Doctor Peters," I said offering my hand.

A thirtyish-looking, rattily-dressed woman stepped up and took it. She smiled, revealing an upper gum of black dental stubs. "Ah'm Sassie, Pearle's sister," she announced. "Pearle's got another one of them headaches."

A taller man slumping against the wall snorted. "Yeah, shore she do." He shifted, leaving an oil smear behind. "She ALWAYS got a headache."

Sassie turned to him and shook a finger. "Hush now." Back to me she explained, "Don't you mind Blake. He's just upset 'cause I made 'em drive us and he's missing his game."

"For nothin'," he groused. "Either she get her shot and pills or she don't. Don't really matter, now do it? Not gonna make any real difference."

"You're Pearle's …?" I held out my hand but after glancing at it, he turned away, staring off at the corner.

"Blake's my fiancé," Sassie said, giving him the evil eye.

I turned my attention to the woman lying on my stretcher. Pearle looked up at me with dull eyes, a large skin scar disfiguring her left forehead. Like her sister, she wore no make-up, her clothes were wrinkled and dirty, and her hair sprouted like a wiry dish scrub. I focused a moment on that hair, easily discerning the dusting of white lice eggs. After Pearle left, we'd have to fumigate the room.

"So, Pearle, it says you have a headache?" I held my pen in readiness, but Pearle didn't speak, just kept staring at me with unblinking eyes. The silence stretched until she responded with a little nod. She pointed to the ugly scar. "Here," she whispered, her voice surprisingly frail.

I reached out and touched the area, a crater that someone with little skill had repaired, leaving ugly mattress lines. Probably an intern. "Car accident?" I suggested.

Sassie shook her head. "Naw, one of her seizures. Happened over in Jacksonville four months ago. She's been having these real bad headaches ever since. Usually when we come to the E.R. she gets a shot and a 'script for more of them Percocets. She takes the tens."

Blake grunted. "Yeah, she shore do. Like candy."

Sassie turned to him, hands on her hips, elbows thrust out and back. "Now you ain't the one with the headache, is you? Your back flared up, you shore did take them pain pills."

He snarled back. "I took 'em once, that's all. Didn't like 'em, and I don't like Pearle bein' on 'em either. Don't do no good. She still got the headaches. And them damn seizures."

He turned to me. "She's just a drug addict, Doc. Tell 'em so we don't have to keep wastin' all this gas money."

I checked the medication list Kris had written on the chart. Besides the Percocet, Pearle took Tegretol, a seizure medication. "How long has Pearle been having seizures?" I asked.

"Couple of years," Sassie replied.

"And has she ever had a work-up? Seen a neurologist, had a CAT scan and an EEG?"

Sassie shrugged. "We ain't never had the money for those kind of things. The E.R. folks say go to a neurologist, and none of them private docs gonna see you unless you got a wad of cash up front. Besides, Blake's gotta have the car to get to work. Cain't you just give her a shot and prescription?"

"Let me look her over first." I washed my hands and began examining Pearle, checking her grips and reflexes and listening to her heart and lungs. Picking up the pen light, I flashed it in her eyes. Her pupils constricted too slowly.

"You said the headaches didn't start until four months ago?" I asked as I worked.

Sassie glanced at Blake who shrugged. "Ah guess 'bout then," she said. "Maybe she was havin' them before Jacksonville, but they been worser ever since. This one the worse she ever got. Couldn't even remember my name this mornin'."

Blake scoffed. "Just means she's wantin' more pain pills."

"And when she had this head injury in Jacksonville," I ventured. "They didn't do a CAT scan then?"

"They wanted to, but Blake wouldn't let 'em."

"Waste of money," he grumbled.

"She's been havin' 'em seizures pretty often," Susie explained. "Mostly small ones, though. Them pills help."

I wrote my findings on the chart and paused a moment, my pen hovering over the order blank. It would be so easy just to order the pain shot and write the prescription. But the story worried me. Possibly she'd gotten a subdural bleed inside her skull during the Jacksonville accident. Maybe we could cure the headaches with a little neurosurgery.

"I think I'd like to get a CAT scan."

Blake swore, and spit on the floor. "Why you wanta do that?" he demanded. "You just tryin' to pad the bill?"

I shook my head. "It's possible we'll find some reason for her headaches. It's the right thing to do."

"We ain't gonna pay for it!" Blake insisted, his jaw thrust out.

I turned to Pearle. "What do you say, Pearle? You want a CAT scan?"

Her flat expression never changed, but a barely perceptible nod made the decision. I wrote the order and left the room. When I got back to the nurses' station Kris grabbed the chart out of my hand and swore.

"Why the hell are you scanning this girl?"

"She deserves one. New onset headache. Never worked up." I gave her a winning smile but she just smirked back at me.

"New? You call three months new? How about you just send her to the neurologist and let them check her out?"

"They don't have the four hundred dollars."

"Cheaper than a C.T.," Kris said with a snort. But when she saw my intransigent expression, she shrugged and bent to the computer to put in the order. "Actually this is a good idea. I'll be curious to see if she actually has a brain. Ought to do one on her family members too."

Being a typical Sunday afternoon in the E.R., I found plenty to occupy my time while waiting for the CAT scan report. Kris made disparaging remarks every time she handed me a new chart. "You going to do a lumbar tap on this three year old with an earache? You wouldn't want to miss a case of meningitis, you know."

"Come on, now," I said. "Pearle needed a CAT scan."

Kris raised one eyebrow. "I've got a headache from all these drug seekers today. You want to order a scan on me?"

An hour later the radiologist called me.

"You ordered the head on Pearle Hammond?" he asked. When I admitted it, he said, "You better call the neurosurgeon stat. She's got the biggest tumor I've seen in years. It's creating a huge mass effect. Looks to me like she's about to herniate her hippocampus."

My mouth went dry.

When I asked Kris to call the neurosurgeon stat she thought I was pulling her leg. I had to pull up the x-ray on the computer where we both stared in amazement at the grapefruit-sized tumor occupying a good third of Pearle's skull cavity. If I had just given Pearle her shot and sent her home, she'd have been dead by midnight. Sometimes the angels look after the innocent.

"At least we know why she's been having headaches," Kris murmured.

The neurosurgeon called back promptly, and we discussed emergency intervention, including steroids and calling in the operating team until he could get there. I arranged the details before going in to tell the family.

Blake had stepped out to smoke a cigarette, so Sassie went to fetch him so I could talk to them together. When I gave them the news both of their faces turned ashen. Sassie's hands covered her mouth. Blake looked at me disbelieving.

"A brain tumor? You shore?"

I nodded. "I can show you the x-ray."

They both wanted to see, and accompanied me to the computer screen where Kris joined us. Tears ran down Sassie's face. Blake just stared in disbelief.

"Ah cain't believe it," he said. "All this time I jest thought she was a druggie. Damn."

He walked out of the viewing room and when he left, Sassie grabbed my hands, holding tightly. "Is mah sister gonna die?"

I looked at the x-ray. The emergency neurosurgery would prevent immediate death, relieving the pressure from the tumor. However, removing that beast in her brain seemed unlikely. "We'll do our best. Why don't you go sit with her and the nurse will bring you and Blake up to the surgery waiting room when they roll Pearle upstairs."

She left, and I watched Kris bend forward to run her finger along the outline of the tumor on the screen. "What do you think?" she asked.

I shook my head. "This thing is so huge, I don't know what they're going to do. Radiation might help. But surgery? The surgeon would have to take out a big hunk of normal brain just to get at the tumor."

"Now that's a shame." Kris sighed. "She didn't have a lot of brain to start with. Well, in that family I guess no one will notice."

I snorted my disapproval and ushered her out.

Back at the station I picked up another chart. Somebody had come in seeking treatment for a toothache he'd had for six weeks. I removed the yellow Post-It with the "POS" Kris had scribbled and turned into the hall. I stopped short when I spotted two women huddled against the door to room three.

It was Kris, holding tightly onto Sassie, the two of them crying in each other's arms.

Brain Tumors

The incidence of primary brain tumors is only three out of ten thousand, making them uncommon. About two-thirds of these are cancerous. Much more common are tumors originating elsewhere; for example, a third of all lung cancers metastasize to the brain. Treatment depends on many factors, such as location, type of cancer, and the patient's condition. Often these tumors respond to radiation, shrinking considerably and making surgery easier. The most common first symptom is a seizure. Thus, the onset of seizures in an adult without history of head trauma or substance abuse (such as alcohol withdrawal) always necessitates a CAT scan for evaluation.

This story is loosely based on a case I had in the emergency room of a thirty-year-old man who had been treated for new onset severe headaches for the prior two months without a CAT scan. On history I asked him if he'd noticed any problems with walking, and he replied he'd noticing he tended to drift to the right as he walked. This change in balance when walking has been one of the big clues for me over the years, with which I've picked out four new brain tumors. This fellow had a huge tumor, like Pearle's.

It's easy to let oneself become jaded as a provider in the emergency room. So it's something I always try to stay aware of— both in myself and my co-workers. I constantly remind myself not considering the more dangerous diagnoses can result in a deadly mistake.

Ready or Not

It was four in the morning, January eighteenth, my birthday. The last patient had just left, and the E.R. nurse, Margaret, had brought out a cake she'd purchased at the grocery store – one of those white things with icing too sweet to eat and topped with little flowers that left your tongue blue. I loved it! I cut myself a small sliver, making allowances for my diet.

A small stream of people dropped by to share cake, give greetings, and talk about life. Joel, my favorite EMT, gave me a present. I groaned theatrically when I pulled out one of those gag gifts, an "over the hill" box containing items like laxatives, muscle cream, and reading glasses. Sadly, they were all things I used!

"How old are you now, Dr. Brandt," Joel asked. "Eighty?" He guffawed.

"Sixty-seven, and feeling every day of it. My knee's acting up, and an hour ago I couldn't remember the dosage for Lipitor. I must've prescribed Lipitor a hundred times, but I had to look it up. Senior moments – not a lot of fun. And working nights in my sixties isn't as easy as when I was a young fellow like you."

Joel wolfed down his extra-large slice of cake, and cut himself another piece. "Sixty-seven? You thinkin' about retiring?"

Margaret shook her finger at him. "You hush now, Joel Kearney. Dr. Brandt's one of the best we got. Why are you trying to make trouble?"

Joel held up his hands in defense. "Hey, I was just asking. He's the one who said he was getting old. Right?"

He turned to me and slammed me on the back. It was a "one-of-the-guys" kind of blows, and it knocked my breath out.

"I said no such thing. In my younger days, doctors were given respect! Nurses stood when the doctor came into the room and young fellas like you would keep their hands to themselves."

Joel laughed and elbowed me. "If you can't take the heat, stay out of the kitchen, that's all I'm saying." We silenced at the crackle of his radio. He picked it out of its holster and held it to his ear. "Roger," he said. "On our way." He signaled to his partner and headed to the door, calling over his shoulder, "Firefighters pulled a guy out of a trailer fire. Those things are death traps."

We cleaned up from the party and prepared the trauma room. I thought about heading to the doctor's lounge and trying to get fifteen minutes of shut-eye before Joel got back, but decided I'd just rest in my chair instead to be on the spot.

It seemed I'd just dozed off when Margaret nudged me.

"Joel's bringing in a crispy. Sounds bad. I already called Life-Flight to send a helicopter."

I struggled awake, onto my feet, and into the trauma room. Margaret and three others fiddled with the devices, readied the IV fluids, and whispered about prior burn patients. *Crispies* were always bad – terrible pain and scary looking. Usually they died. Body fluids leaked out from burned flesh. Giving enough replacement fluid could be nigh impossible.

Joel and his partner rushed in with the victim, the stench of burnt hair and flesh overpowering. Charred from head to toe, blisters popped like bubble wrap. Blackened skin ribbons draped from the fellow's arms and chest. Tugging at the bits of remaining cloth pulled skin off too.

"Jorge Gonzales," Joel reported. "Fifty-three-year-old, probably fell asleep in bed smoking. Empty alcohol bottles all around him. Had a little poodle that escaped out a doggy door flap and woke the neighbors. Smart dog."

"What percent?" Margaret asked.

I did a quick survey; except for some patches of intact skin on his back and buttocks, the burns hit everywhere. "Ninety." Once in medical school I had read that you could estimate the chance of a burn victim dying by adding the percentage of skin burnt to the patient's age. This guy didn't stand a chance.

Margaret looked for an IV site, but with his skin blacked, peeled, and swollen, veins couldn't be found. Meanwhile the guy screamed in pain. Well, he was trying to scream, but it came out as muffled gasps.

"Central set," I called, pointing to the cabinet. Joel pulled out the blue wrapped package and opened it on a standing table. I painted the patient's groin orange with iodine antiseptic and pressed hard to find the pulse. Pushing the needle deep into the inside of the felt artery, I was rewarded with a rush of dark red blood from its neighboring vein.

"Wide open," I ordered, and Margaret obediently hooked up the fluids to the IV I'd started. Under pressure the saline poured in, racing against the leaks.

"Twenty of morphine," I ordered.

Margaret administered the medicine, and the patient stopped thrashing.

"Pulse ox eighty percent," she said, reading his oxygen level from a meter on one of the fellow's fingers. "He needs to be intubated," she said, looking at me expectantly.

I needed put a breathing tube down his throat to pump 100% oxygen into his damaged lungs. I'd done plenty of intubations, but it wasn't my strongest skill. Still, it was my responsibility and I took the laryngoscope that Joel handed me. Forcing open Mr. Gonzales' mouth, I found everything inside seemed like a black swamp. Soot coated his entire respiratory system, from his blackened mouth, down the trachea chimney, and no doubt into his polluted lung air sacs.

When I tried to insert the endotracheal tube, Mr. Gonzales resisted, twisting his neck, biting at the instrument, and gagging.

"This is impossible," I groused.

"You want to put him down?" Margaret asked.

Succinylcholine would take away all his muscle control. I hesitated, knowing that if we paralyzed him and I still couldn't intubate him, he'd suffocate.

She pointed at the pulse ox monitor which had fallen to seventy-five. "He's going downhill quick."

Indicating his burns, I whispered to her, "He's going to die anyway."

She ignored my comment. "Hundred of sucs?"

"Okay."

Joel grabbed an "ambu" bag and began pumping oxygenated air into the fellow's lungs. I watched Margaret pull the paralyzing drug from the dispenser and inject it into Mr. Gonzales' IV. In a few seconds he became totally limp.

Once again I explored the swollen tissues inside his mouth with my lighted metal blade. The swelling and bleeding had gotten worse in the four minutes since I'd last tried. Everything was a spongy mess – black and red bloated tissues hid the tracheal opening. Backing out, I let Joel resume his work with the bag.

After a minute or two I tried again. I failed, and Joel bagged, and I tried yet a fourth time. I repositioned the fellow's head, and held cricoid pressure.

I was trying all the tricks I knew, but I just couldn't find the sweet spot. The alternative, when intubation failed, involved cutting through the tissues of the neck to open a hole directly in the trachea – a dangerous and often unsuccessful procedure, particularly in this case with his distorted neck tissue.

Joel held out his hand. "Hey, old man, give it over."

I looked at the laryngoscope held tightly in my grip. I was the doctor, not this crew-cut young upstart. "No. This is my job."

I turned to the patient again, but Joel laid his hand on my wrist.

"Dr. Brandt. Give me the laryngoscope."

I glanced at the pulse ox. Sixty. I let Joel pull the instrument from my hand. I stepped back.

He repositioned the patient's head and inserted the laryngoscope. I held my breath, counting the seconds. Three. Eight. Ten. I wondered how long he would try. I glanced up at the monitor again. Forty. This guy was going to suffocate. Brain cells were dying.

I watched as Joel danced with both his hands, probing and tickling. With a thrust the tube pushed forward. "In!" he announced, at last.

We hooked up the newly placed tube to the ventilator. With a hundred percent oxygen forced into his lungs at added pressure, the pulse ox rose rapidly above ninety. The security guard stuck his head in the door and announced that the helicopter was landing.

A minute later, the blue suited flight crew rushed in, packaged the patient, and disappeared out the door. Except for the scattered trash and a lingering odor, it was as if the whole thing had never happened. I thanked the group for their efforts and headed to my private doctor's lounge.

Settling onto the couch, I stared at my hands. These hands – they'd never failed me. There had been times I couldn't do what I wanted: a missed lumbar puncture or an inability to reduce a dislocated shoulder. But this time …

"Come in," I responded to a knock.

Joel entered. "Hey. You okay, Doc?"

I gave him a half smile. "Yeah, sure."

He sat down across from me. "Really? You're looking a bit gray, even for an old man."

I sighed. "Maybe you're right, Joel. It's time I took down my shingle. I've been an E.R. doc for forty-one years. Time to call it quits."

He started to laugh, but stopped abruptly. "Nah, Doc. You still got what it takes."

I shook my head. "That fellow almost died. My fault. I'm old. I'm tired. I can't handle it anymore."

He laid his hand on my shoulder. "You wanta quit, Dr. Brandt? Spend more time with the grandkids?"

I thought of little Tommy, now twelve. I enjoyed taking him fishing, sure enough. But is that what I wanted out of life – spending day after day fishing, watching TV, gardening? "I don't know, Joel. I don't want to be killing people."

He snorted. "Hey. You can't win 'em all. My granddad used to say, 'You'll know when it's time to quit.' So, I guess you gotta decide for yourself."

I reflected on the night. I'd seen over a dozen patients: kids with fever, asthmatics, old folks with belly pains. I loved what I did, figuring out the puzzles, making people feel better. Hell, I even saved a life now and then. "I'm not ready to quit yet."

Joel's radio went off, and he held it to his ear. "On our way." He stopped at the door to throw me a wave. "Cardiac arrest at the nursing home. Better get back on your feet – if you can, old man."

I jumped up. "I'm ready. Bring it on."

Getting Old

In his later years, my father would say, "No matter what they count as seniors, I qualify." He suffered a forced retirement at sixty-four-years-old, and for the next six months moped around the house. My mother, fed up, called some of his friends and got him another job, consulting in his field of specialty for another ten years. He LOVED it. At ninety-years-old in the nursing home, he was writing his ex-boss pleading for his job back. He'd reminisce, "The biggest mistake I ever made was retiring."

Retirement is inevitable. As of this writing, I'm the oldest physician working in our emergency room. The powers-that-be decided I was too old to work on the trauma side, so now I fill my days seeing children with fever, old people with belly pain, and the other scattered medical issues that bring the world's population to my door. Perhaps it's not as busy on this unit as on the trauma side, yet busy enough, and at the end of a twelve-hour shift, I'm often exhausted.

But, like my father, I don't yet feel ready to stop. For one thing, I'm good at what I do. Forty years of experience has exposed me to many different diseases, given me a sense of what direction to go with my diagnosis decisions, and, importantly, who's sick enough to come into the hospital and who can safely be allowed to recuperate at home.

Most importantly, I still love my work. I come into the E.R. and settle into the zone ... seeing patients steadily and efficiently. I log in at the upper end of the rate of patients seen per hour in our group. Both nurses and patients have told me I'm their favorite doctor, and, well, it doesn't get better than that.

So I won't be retiring yet. I'm not saying they'll have to pry my stethoscope out of my cold stiffened fingers. I think I'll do a slow descent, maybe into slower E.R.s, or perhaps clinic work. Or maybe I'll chuck it all and spend the days fishing with my grandchild. After all, I'm not my father. Or ... yeah, maybe I am.

www.ingramcontent.com/pod-product-compliance
Lightning Source LLC
Chambersburg PA
CBHW051503170626
46811CB00002B/616